# CRAVING
## CONSTELLATIONS

### NICOLE JACQUELYN

Copyright © 2013 by Nicole Jacquelyn

All rights reserved.

Cover photo by Kara Pesznecker
Cover model Mandy Stockholm
Cover designed by Sommer Stein
Edited by Madison Seidler
Formatted by Jovana Shirley

No part of this book may be reproduced or transmitted in any form or by any means, electronic or mechanical, including photocopying, recording, or by any information storage and retrieval system without the written permission of the author, except for the use of brief quotations in a book review.

This book is a work of fiction. Names, characters, places, and incidents either are products of the author's imagination or are used fictitiously. Any resemblance to actual persons, living or dead, events, or locales is entirely coincidental.

Visit my Facebook page at www.facebook.com/authornicolejacquelyn

ISBN-13: 978-1492164425

To Johni, who told me I should write a book.

I did it.

I wish you were here to see it.

I miss you friend.

# Contents

Chapter 1: Brenna ............... 1
Chapter 2: Brenna ............. 13
Chapter 3: Dragon ............ 23
Chapter 4: Brenna ............. 35
Chapter 5: Brenna ............. 43
Chapter 6: Brenna ............. 55
Chapter 7: Brenna ............. 61
Chapter 8: Dragon ............ 69
Chapter 9: Brenna ............. 77
Chapter 10: Brenna ........... 89
Chapter 11: Brenna ......... 101
Chapter 12: Dragon ........ 113
Chapter 13: Brenna ......... 125
Chapter 14: Dragon ........ 139
Chapter 15: Brenna ......... 153
Chapter 16: Brenna ......... 161
Chapter 17: Brenna ......... 169
Chapter 18: Brenna ......... 179
Chapter 19: Brenna ......... 191
Chapter 20: Brenna ......... 199
Chapter 21: Dragon ........ 207
Chapter 22: Brenna ......... 209
Chapter 23: Brenna ......... 215

Chapter 24: Brenna.......... 225
Chapter 25: Brenna.......... 235
Chapter 26: Brenna.......... 241
Chapter 27: Brenna.......... 249
Chapter 28: Dragon ......... 255
Chapter 29: Brenna.......... 263
Chapter 30: Brenna.......... 269
Chapter 31: Brenna.......... 275
Chapter 32: Dragon ......... 287
Epilogue: Brenna............. 291
Acknowledgments........... 295

## Chapter 1
### Brenna

How could someone make decision after decision attempting to get away from their past and somehow end up right back where they started?

I'd spent the last five years running, and now, it seemed I was going to have to retrace every excruciating step. My heart told me that nothing good could come from heading back to the place I'd grown up, but I knew we had nowhere else to go. Every ache, every pain, and every bruise reminded me that we had to escape. I couldn't lie to myself anymore; there was one place in the world where he'd never reach us. We just had to get there.

I'd grown up rough. I'd seen more than one woman slapped around by her man, and to be truthful, it had never really bothered me much. It was the way of the world, or at least, it was the way of *our* world. It was all I knew.

I wanted a different life though, so I'd gone away to college, and later, I'd tried to carve out a life in the beige community where mothers brought their children to school in minivans and joined the PTA. I wanted a husband who paid taxes and would take his car to a mechanic for routine maintenance. He wouldn't get his hands dirty, wouldn't raise his voice, and wouldn't carry a gun.

I'd never imagined the world I chose would be far worse than the one I had left.

I only had three days to get to where I needed to be, and I wasn't going to hesitate. I wanted to be there and settled before my clean-cut husband came looking for us.

So, for the past week, I'd counted down every minute until his business trip. He had no idea that I was planning to leave, and honestly, I thought he would have killed me if he had. My first order of business was to pack two duffel bags full of things I refused to leave behind: mementos, my laptop, and a necessary change of clothes for each of us. I refused to waste precious space on anything I could easily buy later.

The morning after he'd flown out on his business trip, I raced around the house as fast as someone covered in bruises from neck to thighs could—which wasn't very fast. I'd spent so many hours planning our escape in my head—organizing items in order of importance and deciding what we would take and what would be left—that it only took me an hour to pack everything we needed.

By the time I was finished with the bags, I was in a cold sweat from both pain and nerves. He'd never come home from a business trip early, but I felt like every moment I wasted was one more chance for him to change his habits, and I was strung as tightly as a violin string.

When everything was packed into our car, I picked my girl up off the couch where she was watching cartoons and got her ready for the day as if it were any other morning.

On Tuesdays, we usually went to a Mommy and Me class at a yoga studio downtown. This meant, as I pulled out of the driveway, the neighbor across the street wouldn't wonder where I was going. He wouldn't think about me or even pay enough attention to realize when I left. I also felt comfortable dressing her in yoga pants and a tunic without anything standing out. Perhaps I'd seen too many spy movies or read too many books or maybe it was just my natural inclination toward paranoia, but I was sure that we needed to be as inconspicuous as possible.

Except for Tuesdays, my husband expected my girl to be dressed like an advertisement for some snobby boutique—no jeans, no rain boots, hair perfectly parted into ponytails with elaborate hair ribbons that matched her outfits. She looked adorable, but it was hard watching her sit stiffly on a chair in her frilly dress while other girls jumped and rolled around on the floor in their overalls. It wasn't normal. I had a feeling he had this obsession with my daughter's appearance because she looked nothing like us.

When we moved here from Eugene, new people always did a double take when we were together. My husband had light brown hair and eyes, and his skin was a ruddy pink that I'd originally found extremely attractive. It wasn't until I saw it redden with anger that the pink hue started to remind me of a petulant child's. My skin was pale with a peaches-and-cream complexion. A stereotypical redhead, I have a few freckles and green eyes. This is why, when people commented jokingly, "Wow, she doesn't look like you guys, does she?" about my olive-skinned, dark-haired child, he began to imply that she was adopted.

From the beginning, he had known that the child I carried before we were married wasn't his, but at the time, he'd claimed that it didn't matter. Once he saw her, the bigoted asshole had changed his tune. It was one thing to pretend she was his if no one would know the difference; it was quite another matter entirely if the truth was written across her beautiful face.

God, I couldn't wait to get her away from him. It was so close I could taste it.

We'd gotten on the road at around ten, but I didn't feel my tension ease until Portland was over an hour behind us. About an hour and a half south of Portland, we made our first stop. We had to lose my BMW. We needed something less expensive and far less ostentatious if we wanted to fly under the radar—plus, I hated it.

It was pure luck that the car was even in my name. When we bought it, my husband had been called away for some work-related problem, and by the time the paperwork was finished, the title was in my name only. He hadn't been happy about that turn of events, but once I committed another transgression, his focus had changed, and he didn't bring up the title again. It was one of the few possessions that was mine, free and clear.

Earlier in the week, I had posted the Beemer on Craigslist in Salem, and thankfully, I'd gotten a hit. That Craigslist post was the reason I'd brought my laptop with us. I'd taken down the posting, and if he didn't have the computer, I hoped it would be hard for him to trace our steps.

The buyer was meeting me in a grocery store parking lot in a little town outside of Salem. The post had stipulated *cash only*, and I knew the man meeting me was a sure thing because the price I was asking was so low. It was just enough money for the used Toyota I'd also found on Craigslist.

When we arrived at the grocery store, my nerves were back in full force. What if the buyer didn't show? What would I do with our bags in the thirty-minute lag between selling one car and buying the other? What if the seller didn't show, and I was stranded in this tiny town without even a taxi service? What if we looked suspicious, and the police decided to stop? My mind raced with the possibilities.

I parked the car close to the store entrance and waited for the buyer. He'd said he'd be driving a late model green SUV, and I clocked him the minute he turned into the parking lot. When he and a woman pulled up and parked across from us, I felt a sense of relief. Meeting with a strange man, hours from home, made me a little nervous. Watching his lady grab a screaming infant from behind her seat calmed my nerves even more.

I quickly climbed out from the car and walked to stand in front of my girl's door. While I was comforted to know the man had brought his family along, I wasn't taking any chances.

"Hey! You Kate?" He walked toward me with his hand lifted in order to shake mine.

"That's me," I said with what I hoped was an easygoing smile.

"Man, she's a beauty. Is your asking price the same as when we emailed?" he asked.

He seemed perplexed as he looked at my car that he'd probably expected to be trashed. It was far from trashed. Back in my old life, my car could have been called *cherry*. No crumbs marred the seats, no fingerprints were on the windows, and the rims sparkled in the late morning sunshine. I didn't blame him for being confused. If I were buying a car far below Blue Book from someone I didn't know, I would have been waiting for the other shoe to drop, too.

"Yep. That's it. I'd just like to sell it. I'm not comfortable doing a test drive with you, so if you want it, you're going to have to just, you know, buy it without driving it." I tried to sound confident, but I wasn't sure if this was going to work. "I'm sure you understand. I've got my girl in the car. I'm not driving around with a stranger."

While I spoke, he nodded his head.

"Yep, no problem. With the amount you're selling it for, and since you already drove it here, anything that could be wrong with it, I could easily fix, and I would still be getting a deal."

His face reddened, and I was sure he was wishing back those last few words. Who in the world told someone they were selling something too cheap? Eh. It didn't matter. I just wanted it gone.

"Okay then. Did you bring the cash?" I asked him impatiently. I wanted to get this transaction over with.

"Yep, it's in the car with my wife. Give me just a second."

He walked over to his wife's window, and I watched them banter for a minute before I reached in my purse for the title. I wondered if they were genuinely that happy with each other or if this was a show put on for the outside world. I knew all too well the difference between what was shown in public and what went on behind closed doors. I knew how quickly a charming smile could turn to a scowl the second no one was looking. I repressed a shudder before walking back to meet him to exchange the title for cash. I breathed a sigh of relief when he didn't notice the name on the title.

Once we were done, I grabbed a grocery cart and piled our bags and my girl's car seat inside. We watched him drive away with satisfaction. Well, I felt satisfaction anyway; the girl in my arms, sleeping on my shoulder, hadn't woken up during the whole transaction.

We waited only fifteen minutes before I saw my new car pull into the parking lot. By this time, my girl was awake and begging to get down, so I sat her in the cart and ran my hand through her hair, hoping she'd be patient just a little longer. This transaction was the trickier of the two. I knew my car would be easy to sell without a test drive, but I was also going to have to buy this new car without testing it out first, which meant I was relying on the honesty of someone I hadn't met. This car had to get us to where we were going, or we'd be screwed.

The woman who jumped out of my new Toyota was in her mid-fifties with salt-and-pepper hair in long dreadlocks down her back. She was wearing some type of multi-colored gypsy skirt, and as she walked toward me, she jingled as if she were wearing a hundred little bells.

I slowly stepped toward her as I watched her take in our appearance. I knew we looked weird. I was sure she'd never seen someone show up to buy a car with only a grocery cart filled with duffel bags and a toddler. However, she didn't say a word. If I was judging her correctly, she had an almost knowing look on her face.

"Hi, are you Stargazer?" I asked hesitantly.

I had assumed that, for whatever reason, the name she used in her ad was an alias; however, looking at her now, it was probably her actual name. I could feel the corners of my eyes getting tight, and I was hoping that we could get this over with quickly. Between the stress of exchanging cars and the physical exertion of moving around our bags, my body was beginning to revolt. At this point, I wanted to buy the car, so I could just get in and sit down.

"Hello, there!" she called back. "You must be Lacey! Want to come take a look at my baby?"

"Yep, that's me! I'll be right there," I answered her, nodding my head, as I struggled to push our bulging cart across the pavement, my movements stiff and awkward.

"Ooh, your little girl sure is a cutie!" she said with a smile on her face. "Hello, sweetheart!"

I inspected the car while she chattered away about how long she had owned it, what the mileage was, and how she had just come from vacuuming it out and putting in a vanilla-scented air freshener that she'd made herself—detailing the whole process with words like *infusion* and *scented oils*. She was super nice, but she was driving me crazy as she prattled on and on. The longer we stayed in one place, the antsier I became to get on the road. When she finally got around to handing me the title, my girl was fidgeting with impatience, but she sat silently, waiting for me to put her in the car. She was used to staying quiet while around any other adults, except for me. She knew the punishment that could come from speaking up at the wrong time.

We got on the road about twenty minutes later, driving away in a car that smelled strongly of patchouli oil and vanilla. I didn't mind the smell though. All that mattered was the car worked like a dream. I just hoped it continued to do so.

After a quick stop to get us fast food for a late lunch, we got back on the interstate and headed south. There were no more errands to run and no other stops to make. I was almost home, and I was worried that once we got there, life would become even more complicated.

I grew up outside of a town called Eugene. Its biggest claim to fame was the state university and, more specifically, the university's football team. It was where I'd met my husband although I never brought him home to meet my father. I'd been trying to distance myself from that life, so I'd pretty much just pretended it didn't exist during my four years of college.

My husband strangely never asked to meet my pop. For a while, I'd wondered why he chose to completely ignore that part of my life. It seemed to me that someone would want to know his or her future spouse's family. Eventually though, I'd chalked it up to total self-absorption. He didn't care about my previous life because it didn't directly impact him. That had worked in my favor, so I'd been happy with the status quo.

I'd gone home only a few times during college, and the last weekend home during my senior year had changed the course of my life forever. After that, I'd refused to look back.

We got to Eugene at about three in the afternoon, and I'd left the city, taking back road after back road on my way to where I'd find my father. I wasn't sure where he was living, but I knew exactly where he'd be at three o'clock on a Tuesday. It was the same place he'd been every Tuesday my entire life and where he'd be every Tuesday until he died.

As we pulled up outside the gate, I was filled with a jumble of emotions I didn't even bother to sort through. It had been a very long day, and my body was so weary that I wasn't sure how I'd even make it out of the car. Maybe I should have waited, grabbed us a hotel room, and returned bright and early the next morning, but as soon as I brought the car to a stop, the guard at the gate was walking toward me. There was no time to back out, so I sighed quietly and rolled down my window.

"Whatcha need, beautiful? You lost?" he asked me with a smile pulling up the corner of his mouth.

"Nope. Looking for my pop. Can you let us in?" I muttered distractedly, rubbing the bridge of my nose with my fingertips. A headache was building in between my eyes, and I didn't have the energy to care how annoyed he looked that I was neither nervous nor trying to flirt my way in.

This guard was new. He hadn't been here five years before, and it looked like he was a recruit. No patch yet.

"Well, who's your pop? Is he expecting you? This is private property." He was smirking with a cocky look in his eyes that hadn't been there seconds before.

Five years ago, I would have put him in his place, but I was too tired to fight. I just wanted to get to my pop, so I could finally rest.

"Poet," I answered him shortly. "Look, just call him, okay? No, he's not expecting me, but it won't matter. You're new here, so I'll give you a little heads-up. You don't want to keep me waiting."

He looked at me quizzically, and then he stepped away from the car and pulled out his cell phone. Soon after that, his hand came up to rub the back of his neck, and he turned to face me as he disconnected. "Sorry about that. I'll just get the gate open, and you can go on up."

It was obvious that whomever he'd spoken with wasn't happy to hear that I was waiting at the gate.

When I pulled up at the clubhouse, there were a few guys outside, working on motorcycles and sitting at picnic tables, shooting the shit. All of them turned my way as I parked and got out of the car, holding tightly to the doorframe to steady myself. I recognized a few, but I didn't acknowledge any of them. I was here for Pop, not to socialize. These weren't my people anymore. I was surprised to find my backbone returning though, the longer I stood in the yard of my childhood. I was the princess here. It may have been long ago, but I knew my status had not changed.

My thoughts went blank as I saw my father walk quickly out of one of the garage bays with two men on his heels. I didn't even glance at the men; my eyes were eating up my father as he paused for a few moments and then took long strides toward me. He hadn't changed a bit. His gray long hair was parted down the middle and hanging down his back in a ponytail. His beard, which had always reached his chest, was cut short, but his smile and shining green eyes, which were just like mine, were achingly familiar. He was smiling at me up until we made eye contact, and then his face changed to one of concern. I wasn't sure what emotion was showing on my face, but he knew that something was wrong.

My body sagged in relief as he reached me. We were safe. He was here, and we were surrounded. Nothing and no one could touch us now.

"Pop," I whispered as he wrapped his thick arms around me.

"My Brenna girl. Where have you been, lass?" He squeezed my middle in a tight hug.

My relief was unfortunately short-lived because the moment he squeezed, my body tensed in pain. I promptly lost consciousness and felt nothing.

## Chapter 2
### Brenna

I woke up, bleary-eyed, to someone prodding at my ribs. At first, I wasn't aware of my surroundings, so I began to panic, frantically pushing those roaming fingers away.

"Brenna! Stop! Let Doc look at you."

I heard my father's voice from across the room. The past week came back to me instantly, and panic rushed in for another reason.

"Where's my girl? She was in the car! Where is she?" I feverishly looked around the room, not spotting my daughter anywhere.

"Ach. I found her. Don't be worrying about that. I left her outside with the boys, and she was just fine. Now say hello to Doc. Let him finish looking you over, and we can have a bit of a chat, yes?" he admonished me.

I looked to Doc, who hadn't seemed to age since the last time I saw him—well, except for the fact that he seemed to have lost about thirty pounds. I wasn't sure he ever had an actual medical degree, but he'd been fixing up members of the club and their families for as long as I could remember. He'd always seemed like such a contradiction to me. He could gently set a five-year-old's broken arm (mine) and beat the hell out of someone (some huge guy that I had never seen before) all in the space of an hour. He was old as dirt when I was a kid, and I wasn't sure how he was still alive and kicking.

"Hi, Doc. It's been a while," I said with a sheepish smile. "I'm not used to waking up to someone coppin' a feel. I thought you were just getting handsy. Sorry about that."

He started to guffaw in his deep baritone, and I found myself smiling at its infectiousness. His looks were deceiving; the man's voice was as strong as ever.

"Glad to know you still got some fight in you. Although, I'm wondering where that fight went when whoever it was cracked these ribs," he replied with a raised eyebrow. "You're going to need to take it easy, girl. I don't know how you've been getting around like this." He shook his head. "I've wrapped your ribs, which doesn't do a whole lot other than keep you aware of things, so you don't move the wrong way. There's really nothing I can do for you at this point. I'll leave you some pain meds, but with the way you react to them, you may want to stick with something over-the-counter."

I'd always had a very strong reaction to pain medication. For some reason, they just seemed to hit me harder than they did everyone else. When Doc had given me one for cramps when I was a teenager, I'd slept for thirty-six hours. It'd freaked Pop way the hell out.

With a nod, Doc packed up his bag and left, closing the door behind him. I closed my eyes for just a moment, preparing for what I knew was going to be an extremely hard conversation. When I opened them again, Pop was sitting on the edge of the bed. I realized I was in his room, and it was freshly painted in a garish shade of yellow, but before I could say a word, he started to speak.

"Brenna, what the hell is going on? You show up here after five years—and believe you me, lass, I'm grateful—but the minute I hugged you, there you went, fainted dead away in my arms. So, I lifted you up to carry you inside, and out of the corner of me eye, I found your wee lass sitting in the car bawling her eyes out."

Even after all these years, if Pop was upset about something, his accent got thicker. I found that comforting in a way that I couldn't explain.

"She wasn't making a sound, Brenna! Tears were falling down her face, and she wasn't making a bloody sound! She couldn't be more than four years old, and she doesn't say a word when her mum collapses? I handed you off, and as they took you inside, I grabbed your girl. Now, she's crying, mind you, but no matter what I said, she just kept on crying, but she was completely fuckin' silent."

He raised his arms in exasperation, and I forced myself not to flinch from the sudden movement.

"She was stiff as a board! I can understand the lass being afraid of a scary old man like me who she don't know from Adam, but she didn't fight me! Oh no, I lifted her up, and her back just snapped stick straight, but she kept on crying. Then, when she finally stopped, I left her with the boys outside. I came in here and saw Doc checking out that bruising you have all over your body. Tell me what the fuck is going on."

As he spoke, his face got redder and redder, and by the time he finished, I could see the tendons in his neck straining under the skin. I took a deep breath to try and calm my nerves. The conversation could end in one of two ways: Pop would be mad as hell at me, or he'd be ready to kill my husband. I knew it would be the latter.

"Now, Brenna!" he growled.

"It's a long story," I said, trying to find the right words. I was already starting to cry.

His voice was softer when he spoke again. "Start at the beginning, lass."

"I'm married. I'm sure you already know that though. Um, we met in college, and he seemed like a really good guy. We dated for a while, and eventually, he asked me to marry him, and I agreed. By then, I was pregnant, so we just did a quick Justice of the Peace thing, ya know? Things were fine for a while. His family is from Salem, and they're really into politics although I'm not sure what his dad does. He makes a lot of money though because, Pop, seriously, his mom lunches. She spends her days doing all of this charity shit, and she doesn't work. Ever. She's never worked. Plus, she's a bitch."

Pop nodded his head as I kept talking. "Anyway, we finished up college, and then lived with his parents when Trix was born. She was so tiny, Pop. She was early, and there were all these problems. After she was born, I spent the first two months with her in the hospital. I rarely saw him, and we never saw his parents. He rarely came to see her even though he didn't have a job and spent all day doing nothing. It was weird, but I really didn't care, ya know? 'Cause I had Trix taking up all of my energy."

I stopped to take a shuddering breath. *I had to just get this part over with. Just give him the story—no exaggerations, no emotion. Just get this shit over with.* "He finally got a job up in Portland, so we moved up there. I'm not sure why, but he started getting pissed all the time. Everything set him off, but I just figured it was shit with his new job. I thought things would get better. I was so caught up in the move and getting Trix situated that I just didn't see it coming." I shook my head. "One day, he came home, and the living room was a mess because my girl was fussy. I remember that toys were all over the floor, and laundry was all over the place, too, because I was trying to catch up. He came in and just started talking in this soft voice. It was eerie because I could tell he was pissed, but his voice never changed. Before I knew it, he walked over and punched me. Right in the stomach."

By this time, I was breathing hard but trying to keep it under control because my ribs were on fire. I didn't even notice the tears streaming down my cheeks and into the hollow of my neck until Pop handed me the handkerchief he always kept in his back pocket.

"You know I can take a punch…you know I can. It's not even a big deal normally," I insisted as I wiped my face.

I was raised in the life. There was honor in being able to take whatever someone threw at you.

"It wasn't even that I was surprised really. I mean, I knew it was coming. I could tell by the way he was standing, the way every single muscle in his body seemed to tighten up. But Trix was less than three months old, and I had a C-section. I don't think I was totally healed yet…or something…because it was the worst pain I had ever felt. Ever. It knocked me off my feet. He didn't care, and he wasn't sorry. It wasn't like I had done something wrong, and he was punishing me for it. He wasn't pissed at me. It was like he enjoyed it. After that, it was like he knew he could get away with it, and no one would know. Every single thing I did. Everything set him off. It was like it wasn't even about me, you know? He just needed an outlet, and I was his personal punching bag. He didn't scream or trash the house. It was only me he went after."

I paused again and closed my eyes as I remembered every punch, every kick. "I could take it. I was strong, and I knew I could just deal with it—at least until Trix was a little older and in school. I figured if I could just make it that long, then I could figure something else out. He's a stockbroker; it's not like I couldn't take anything he dished out."

As I told Pop the abbreviated story of the last five years of my life, I felt like an idiot. Who stays with a guy that beats her bloody more than once a week? What the fuck had I been thinking? I scooted myself up carefully on the pillows. I didn't want to tell Pop the last of my story while lying down although I wasn't sure why it would have mattered.

"Last week, Trix didn't put her toothpaste away after she'd brushed her teeth before bed."

I saw my father's body, which had been tensed to the breaking point before, turn to forged steel.

"He grabbed her out of bed. She had already been asleep when he got there. I came running into the room as he started to shake her. Pop, she looked like a fucking bobblehead! Her poor little neck was just jerking with every shake, and there were tears running down her face. When I got there, her eyes just sort of shifted to the side, and I know she saw me because she started to whimper. It was like she was asking me to make it stop." I clenched my hands together on my lap, realizing they had begun to shake. In fact, my whole body was shaking, and I had been so engrossed in my story that I hadn't noticed. "I charged at him and tore her away. Before I even set her down, he was punching me in the back. She knew if he was angry that she should go sit in her window seat, and she did. Thank Christ. She sat there, trembling, as he turned on me."

I closed my eyes as I remembered that night. "He beat the holy hell out of me, Pop—right in front of my four-year-old daughter. I thought he was going to kill me. I couldn't get out of bed for two fucking days. I've been peeing blood for a week. Trix made kitchen runs because I couldn't make it down the stairs. When he would leave for work in the morning, she would crawl into bed with me and lie there all day. She tried not to move because every time she did, it was excruciating for me." I shook my head. "I couldn't let her see that again. I thought I was being so sneaky, but you've seen her. She's so fucking quiet."

I had done it. I made it through my entire story without breaking into hysterics. Now, I just had to brace myself for my father's reaction.

"That motherfucker. I'm gonna kill him. But first, he's going to hurt," he replied calmly.

I knew that this wasn't just an overwrought father who was talking big about avenging his daughter's honor. My father never made threats, and while I had never feared him once in my entire life, I knew everyone else did. I always knew that Pop was different from the other dads. It was why I had run as far and fast as I could, why I'd married the first guy who asked, why I'd never told Trix's biological father that I was pregnant. Ironically, I had decided early on that his life was not the life I wanted, and yet, when I needed a safe haven, this was the only place I wanted to be. I was slowly figuring out—five years too late—that this was where I belonged.

My father belonged to the Aces MC. The Aces controlled the gun trade on the West Coast from Fresno to Vancouver. All of them had rap sheets, and many of them had outstanding warrants. They lived by their own rules—the law of the club—and once you were in, you were there until you died.

Pop wasn't just a member. He was the vice president.

"Why didn't you come home, love? You know I would have taken care of you," he said.

"I couldn't, Pop." I looked down at my hands, so he wouldn't read anything on my face.

"Well, it's water under the bridge now, I suppose." He sighed but looked at me knowingly. "I don't want you to worry anymore. It'll be taken care of."

I wanted to argue, but this was what I came for, wasn't it? I knew what the Aces were capable of, and I also knew that I belonged to them. No one messes with an Ace.

After a few tense moments, he spoke again. "Tell me, why would you give that beautiful granddaughter of mine an awful name like Trix? What the fuck is that? A cereal?"

I giggled softly. "It's short for Bellatrix. Bellatrix Colleen."

"Ah, Colleen is a good Irish name. Where the hell did you find Bellatrix?"

A raspy voice that I thought I'd never hear again answered from the doorway. "Bellatrix, a star on Orion's belt. It's Latin for female warrior."

I was afraid to look up. I knew he would be here, but I hoped against hope that we wouldn't cross paths. It seemed silly in hindsight since the clubhouse wasn't really that big. The odds of us completely missing each other were slim at best. I clenched my hands so tightly that my knuckles turned white before I finally glanced up at the man I'd thought I knew so well five years ago. If I thought I could get through this without my secret becoming known, I was mistaken.

For there, standing in the doorway, was Dragon, and he was holding our daughter in his arms.

## Chapter 3
## Dragon

I hadn't seen her in five years. The minute Poet got a phone call from the gate, I felt the hairs on the back of my neck stand straight up. I knew it was her. I was instantly brought back to when we'd first met. It was at my party—the night I'd gotten my cut.

*I was well on my way to being shitfaced the first time I saw her. Not the best beginning, but I swear, the minute I saw her, I sobered up pretty fuckin' quick.*

*I had spent the first few hours at the party doing anything I could to ignore the pain from the recent and massive tattoo on my back—a reminder I would have forever. I was an Ace for life. There would be no running, and my brothers would kill me rather than turn their backs. I knew shrinks would have a field day with my abandonment issues, but I didn't give a fuck. It felt good to be somewhere solid. If I were being honest, I was really fuckin' proud of it. After a year of probation, and even more time before that just hanging around, I was in.*

*I could feel the blood on my back sticking to my T-shirt, and every time I moved, my cut dragged against both. My fuckin' back was on fire. This was why I had been carrying around a fifth of Jack, and I was already more than halfway through it.*

*She was spectacular—all legs and tits. I wasn't sure why her legs looked so long 'cause she was actually pretty tiny, but I was sure her almost nonexistent shorts and high-heeled sandal things* had a lot to do with it. She had a torn T-shirt on, and Jim Morrison's eyes were staring at me from across her tits. Damn, the old boy had never looked so good. She walked in like she owned the joint, and I was surprised when she stopped to talk to some of the guys and their old ladies. I sure as hell had never seen her before. She didn't look like one of the girls that hung around—too little hair and too little makeup—but she really couldn't be anything else. This wasn't Sunday brunch; good girls didn't just show up in the middle of an Aces party. Didn't happen.

She seemed like she was looking for someone, but she didn't find whoever it was because, eventually, her head turned back toward me. I won't pretend like we held gazes or any of that stupid shit. She was across the room, and I couldn't even tell what color her eyes were for chrissake. I could tell she was looking at me though. After a few minutes, she turned completely away from me, and I got hard, just like that. The back of her T-shirt was cut down to her waist, and I could see a lacy green bra strap across her back.

Fuck. Me.

I just stood there, watching her, looking like a tool, as she gave hugs to the women around her—wondering how that fucking shirt stayed on. She actually hugged the boss's old lady, Vera. Shit, that bitch was hard as nails. Who the fuck was this girl?

I followed her ass out of the clubhouse. It was like she was one of those sirens who lured men to their deaths. She was holding some sort of invisible leash, and I was tagging along behind her like a goddamn puppy. When I made it outside, she was sitting on the hood *of her car with her heels resting on the front bumper of a 1969 red convertible Beetle.*

*I instantly pictured her naked and spread out over the hood of the bug while I feasted on her. Did the carpet match the drapes? Yeah, I was pretty sure she had that fiery red hair down below. No way that mop of curls on top of her head wasn't natural. Or maybe she was bare—fuck, I bet she was. Most of the bitches that hung around here kept things bare or at least trimmed short. I loved it when women kept everything waxed. It felt so much better against my face and made them way more sensitive to the scratch of my beard.*

*She seemed surprised to see me when I walked up and stood right between her legs. The girls around the club knew the score. It wasn't like I instantly crawled on top of her, but she acted like I had. She scooted back as far as she could until I caged her in with my hands resting on each side of her hips.*

*"Um, hey. Have we met?"*

*Christ. Her voice was sugar and spice and every fuckin' fantasy I'd ever had.*

*"Nope. I would've remembered that. You're fuckin' gorgeous." God, could I be more of an asshole?*

*"Ha. Thanks. You mind moving back a little? The hood of the car is still a little warm, and I'm burning my ass here." She blushed.*

*Holy fuck. I was amazed that she actually just blushed at me. Then, I realized that her ass was still on the hot car. I quickly took a step back, but not before I hooked my hands behind her knees so I* could pull her forward. She made a startled noise and grabbed my shoulders as her ass cleared the end of the hood. Perfect. She wrapped her legs around my middle, trying to get her balance, and I slid my hands up the backs of her smooth thighs, finally resting them just underneath her shorts on her ass cheeks. She was exactly where I wanted her. Now, I just had to get her horizontal or against a wall. It didn't really matter to me at this point.

"Uh, I'm good, you know? You can, uh, just put me down anywhere. I mean, set me down. I can stand. No permanent damage." She laughed nervously. "Really, we're all good."

I tilted my head down, so our faces were just inches apart. Damn, she was small. At around six feet tall, I was no giant, but I felt massive next to her. She was looking at me with these wide green eyes, all innocent. Her face was still rosy from her blush, and her bottom lip was snagged between her teeth. Damn, she was sexy. I knew I was freaking her out, but I couldn't stop myself.

I lowered my head farther, and just when she thought I was going to kiss her, I turned my head and ran my beard and then my mouth down her neck. She smelled like cinnamon, and she tasted all tangy and fantastic. I wanted to fuckin' consume her. So, I started with her neck. I bit and licked and sucked on her from her ear to her collarbone.

At first, she pushed at me like she was trying to get away, but I knew that wasn't the case. These girls came here for this. They came for a chance to fuck an Ace—or twenty—and carve a few notches on their tiny belts. I was sure some of the bitches were hoping to find a man, but that didn't happen often. Brothers didn't want sluts for old ladies. Fuck, with this girl though? I probably wouldn't care if she'd fucked every brother in the club.

I ignored it when she was pushing at me, but I sure as shit felt it when her body relaxed against mine, and her legs tightened around me. I had her. I strode to the corner of the building, still worshiping her neck and ears until we ran straight into a wall. And I mean, we ran into it. I was afraid for a second that I had hurt her until I heard a husky giggle in my neck.

"In a hurry?" she asked with a smile in her voice.

Fuck yes, I was in a hurry. Not only did I not want her to change her mind, but her legs were also wrapped so tightly around my back that they were digging into my tattoo. Her hands didn't feel any better hanging on to my shoulders. I needed to pin her up against the wall to take some of the fuckin' pressure off.

"I'm Dragon."

I figured we should get the whole name bullshit out of the way. I wanted her to be screaming my name when she came—none of that generic shit and not the name I was given at birth. Everyone around the club started calling me Dragon the year before. The name came from a throw down I had with a local dealer. Dude's name was Jorge, and I fucked his shit up. Bad. I did it quick, too. After that, the vice president of the MC, Poet, started calling me Dragon. Some shit about a story of St. George and the Dragon. I was fine with it. I earned it. New name. New life.

She'd call me Dragon, and she'd know exactly who was fucking her. "I've got a room in the house. Why don't I take you in there and make you scream it?"

She blushed again even brighter than the first time and cleared her throat. "I don't think that's a good idea, Dragon. I don't know you. You don't know me. This was stupid. I don't know what I was thinking. I don't sleep with guys who I don't know. I'm sorry. I'm sure I look like a total cock tease right now. Can you put me down?"

She was wiggling around, and her legs had dropped from around my waist, so I was holding her by her knees again. I probably would have decided she wasn't worth the hassle. I didn't have to beg women or even seduce them to fuck them. They came to me, always had. Now that I got my cut, I had a feeling they'd be even thicker on the ground. Yeah, I would have decided that she wasn't worth the trouble, but then the word cock came slipping out of those rosy lips. It didn't fit her; she didn't look like she'd even said the word before, but it was erotic as hell to watch it form on her lips. Plus, who the hell said cock tease? Fuckin' adorable.

"Christ, you're sweet," I mumbled, and I dove straight for those lips.

She had some sticky sweet lip gloss on, and I licked it off before pushing inside her mouth. I had barely gotten my tongue inside before she started whimpering and grabbing at my hair. It was like she couldn't get my face close enough to hers even though she was barely moving her lips. There was something about the way she did it though—the desperation—that made my dick twitch in *anticipation. She needed it, and she was waiting for me to give it to her.*

*As far as I was concerned, kissing was overrated—the kind of thing a man does to get a bitch in his bed. With her though, I could have tasted her mouth for days. She tasted slightly of beer, which I hadn't noticed that she'd been drinking, and her tongue kept shyly reaching out from her mouth to rub against mine.*

*"Let me have your tongue, baby," I whispered against her mouth.*

*I needed more of her. Where she was shy, I was greedy. I bit at her lips, sucking the top one and then the bottom. I groaned when she finally got more aggressive. When she sucked my tongue in her mouth, I thought I was going to pass out. Images of her sucking my cock the same way raced through my mind until her hands slid down my back. Even through the leather of my cut, her fingers felt like knives slicing through my skin.*

*I hissed. "Fuck!"*

*"What?" She looked up at me in confusion as I tried to ignore the tiny black spots dancing in my eyes.*

*"Nothing. Come on, we're going to my room. I want you naked in my bed." I dropped her legs and grabbed one of her hands, dragging her behind me to one of the side doors.*

*She tried to argue with me, but I didn't pay attention. My back was on fire, my dick was hard as a fuckin' rock, and I didn't want anyone stopping us before I could get her naked.*

*Thankfully, the door closest to us headed directly to the back hall where my room was. The clubhouse was a rectangle with garage bays on the west side that connected to a large room where we congregated. Behind that space was a long hallway lined with doors that ran the length of the room. Mine, thank fuck, was only three doors in, but we passed Grease on our way there. He did a double take as we passed and then called my name as I opened my door.*

"Stay here." *I pushed her inside, flipped the light, closed the door, and walked back toward him.*

"What's up, man?" *I asked him distractedly.*

"Hey, you sure you want to go there? Poet's gonna fuck your shit up if you go there." *He was staring at my door.*

"You really asking me about where I put my dick? Want to get a latte and fuckin' gossip, too?" *I shook my head.* "I'll see you later…hopefully, not until morning. Don't come knocking." *I gave him a look that promised retribution if he ignored me.*

*I knew Poet didn't have an old lady, and he didn't seem to have a favorite with the other bitches either. Why the fuck would Poet care? I was just drunk enough and thinking with my dick, so I ignored the questions running through my head.*

*Then, I went back to her.*

Boss dragged me back from five years ago with a few quick words.

"Dragon, quit fuckin' daydreamin', and get your ass out there with Poet. See what the fuck is going on," he snapped at me. "You too, Grease."

I shook my head and walked away from the Chevelle I was working on and out into the sunlight. I caught up to Poet pretty quickly because he had stopped in the middle of the forecourt, staring at a woman standing next to an old Corolla. *What the fuck?* That couldn't be her. The lady was wearing a fuckin' cardigan. Her hair was not the bold-as-hell red that I remembered; it was more of a strawberry blonde and sleek with no curls in sight. It wasn't her. No way. This lady would never cut up an old Doors T-shirt, making sure that she didn't mess up Morrison's bone structure. She'd never fuck a man the first night she met him. She'd never spend hours lying on his chest, telling him about the constellations and their meanings. And I could never, ever see this lady down on her knees sucking a man's cock like it was the best fuckin' lollipop she'd ever tasted.

I didn't realize how hard I'd been breathing until it started to slow. Poet was just standing there. This bitch must be lost. I thanked Christ and all the apostles. Poet mocked my thanks when he started moving—fast. He was across the forecourt in a matter of seconds, and as I watched, her mouth formed one word—*Pop.*

*Fuck. Fuck. Fuck.* I could hear my pulse pounding in my ears. Five years later, and she showed up out of the fuckin' blue. No warning and no word for five goddamn years, and she just drove in like it's nothing, like she didn't leave her dad—or me—high and dry. Fury raced through me, but I couldn't ignore the fact that my heart was beating hard against my ribs as Poet wrapped his arms around her. Then, I swear to Christ, I felt it stop as I watched her face pale and her body go limp.

After Brenna passed out, everything happened in a blur. Poet caught her, but as he started to walk past her car to bring her inside, his eyes caught on something in her backseat, and he hesitated.

"Dragon! Come get Brenna! Take her to my room, yeah?"

I was stepping forward to grab her when I realized exactly what Poet was looking at in the backseat—a kid. A kid who didn't look anything like Brenna. At first, I wondered if she'd fuckin' lost it and stolen someone's kid. Why else would she be here? Shit. Not my problem. But I couldn't move. I was frozen, standing by that piece of shit Toyota. Poet's voice was nothing more than a buzz in my ears.

I think Grease ended up taking Brenna inside, but I couldn't take my eyes off the little girl. After what seemed like hours later but had to be only minutes, Poet opened the back door and unbuckled the kid from her seatbelt. It was the strangest thing. She was crying, but she wasn't making any noise or trying to get away. She just sat there on his arm. Stoic. She was a fuckin' statue, except for those tears.

I couldn't figure out why the fuck I was frozen. I was just standing there like an asshole, a lot like the way I had reacted to seeing Brenna for the first time. Poet just kept talking to the girl, trying to get a response, but she was as closed up as a bank vault. Her eyes were darting around the yard though, so I knew there wasn't anything wrong with her. She was assessing the situation like a little general—finding all of her escape routes and possible enemies.

When her eyes lit on mine, I finally understood why I couldn't move, why my chest felt like it was going to explode, and why I was as silent as she was. I knew the reason she didn't look like Brenna. She surprised everyone in the courtyard by reaching her hands toward me. She didn't say a word, but her intention was clear. Poet looked back and forth between the two of us several times before realization dawned. The fury on his face would have concerned me if I was aware of it, but as I took her into my arms, she was my sole focus. Her face was mine. Her dark brown eyes were mine. The dimple that showed when she bit the inside of her cheek was mine. She was mine. She didn't look like her mother because she was a replica of me.

Fuckin' Brenna. The fuckin' bitch had kept my kid from me.

## Chapter 4
### Brenna

When Dragon and Trix walked through the door, my breath caught on a painful gasp. How many times had I dreamed of this? It was both a nightmare and a fantasy. I'd ached for him while my belly grew, when I felt little arms and legs reaching for the surface, when I went into labor far too soon, when they put my face under the mask and asked me to count backward, and when I woke up after my emergency C-section. The first time I'd held our child to my breast, and every moment, every milestone, every smile Trix had given me reminded me of him.

He'd been the face I sought in my memory every time my husband hit me. Every time I thought I had reached my breaking point, I'd pictured the crinkles at the sides of his eyes and the feel of his beard on my neck. He'd been my strength but also the reason I had waited so long to leave. I'd used him to keep me strong because the man I had known would have been everything I needed. He was also everything we had to stay away from. This life was not what I wanted for my girl, and I knew once he saw her, we would never be able to leave—ever.

I sat motionless as I watched Trix with her arms wrapped tightly around Dragon's neck. Had she ever held anyone but me like that? I didn't think so. As soon as she caught a glimpse of me, she wiggled to be let down. Dragon held her a little tighter, and she turned to him with a questioning gaze. He finally gave her back a little rub and set her on the hardwood floor.

"Mama!" she called quietly as she ran to the bed.

Before she could reach me, Pop raised his arm as if to slow her down. "Be careful, lass!"

Trix stopped instantly. It would have been comical if not for the sheer terror on her face, her little arms quickly shielding her head. She looked at me for direction.

"Aw, Pop," I whispered, "my girl is always careful. Aren't you, baby? Climb on up here with Mama. I need a snuggle from my favorite girl."

She hesitated for a moment before rushing toward me again. I felt Pop's body tense as she stumbled, but she did exactly as I knew she would. As soon as she reached the side of the bed, opposite of Pop, she slowed to a crawl and gingerly climbed up next to me.

"There's my girl. Mama fell asleep. Did you see that outside? I'm such a dork. We've been driving so long, and once we got here, I just fell right asleep in my pop's arms, just like you do with me! I'm sorry if you got scared, honey. Did I freak you out?"

She was so snug against me, and I couldn't see her face, but I felt her slowly nod her head into my side.

"Ah, well, there's nothing to be scared of here. This is my pop's house. Remember I told you about him and his long beard that's just like Santa? You can just stay right here by me for a while until you get comfortable, yeah? Then, maybe we can go outside and play for a bit," I whispered to her.

While I spoke softly to Trix, Dragon watched us from the doorway. I could feel his gaze on me, but I stubbornly refused to look up. Call it cowardice, but I wasn't ready to see his reaction to Trix. I knew he was pissed, and frankly, I had enough on my plate at the moment.

For a couple of minutes, we all sat in silence, and I used that time to take inventory of Pop's room. Other than the god-awful yellow walls, things hadn't changed much. While I was growing up, we'd had a house in town, so I'd rarely seen the inside of this room. The few times I had been in here, I'd tried to memorize everything.

Pop had bookshelves filled to overflowing with everything from Tolstoy to Kerouac. That was how he'd gotten his name. I never knew what he did in Ireland or how he'd ended up here. We didn't speak of it, but I knew that the old president had started calling him Poet because of the books he carried around folded in half in the back pocket of his jeans. The man may have spent his life running guns, but he sure as hell was well-read.

Trix finally raised her head from my armpit and started talking. I thought she was trying to whisper, but as any parent with a four-year-old knew, four-year-old whispering was her talking at a normal level with her hand covering half of her face.

"Is that Dragon? Like you told me? The Dragon that rides on a motorcycle? He said his name was Dragon." She paused for a second, her little eyebrows raised to her wispy hairline. "Is it?"

At her words, Dragon took two steps into the room and then stopped. I slowly lifted my head and met his eyes, but I couldn't read his expression. "Yeah, baby," I replied, not looking away from his face, "he's the one I told you about." For a moment, I thought I saw surprise and a flash of pain, but whatever emotions he was feeling were quickly masked.

"Okay. Who's that?" she whispered again, pointing at my father.

"Ah, that's my pop. Your gramps. I bet if you said hello he'd give you a licorice."

As long as I could remember, Pop had carried around little ropes of licorice, and I hoped that little habit hadn't changed. Licorice was Trix's favorite. I loved it that she shared that with Pop, and I'd been giving them to her since she could chew them. When we were away, it made me feel like they had a connection somehow even though I'd never expected for them to meet.

"Well, now, I do believe I have a piece here somewhere…" he muttered, patting his pockets as if searching.

I could tell that Trix was trying to work up the courage to say something. Her little body was wiggling in anticipation as she sat at my side. Finally, Pop grabbed a piece of candy off the top of his nightstand and looked expectantly at Trix.

"Hi, Gramps," she said quietly and then held out her hand, waiting for her treat.

"Well, there you go, pretty girl. You want another, you're going to have to get out from under your ma's arm there. Ya can't be getting the sheets all messy, or I'll be sticking to them for a month!" he exclaimed with raised eyebrows.

Trix giggled softly next to me. It was my absolute favorite sound in the world, and I could tell Pop was thrilled he was wearing her down. Trix was funny. She had always been very shy around people she didn't know until I gave her the all clear. Once that happened, she warmed up to them pretty quickly. Her trust in me was absolute, and after the week we'd had, I wondered if her trust was misplaced. It had always been harder for her to warm up to men for obvious reasons, but the fact that I was so comfortable with Pop must have made her feel secure. She had surprised me with Dragon though. I was definitely not comfortable around him. However, since they walked in and he put her down, she'd been glancing his way as if waiting for him to speak. I couldn't even wrap my head around the fact that she had been clinging to him like a damn spider monkey when they walked in.

After a few minutes of talking to each other, Pop and Trix decided it was time to go get a soda and find something to do outside.

"Give your mum a kiss there, Trix, and we'll go find ya something to play with. Your mum needs to rest."

Panicked, I looked at Pop, trying to find a reason for them to stay with me. I opened my mouth to say something, anything, but Pop stopped me with one look. *Shit*. He wasn't going to let me put this off. I realized then that Pop had said Trix was "out with the boys" earlier, but she had really been outside with Dragon. He had lied, and I knew there had to be a reason. He knew. I thought I'd have more time to prepare myself—to prepare Pop—and then ease my way into telling him. He must have been pissed when he realized. Screwing a member's daughter was one of the worst things a brother could do, right behind being a rat and screwing their old lady. It was an issue of respect. You didn't touch something that didn't belong to you. Dragon was in huge shit, and I'd just put him there. Well, to be honest, I'd put him there five years ago.

Once Trix and Pop left the room, the silence was deafening. I wasn't sure what to say without sounding like a complete idiot, so I just kept quiet. However, the longer I stayed quiet, the more oppressive the quiet became. I looked anywhere but at the man standing inside the doorway. I was hoping if I just ignored him, he'd go away, and I wouldn't have to deal with anything yet. When he finally spoke, I jumped in surprise and clenched my teeth.

"She's mine?" His voice was low and guttural.

"She…" I whispered then cleared my throat. Then, I cleared it again. Why couldn't I just say it? "She's…yes, she's yours."

We both knew the answer before I said it. It was obvious by looking at her, but when he heard my confirmation, he lost it. He swung around and punched right through the drywall next to the doorway. He punched it twice more before turning back around. Then, he stalked toward me. I had never been afraid of him even though I knew the life he'd lived. This club was my home, and anything that happened behind the barbed wire fences was familiar. Violence was a way of life here, but it wasn't the out of control madness I had been living with. It was passionate, not methodical, and always, always under control. It was a violence that I understood. Only the strong survived here, survival of the fittest. That was why when he grabbed me by the throat and pushed me against the headboard, I just swallowed nervously and waited.

"You fuckin' cunt! You come back here, shaking your college ass, begging for a fuck. You don't tell me who the fuck you are. So, I wake up the next morning to find you out with your fuckin' daddy, who happens to be my vice president. That shit is so fucked. It might as well be a death sentence, and you fuckin' knew it. But as scared as I am, I'm willing to fuckin' lay it all out. Make you my old lady. Make it right. All of a sudden though, you're fuckin' gone. You just leave without one fuckin' word to me. I'm left here, holding my dick and thanking fuckin' Christ that I didn't say anything to Poet. Fuckin' gone for five years. No one hears from you. Now, you come back, and I find out you had my daughter and didn't tell me FOR FIVE FUCKIN' YEARS?" His voice was steadily rising, and by the time he finished, he was roaring in my face.

"Some other guy has been playing Daddy to my daughter?"

I could feel my pulse pounding under his fingers where his hand had slowly tightened. In all my years growing up surrounded by badass bikers, I'd never seen anyone so angry. Tears were silently rolling down my face. I knew why he was so angry. I knew, and I had always known what I'd done when I left. He'd never had a family until the club, and when I left him, I'd left him not only on shaky ground with the only family he had, but I'd also taken his unborn child with me. It was an unforgivable sin, and in that moment, I was completely ashamed.

His hand was still around my throat, his face inches from mine when we heard a throat clearing from the doorway. I was afraid to look away from Dragon's face as I heard an old familiar voice.

I could barely see Grease from the corner of my eye, and with what little thought I could spare, I was surprised at how big he'd grown. The boy I'd remembered was never scrawny but definitely lean in build. The guy was now built like a tank. His shoulders barely fit in the doorway.

"Dragon, brother, we need to ride. We need to be in Boise by morning. We just got the call." Grease paused like he wanted to say something else, but instead, he just told Dragon, "I'll meet you outside."

The hand at my throat loosened a little and then tightened again as if it had a mind of its own. Then, I felt each finger slowly loosen again until he completely let go.

"Don't you fuckin' go anywhere, Brenna." He pointed a finger inches away from my nose. "I might have let you go before, but that was before I knew about her. If you leave, I'll find you. You don't want me to fuckin' chase you. You don't wanna see what I'll do if I have to chase your ass."

With those parting words, he stormed out of the bedroom.

It was official.

I was screwed.

## Chapter 5
### Brenna

Trix and I spent the next two weeks living out of Pop's room at the club. When I made my plan to move in with Pop, I'd had no idea that he'd sold our little house on the outskirts of town two years ago. He'd been living in the clubhouse indefinitely because he couldn't think of a reason to keep up a house that he never spent any time in. I understood his reasons, but I was still a bit sad that the house I'd grown up in was gone. I'd dreamed about Trix swinging in the old play structure in our backyard, jumping on my old bed, taking a bath in our old claw-foot tub. The whole situation was nothing like I had planned, and I felt like I was on a merry-go-round that wouldn't stop.

The first night, right after Dragon had left, we'd had dinner with the club president and his old lady. The man who was feared all along the Western seaboard was nothing but an uncle figure to me, and I was actually pretty excited to see him. When I was growing up, his old lady, Vera, had been the only mother figure in my life. She'd taught me about tampons and bought me a bra, and I couldn't wait to show Trix off to them both. Unfortunately, dinner didn't go quite as I'd planned—at all.

Their house was right outside the compound, but in order to get to it, we had to drive. This was done so in the event of any warrants being written for club grounds, their house would be exempt. I didn't even know if the deed was in either of their names. Probably not.

The house wasn't anything fancy, just a two-story, wide front porch, regular-looking house. All of the upgrades were invisible to the untrained eye. They had video cameras, bulletproof glass, a panic room, and God only knew what else. When you drove up though, it looked like any other house in the middle of nowhere.

When we got to the house, Vera came rushing out to give me a hug. I knew she would. She was a bitch to most people, but if you knew her well, like I did, you knew that underneath all of that hardness was the clichéd heart of gold. When she got done hugging me, I reached down and pulled Trix to stand in front of me.

"This is my daughter, Bellatrix. Trix, this is Auntie Vera. Can you say hello?" When I introduced them, I prayed that Vera wouldn't see what I did when I looked at Trix.

I knew my prayers were in vain when she raised her eyes to me. All softness was gone out of her face, and for the first time, she looked at me with the hard eyes she showed to everyone else. *Shit.* This wasn't going to go easily.

While I introduced Vera to Trix, Pop was busy walking toward the front door where Slider, our president was standing. I looked up to catch them talking in low voices before they went into the house. He didn't even say hello to me—not even after five years. *Fuck me.* He was pissed.

I hoped that word hadn't reached him yet about Dragon and me, but I should have known better. Bikers gossip like teenage girls. He'd obviously not yet told Vera, and I was glad that I would be gone long before they had that discussion later. Some old ladies felt free to bitch and moan at their men in front of anyone, but Vera never did. I didn't know if it was just her natural reserve or the fact that she was married to the president—probably a little of both.

Dinner was awkward. When Vera brought out her pot roast, which was my favorite, my mouth watered at the smell, but looking at her face, I wondered if she was going to refuse to let me eat it. She hadn't said one word to me the entire time I'd been here; she just stared me down. I knew she was pissed, and I knew she was disappointed, but I wasn't willing to explain myself. For one, Trix was right there with me, and she had no idea what was going on. And two, I knew I was going to be interrogated by Slider later. There wouldn't be any evading it, and I was going to have to answer every humiliating question. I only wanted to do it once.

Trix was the baby elephant in the room, and she had no clue. She never noticed that only Pop spoke to me. Both Slider and Vera reserved all of their smiles for her.

Pop and Slider spoke about club business as usual, and listening to them made me wonder if Trix's vocabulary was going to double by the end of the night. She had never heard so many different variations of swear words before. It didn't bother me too much though. She would've learned far worse things if I had stayed with my husband. This was definitely a lesser evil.

I tried to picture my name-brand baby growing up in the life, and I couldn't do it. I couldn't imagine her in ratty jeans or band T-shirts, playing in the hose next to the compound, all dirty. I wondered if this would change her entire personality. I started to imagine my innocent Trix with tattoos and facial piercings, and I had to stop a giggle in my throat. The tension at the table was killing me, and I was getting so anxious that it began bordering on hysteria. When I started to seriously wonder if I was going to have to buy some non-toxic soap in order to wash Trix's mouth out, Slider finally stood up from the table.

"Vera, why don't you and Trix see if you can find a movie to watch? Poet, Brenna, and I are going into the office for a bit." He looked at Trix. "See if you can find a good one, yeah? Then, maybe you can have some ice cream or somethin'."

Trix looked to me for permission, and even though I didn't want to, I smiled and gave it to her. *Dammit.* Once Trix and Vera left the room, I followed Pop and Slider into his office. It was a medium-sized room that should have been a bedroom, but Slider had converted it into his cave. A walk-in closet was transformed into a large safe, and the windows were covered in dark curtains. Growing up, I had always wondered what he kept in that massive safe until I realized the business he was in. Then, I'd avoided it at all costs.

"Take a seat, Brenna. I think we have some things to discuss."

I took a deep breath as I sat on a black leather chair facing his massive desk. Pop walked around and stood at Slider's shoulder, and my stomach clenched even though I knew that he was standing in his designated place. He always stood at Slider's left during business meetings. It still hurt like a bitch that he wasn't standing by me though. He was making a point. His allegiance was to Slider.

That was when I knew I was going to like this conversation even less than I had envisioned.

Slider didn't hesitate before he started speaking. "You fucked up, Brenna. You fucked up in so many ways I'm not even going to list them all because we would be here all fucking night. Let's just discuss the biggest transgressions, shall we?"

This was not the man I had known all my life. This was a stranger. He had never before talked to me in this tone of voice, and I knew that just as with Vera earlier, I was finally seeing the man that everyone was afraid of. I was suddenly more scared than I had ever been in my entire life, ironically, while I was in the same room with the men I'd thought would protect me. My throat clogged with tears, but I raised my chin. Never let them see you sweat. Predators fed on the weak.

"You left your pop, my vice president, with no notice and no backward glance. You showed no respect for this club and the family that raised you. You fucked a member, putting his life in jeopardy. You lied to that same member about who you are and who your father is."

At this point, I tried to speak. "I didn't—"

But he quickly stopped me by slamming his hand down on the top of his desk.

"Do not speak unless I tell you to!" he growled. "You left your family, your club, your father, Vera, and your president without a word. You left the man you fucked over without a word. And you left carrying that man's child and didn't disclose that information until today. Correct?"

I wasn't sure if I was supposed to speak yet, so I just sat there while he stared at me. I figured silence was my best course of action.

"Answer when I ask you a question."

I looked back and forth between my pop and Slider, but their faces held no emotion. I couldn't read them. I had never seen this side of either of them before. "Yeah." I cleared my throat. "That's correct."

"Fuck, Brenna. If you were any other woman, you'd be beaten black-and-blue for this stunt you fucking pulled. I wanted to go after you when you left, but your pop stayed my hand. Said if you didn't want this life, that it was your choice. I didn't agree with him, but I didn't push it either. Now, it seems as if I should have pushed it. 'Cause you fucked and then fucked over one of my lieutenants. Left him with his baby planted in your belly and then married some dumb fuck. Fucked over a man I respect. A good soldier. Made him lie to his brothers. Made Grease lie for him." He looked down at his hands as if searching for patience, and when he lifted his head, I could tell he had found it. "You're here now. What? You decided now that your life isn't all rainbows and butterflies and that maybe you're not too good for this club all of a sudden?"

I knew his question was rhetorical, so I kept my mouth shut.

His next words made it drop back open though. "You're not leaving again. We let you go off on your own, and it was a mistake. I only make mistakes once. If you pull some shit like this again, I'll wash my hands of you. I won't let Vera at you as a matter of respect for your father, but you will not be allowed on club grounds again. You will no longer have the protection of the club that has protected you all of your life. Do you understand me? You will be fair game to every fucking cartel and rival club in the continental United States. You're Poet's daughter. Men will try to use you to get to me, and you know what they will to do to you. If you step foot off club grounds with the intention of taking off, I will leave you to the wolves. Are we fucking clear?"

My mind spun with scenarios, and none of them were things I wanted to contemplate. I had to stay here? I had planned for this to be a stopping-off point—a place where I could get my troubles taken care of and get my daughter protected. Then, I could leave and start a life somewhere new—safe from the monster I was married to and away from this life that I had never wanted.

I'd never imagined these sorts of ramifications. I'd never guessed that my desertion would have such a widespread impact or that my safe haven would become a prison. Could I just leave now? Pack my shit and take off? I might be able to hide for a while, but I knew someone would find me eventually. As afraid as I was of what Dragon would do when he came back, I knew having him track me down would be the best-case scenario. Without the club protection, a giant bull's-eye would be painted on my back. I started to panic, and I stood up, but Slider's next words had me dropping back into the chair.

"Brenna. If you leave, your daughter will not be going with you."

I looked at Pop for reassurance, but his face was completely blank, and he was staring over my shoulder. I couldn't believe that he would let them take my daughter from me. This was my father. He loved me. He'd never allow something so heinous. Right?

"Pop?" I whispered. My throat was clogged with tears.

When he looked at me, I knew I would get no help from him.

"You are my daughter. For that reason alone, I have tried to protect you from the ramifications of your actions. I can no longer help you. You chose this. You knew what would happen before you left. You knew the consequences of coming back. Never have I been so ashamed as when I found that child in your car. I knew from the moment I picked her up who she was. You have lived this life. You were raised in this life. Five years ago, you decided to completely disregard anything I have taught you. You fucked a member. You knew what would happen, yet you continued on your course. I am the vice president of this club."

I could tell he was keeping his temper in check by the very precise language he was using. His voice was so calm it was eerie.

"The minute you drove in with a member's child in your car, every brother in the club knew. My daughter had fucked a lieutenant, and I, her father, had done nothing about it. I had known nothing about it. With your actions, you have fucked the respect that I have earned. You fucked the respect that Dragon had earned. You put Grease in the intolerable position of choosing between his brothers.

You have compromised the trust that the brothers in this club must have in order to survive and do their jobs. You, who knew the consequences more than most, have caused dissention among the members."

By this time, tears were rolling down my face, and my breath was hiccupping in my chest. I couldn't meet his eyes, and I couldn't even tell if he was looking at me because my chin was tucked so far into my chest. The shame I felt was multiplied tenfold by the shame I heard in Pop's voice. What the fuck had I done?

"I love my granddaughter. I bear no ill will toward Trix; she is completely innocent in this. But you, Brenna? You made your bed, and you will fucking lie in it."

Pop calmly walked to the door and quietly left. It would have been far easier if he had yelled at me, if he had thrown things or hit me. The controlled movements and calm voice had freaked me out far more than any outburst ever would.

"Brenna, look at me," Slider called from across the desk. He waited until I raised my face before he spoke again. "This subject is over. If we have an understanding…" He looked at me in confirmation, and I nodded my head. "We don't have to speak of it again. However, we do have other matters that need attention."

"What other matters?" I asked in a gravelly voice.

"The matter of where you and Trix will be living. You know you can't stay in the clubhouse. Bitches don't live in my clubhouse. I let you stay there, and the boys will want their fucking whores staying there, and then old ladies will be wondering why they can't stay there, and then I'll have catfights and screaming in my place of business. There's a small house that is currently not in use on the east end of the property. I've already sent some bitches over there to see what needs to be done before you can move into it."

Well, that was a surprise. Even though he was angrier than I'd ever seen him, he was still watching out for us—sort of. I understood about the clubhouse though. I was so grateful that I almost missed his last words.

"You'll let Dragon stay with you if that's what he chooses. I don't know what the fuck he's gonna do when he gets back. He's got his old lady living with him though, so I can't move your ass in there."

Even after all the turmoil of the past hour, his words were still enough of a surprise that I felt like I had been kicked in the stomach. Dragon had an old lady. Well, fuck, that hurt. Bad. I guessed I shouldn't be surprised. I'd left him. I'd been gone five years. I had absolutely no hold on him. That didn't mean it didn't hurt like a bitch though. Thoughts of his old lady raced through my head. What did she look like? When did they get together? Was she a bitch? Was she nice? What was their relationship like? How did he treat her? Where did they meet? How long after I left did they hook up? Was he with her when I was here before? What would she think about Trix? Would she even want to meet her? Would Trix have to visit them at their place? Fuck, would she want to be a stepmom to Trix? In all the scenarios I had imagined before I got here, Dragon having an old lady never factored into them. As I was trying to process this information, Pop walked back into the room and sat next to me.

"Brenna, you need to tell Slider what you told me. Everything. Don't leave anything out. We need to decide what to do."

I really didn't want to do it. The Slider I knew before, the uncle, I would have had no problem pouring my heart out to. He was a confidant and a protector. This Slider? Well, I didn't know what he was. I didn't know how he would react. Would he think I deserved everything I got for what I'd done to the club? I didn't think I could handle that. I decided to give him an abridged version of my story. I didn't omit anything, but I also didn't let myself feel any emotion. I told the story as if it had happened on some Lifetime Movie-of-the-Week, not to me and not to my daughter. Halfway through my story, Slider stood up and started to pace. He didn't say a word, just walked back and forth in front of Pop and me until I finished. Once he knew I was done, he sat back down.

"Who is this fucker? We'll take care of it," he said firmly.

That was all he said, and I was brought back into the fold. I held back my tears of relief and finally told him the name that I had refused to say since I left our house in Portland. I had some sort of weird belief that if I said his name, he would appear...sort of like Beetlejuice. I knew it was stupid, but I held on to that belief.

"His name is Anthony Richards."

"Is he gonna cause you problems? Follow you?" Slider asked me, seemingly unconcerned.

"Probably. He's going to be pissed I took off. He's going to be livid when he figures out where we are. *If* he figures out where we are…"

"He don't know where you came from, Brenna?" Pop asked incredulously.

"Uh, no. He didn't. I didn't bring it up, and he didn't ask." My face blushed with shame.

I never wanted them to feel like I was ashamed of them, but the truth was that I used to be embarrassed by our life when compared to Tony's. His family was wealthy and very clean-cut, and so different from ours. I hadn't wanted to bring him back here in his preppy clothes to see my family covered in tattoos and leather jackets. Not to mention, half of the boys on the property had outstanding warrants in more than a few states.

Looking back, I wished I had brought him here. Maybe someone would have noticed what I hadn't. Maybe seeing me surrounded by men that most people would cross the street to stay away from would have given him enough incentive to keep his hands off me. Maybe he would have dumped me and never looked back. Maybe the last five years would never have happened.

## Chapter 6
### Brenna

The day Dragon got back started out normally or as normal as it could when I was sleeping with my four-year-old daughter in my pop's bed at a biker compound. Slider refused to give us our own room because he didn't want to set precedence, so Pop took one of the empty rooms while Trix and I stayed in his room. This seemed a little ridiculous to me, but I guess I could see his point. He wanted to make it very clear to the members and their bitches that this was a temporary situation. Bitches could stay the night in the guys' rooms; however, they were not moving in. Ever. He didn't want the drama of old ladies and club skanks fighting it out over living arrangements. What a clusterfuck that would be.

By noon, Trix and I were sitting at a picnic table eating sandwiches in the sunshine. It was mostly quiet around the club these days with so many of the boys gone with Dragon and Grease. I couldn't remember the last time I had felt so calm. Not at peace as there were too many unknowns for that, but I felt safe. Trix and I hadn't left the compound once since that first day. Vera had offered to go to a local Walmart to get us some clothes and toys for Trix, so we didn't have to leave. Thank God because I wasn't sure that I could have made myself go outside the gate.

When I heard the roar of pipes coming up the driveway, I was instantly alert. There were far too many for it to be just one of the boys who had left on some errand. It was at least six or seven.

Dragon was home, and it was time to face the music. I didn't want to freak Trix out, but I really wanted to get inside before they reached us. It was too open out here, and most everyone was inside at this time of day. I was really hoping that Pop would take Trix while Dragon and I had our little conversation. I quickly picked up our garbage and swung Trix down from her seat, but I wasn't quick enough. The boys rolled into the forecourt followed by a dark gray sedan with tinted windows. Dragon was parked closest to us, and we immediately made eye contact as he climbed off his bike. His face was completely emotionless as he started in our direction. He didn't make it far before I heard a voice behind him and felt Trix's body push hard against the side of my leg.

"Ah, Brenna, my wayward wife. Come give me a kiss, love, and then it's time to go."

I slowly turned my head in the direction of the voice and felt my heart begin to race. Standing beside the sedan was my husband, flanked by two massive boogeymen with no necks. Tony looked the same as ever—expensive suit, loafers, and not a hair out of place. However, I could tell by the look on his face that he was livid.

How the FUCK did he get in here? Was Slider giving me back? Thoughts raced through my head, and for a moment, it was as if I had tunnel vision. All I could see was Tony, and all I could hear was his voice over and over. *Come give me a kiss, love. Come give me a kiss, love.* This couldn't be happening. I snapped back into reality when I heard Trix's whimper. I glanced down to see her watching the scene unfolding before us with unblinking eyes.

Dragon was striding toward Tony. His back was to us, but by the set of his shoulders, I knew he was pissed. Just then, Slider and Pop came out of the clubhouse followed by a group of the boys. This was not going to end well for anyone. Tony was outnumbered, but by the look on his face, he knew he was safe. I wasn't sure if he thought I would just willingly leave with him or if Slider would hand me over, but I knew he thought this was going to end in his favor.

When Dragon was about five feet from Tony, Slider finally spoke up.

"Dragon, stop! Grease, grab him!"

By now, the goons had pulled weapons, but so had the brothers. It was a standoff between them with Trix and me in the thick of it. Dragon didn't act like he'd heard Slider as he strode toward Tony. He was moving at the same steady speed as before, completely ignoring the guns pointed him. Before Grease could grab him, Trix called out from beside me.

"Papa!"

I was pretty sure my jaw dropped. What the fuck? I knew she wasn't talking to Tony. She only ever called him Daddy. She never made noise around Tony, especially when he was in a mood. She called my Pop Gramps. This was fucking weird, and even with everything going on around us, I was completely focused on her as she called out again.

"PAPA!"

Dragon finally pulled himself to a stop about two feet from Tony. Only his head turned when he glanced back at us. As soon as he made eye contact with Trix, she took off running. I tried to catch her, but she slipped past me and weaved her way through the bikers like they were obstacles on a jungle gym. The kid was fast, and I was practically chasing her through the bikes. Once Dragon saw what she was doing, he quickly turned and started toward her. Within seconds, he swung her up on his arm, and she buried her face in his neck. You couldn't even see it behind his beard. I slowed to a stop a few feet from them, out of breath and freaking the fuck out. What the hell was that? All of a sudden I realized that Tony had seen the whole thing, and my head slowly turned to catch his reaction.

He was laughing, but it wasn't genuine. It was sinister and mean, and I thought for a second my sandwich was going to force its way past my throat.

"Ah, so you finally told her who her daddy was. Interesting timing although I guess you really couldn't help it, could you? The little spic looks just like him."

I was shaking so badly I thought my knees were going to give out. Dragon strode over to stand next to me as I faced Tony, and he lightly rested his hand at the small of my back. I could feel his body thrumming with energy, and I knew that if he weren't holding Trix, Tony would already be a dead man—goons or no goons. I wasn't sure where to look, what to do, or if I should say something. Tony was here in my safe place, and I just wanted him gone. Why couldn't he leave us the hell alone? He stood there with that arrogant grin on his face and called my daughter a spic. I couldn't even wrap my head around it, not to mention the fact that she wasn't even Hispanic. Dragon was Native American.

"Look at that, a perfect little family. You fucking him yet, Brenna?" His eyes turned to Dragon. "She's really good once you've knocked her around a bit. All that moaning and groaning. She hardly ever makes noise otherwise. Boring as hell, really. I guess you already knew that though. It was so satisfying, you know? Fucking her after I knew she went slumming here. Knowing that I had her, and some white trash piece of garbage was waiting around for her. I didn't know who she slept with when she came back here, and I really didn't care. But the kid looks just like you, so you must have been the one. Unfortunately."

Dragon slid Trix off his arm and handed her to me, never taking his eyes off Tony. "Take her inside, Brenna."

"Dragon, don't—"

"NOW, Brenna. Go now." He gave me a little shove.

I wasn't about to watch what Dragon was going to do, and I really didn't want Trix to see it, so I did as he told me.

As I passed Pop, he grabbed my arm lightly. "Bring her to Vera and come back out here, lass. I don't think we'll be able to control the situation otherwise."

Vera was right inside the door as I rushed in, and I almost didn't see her. She stood at an angle facing Tony and the goons with a shotgun propped in a little notch in the doorframe. You couldn't see her from outside, but I was surprised I didn't remember where she would be standing. This was her place during anything that went down in the forecourt. She could easily shut and bolt the door from this position, but she would still be able to protect Slider's back. Slider hated it, but eventually, he came to accept it. He was the one to notch the doorway, so she wouldn't have to support the shotgun for long periods of time.

"Vera! Can you take Trix?"

"You goin' back out there?"

"Yeah, Pop told me to come back out."

"Sure. Come here, Trix. Let's let your mama go bust some heads."

I handed Trix off to Vera and took a deep breath before going outside. I wasn't sure what Pop was expecting me to do once I got there. I had no control over either of the men in my life—obviously or I wouldn't be in this damn position in the first place.

## Chapter 7
### Brenna

When I got outside, I glanced at my surroundings. Tony was still by the car, Dragon was still facing him with no expression on his face, Pop was standing closest to me by the doorway, and Slider was a few feet in front of Pop. He sounded like he was trying to diffuse the situation without freaking the fuck out. I couldn't quite hear what he was saying. My ears seemed to be buzzing, but I had a pretty good idea. The fact that Tony had come onto Aces' property uninvited was huge.

This fucking mess was getting worse by the minute. It wasn't like the boys could just take Tony and his henchmen out. The Richards family had a lot of connections, probably not as many as the Aces, but definitely enough to cause them more trouble than the boys wanted to deal with. Police and FBI could be swarming all over the compound by the time the sun went down if Tony made one phone call. Slider was livid that Tony had come onto the property, but he was also in the very awkward position of harboring a Richards…even if it was just a wife.

While I tried to figure out what exactly Pop was expecting me to do, I saw a flash out of the corner of my eye and realized that another car was racing up the driveway. Who the hell was that? I was pretty sure that it was a woman. I couldn't imagine one of the boys driving a little silver convertible. Why the hell was she driving so fast? I could see brown long hair flying around her face, but that was pretty much it. I was curious, but I needed to focus.

Pop glanced over at me, and I figured it was now or never. I slowly walked toward Dragon, trying to remain unnoticed, making no sudden movements. There were a lot of guns pointed at the little piece of ground I was walking to. The tension was so thick, I felt like I was going to choke on it. Both Dragon and Tony turned their eyes to me as I walked between them. I was keeping my back more toward Dragon because I was close enough to them now that I couldn't face them both at once. As pissed as Dragon was at me, I would rather have my back to him. Tony was unpredictable. Dragon was solid. I also wanted to make clear that my alliance was with the Aces. I could still hear Slider droning on behind me, trying to smooth things over…well, sort of. He was telling Tony to get the fuck off of his property before he buried him. Well, that was not what I was expecting to hear.

I had barely reached Dragon when the driver of the little silver convertible bounced up between us. She was gorgeous. Her hair hung to her ass and was silky, like one of those shampoo commercials. And the ass her hair was swishing across was fantastic. She was wearing leggings and a snug, little T-shirt, and I could tell that her tits were fake—very fake and very perky. She was a freaking goddess.

"Baby! What's going on?"

And she was obviously stupid. All of these thoughts rushed through my head in a matter of seconds before I realized I was standing next to Dragon's old lady. His beautiful, built, idiot old lady. Fuck me. Was I in a comedy of errors for fuck's sake? Seriously? She shows up now? Yeah, I really should not have been surprised. This was how my life went. Just when I thought things couldn't get worse, they did. She wrapped her arms around his waist, oblivious to the fact that his hands were still hanging down at his sides, and his face was like stone. Every single person had gone completely silent. Was this bitch insane or just completely self-absorbed? I couldn't tell.

Tony began to laugh. "Ah shit, Brenna. God, and here I thought you were fucking the spic again. Shit. No way in hell is he leaving her for you. There is no comparison. Damn." His eyes darted between her and me and then settled on me. "You don't want to leave yet. Okay. You won't be here long. You thought you'd just come back here and have your little family? Run back to this guy and start up all over again? That bitch has got a ring on her finger. There isn't shit here for you. You'll come back, baby. You'll pay for it, but you'll come back." With a nod to his goons, he climbed back into the car.

I didn't say anything back. I didn't refute it. I just stood there, completely still. If I moved, I knew my body would shatter into a million pieces, and I'd never find them all. All these boys knew me. Even the ones I hadn't grown up with, I'd met in the past two weeks. They knew I had left my husband. They knew he was crazy, and Pop and Slider were giving me sanctuary. They knew Dragon was Trix's father. However, as I stood there, I also realized that they knew how hot Dragon's old lady was, that he was married. They knew that I never stood a chance with him, which shouldn't have even mattered because I'd told myself over and over that I didn't want him.

But I did. I did want him, and now, I felt hollow. Tony insinuated that I'd come back to find Dragon, and he was right. I'd told myself I was running to my Pop, but I wasn't. I was running to Dragon the same way I had always run to him in my mind when I needed him. Every time Tony beat me and every time he raped me, I'd closed my eyes, and I was with Dragon. I didn't see anything, but his face close to mine, whispering like the night we met. And now, all of these men knew that my own husband looked at me and realized I wasn't even in the same league as Dragon's wife.

I didn't know how long I was there before someone grabbed my arm, and I realized I had just been standing, eyes closed, in the middle of the forecourt, slowly falling apart while Tony left and the boys dispersed. It was Pop.

"Let's get you inside, lass. You're shaking like a leaf."

I let Pop drag me toward the clubhouse even though I really didn't want to go in there. The silver convertible was still parked in the yard, and I knew she was still around here somewhere. I also didn't want to face everyone after that parting gift from Tony. What a fuck. He knew just what to say to inflict the most damage, and as usual, he had perfect aim. God, I was humiliated. I must have looked so pathetic, standing there in my own world while everyone left. Fuck.

The clubhouse was noisy when we walked in, and thankfully, no one seemed to notice us arrive. I glanced around to find Trix, but I couldn't see her anywhere. She was supposed to be with Vera, but Vera was on Slider's lap near the bar. No Trix. Pop had gotten a few steps ahead of me, but he stopped when he noticed I wasn't moving. I was twisting from side to side, frantically searching for my girl in this room filled with bikers, and I couldn't see her anywhere.

Had Tony somehow gotten ahold of her? No, he couldn't have. She was with Vera; there was no way he took Trix. But where the hell was she? I'd only been outside for fifteen minutes tops. What the fuck was Vera doing with Slider? Where the *hell* was my child? My heart was thumping in my ears, and I was breathing so fast I could see black spots dancing in my vision. Oh god. Where was she?

I felt Pop come up behind me, and his arm stretched out over the top of my shoulder, his finger pointing to the corner of the room where a few leather chairs sat. He didn't say a word, but I instantly saw what he was pointing at—Trix. Thank God.

My relief was short-lived when I realized Trix was on Dragon's lap, and his bitch was seated beside them. She had a confused look on her face as she was watching Dragon talking to my girl. After a few seconds, her eyes turned cold and mean.

Oh, hell no. He was out of his fucking mind bringing that bitch around Trix, and she was out of hers if she thought she could glare at my girl that way. I made my way slowly and calmly through the clubhouse, trying in vain to get by unnoticed. I really didn't need every member of the club seeing our little family drama unfold like a daytime soap opera. I should have known that they would be watching though, especially after the show outside.

As I reached where they were sitting, I could hear her voice. It was annoying, a little high-pitched and babyish, which was more than a little disturbing, but the words coming out of her mouth stopped me cold.

"Baby, she's just precious. Look how beautiful she is! I can't believe you have a daughter! Well, I guess *we* have a daughter, huh?" She glanced up through her eyelashes.

Was she fucking serious? I ignored her for the moment and walked directly to Dragon and Trix.

"Mama!"

Trix launched herself at me, and I caught her up in my arms, sniffing her hair that smelled like a mix of baby shampoo and Dragon, and feeling grateful after the scare I'd had when I first walked inside. I really shouldn't have worried. I knew Vera would guard her like a lioness, but after all of that shit outside, I was feeling a little jumpy. I couldn't imagine something happening to Trix. What would I do without her? She was my everything.

I set her down and pointed her in the direction of Pop on the other side of the room. "Go see Gramps, yeah? I'll be over in a minute." I gave her a little shove, and she went skipping happily over to Pops, completely unaware of the undercurrent flowing between the three adults she was leaving.

Once I saw her off, I didn't even hesitate. I turned around, swung my left arm up, and caught Dragon's old lady under her chin.

Then, I swung with my right and busted my knuckles across her teeth. She went down easily. Obviously, the bitch wasn't from around here. Dragon stood up as if to stop me, but he didn't move when he saw the look on my face. He just tilted his head as if wondering what I would do next.

I stood above her, and she was lying on the ground with her mouth bleeding and a dazed look on her face. I crouched down close to her head, grabbed her hair, and told her in a low voice, "My daughter has a mother. She is not and never will be yours. You stay the fuck away from her. And if I ever see you look at her again the way you were earlier, I'll fucking cut your eyes out with a dull spoon." I dropped her head and stood up, looking around the room.

Everyone was watching. Most were looking at me with respect, some in surprise, and Vera had a big-ass grin on her face. I didn't care. I just wanted to get the fuck out of there. I walked to Pop and grabbed Trix.

"Come on, baby girl, it's nap time. Want Mama to lay with you for a bit?"

I walked toward Pop's room, nodding along to Trix's chatter, but I didn't hear a thing. The whole time I thought, *Shit—right back where I started.*

I was the princess of the Aces MC, and I had the bloody knuckles to prove it.

## Chapter 8
## Dragon

The trip to Boise went pretty well. Thank God we didn't have any problems because my head just wasn't in it. I didn't want to leave the compound, but I had a job to do. There wasn't a whole lot that would stop Slider from sending me where I was needed, and having Brenna show up with my kid sure as fuck didn't rate a day off. I understood it even if I didn't like it.

It took us close to two weeks to get the shit loaded and moved—longer than usual, but not enough to cause any problems. The buyers would pick it up at the new warehouse after a sit down with Slider, but I didn't deal with that shit. I just moved things and dealt with other problems as they came up. We didn't shit where we lived, so I was always moving stuff from one place to another. Buyers never showed at our warehouses; we always found a neutral zone to make the drop. Slider had called a couple of times to get an update, and each time, I could tell there was something on his mind. At one point, I'd asked about it, but he'd made it clear that we would talk about it when I got back, so I dropped it. He'd tell me if it were important.

By the time I got back to the compound, I was sweaty, tired, and hungry. I wasn't looking forward to talking to Brenna. I couldn't wrap my head around the fact that she'd kept my kid from me. Who the fuck did that? I also wasn't looking forward to the retaliation from Poet. It was going to fuckin' hurt. I knew he wouldn't kill me, but I'd probably wish he had by the time he was done. Fuck. I couldn't wait to see my girl though. I hadn't planned on having kids. I just didn't see the point. Sure, with Brenna, I'd thought about it—during that one night we'd had. But since her? No way. I didn't need that shit complicating my life.

Kendra, the bitch I'd been with for the last year, sure as hell wasn't mother material. The chick could barely tie her fuckin' shoes. She worked though. She had a banging body. She let me do whatever the fuck I wanted to her, never complained, and seemed completely ignorant to anything outside her little bubble. Plus, she was a freak in bed. Fuckin' crazy.

About two months ago, she'd started bitching about a ring, so I'd bought her one. She'd wanted to think that meant I was going to marry her, but I wouldn't. Only one woman ever had the chance of that, and she had taken off for parts unknown for five years.

As I pulled up to the gate, a guy in a dark gray sedan pulled up behind us and rolled down his window. He looked like some kind of businessman, but he had some heavy-duty guards with him.

"Hey, I need to speak with Slider. Can we follow you up?"

The douche was smiling at me. Fuck it.

"Yeah, sure."

If Slider had a problem with this guy, I would have known. I didn't recognize him, but I could tell he wasn't a cop. After all these years, I could smell a cop from a mile away. I didn't see any reason to lock him out.

We pulled up to the garages, and I saw Brenna and Trix walking toward us from a couple of picnic tables in the grass. God, she was beautiful. She hadn't straightened her hair, and all of the little corkscrew curls were everywhere. She and Trix were both wearing sundresses, and they looked like they had gotten a little sun. Brenna looked at me nervously. I heard the douche start talking behind me, but it took me a second to realize what he'd said because Brenna turned her head, and the blood drained from her face. I glanced down at Trix, who was trying to climb under Brenna's skirt. It took me a moment to understand what was happening. They were shrinking. Right in front of my eyes, my beautiful girls were pulling into themselves—as if they would disappear if they could just get small enough, quiet enough, still enough. Then, it hit me. Only one reason why the guy behind me could get a reaction like that.

I didn't even think. This had to be the guy who had beaten the hell out of Brenna. The guy she was running from. The guy who had made my girl so scared she went completely silent at the first hint of a threat. I didn't know how the fuck she'd gotten caught up with this douche, who was so different from us in his expensive suit and fuckin' comb-over, but it didn't matter.

I was going to fuckin' kill him.

I got within about five feet from him when I heard Slider start yelling for Grease. Two steps closer, and I noticed his men drawing down on me. It didn't matter. They could fuck off; my boys had my back. There wasn't a fuckin' thing anyone could do, short of killing me, that would keep me from killing him where he stood. Then, I heard Trix yelling for her papa. Who was she yelling at? She couldn't be running to the dick in front of me. That didn't make any sense.

I turned my head to look at her, and she started running right toward us. What the fuck was Brenna doing, letting her run through this shit? I glanced quickly up at Brenna but couldn't meet her eye. She looked shell-shocked. Then, she started chasing Trix. Right as I looked back at Trix, she ran as hard as she could and leaped onto me like a fuckin' monkey. As I lifted her up on my arm, she buried her face in my neck, and I could feel her soft, warm breath against me.

"Papa, Papa, Papa, Papa."

My little warrior was fuckin' whimpering in my ear. I heard Brenna run up behind us, and I took a couple steps back, so Trix was closer to our boys and farther away from Brenna's husband and his goons. I didn't want her anywhere near the fucker.

We ended up right next to Brenna, and I could feel her shaking, so I slid my hand to her lower back. I might be pissed as hell at her, but I couldn't stop myself from trying to comfort her. She was scared shitless, and I needed to touch her. I wanted to wrap my arms around her and promise her he'd never touch her again—that I'd take care of her, that she didn't have to be scared. Instead, I just put my hand above her ass. She didn't seem to notice the move. She just stood there. Every man in the forecourt knew what it meant though. It was possessive, claiming.

This motherfucker needed to know I was never giving them back. He started spewing fuckin' garbage, and my stomach clenched so tight that I thought I was going to vomit all over the pavement like a fuckin' pussy. Jesus Christ. Brenna was still as stone beside me, and I knew I needed to get her and Trix away from here. She needed to go now before I pulled my gun and shot this fucker. As soon as I pulled my piece, all hell was going to break loose, and I didn't want them in the middle of it. I handed Trix to Brenna and told her to get the baby inside. She tried to argue, but I gave her a little shove to get her moving. I didn't know how long I was going to last before I lost it.

As soon as she stepped through the doors of the clubhouse, I pulled the gun from the back of my pants, but before I could raise my arm, Slider was there. I'd never seen him so pissed. I couldn't shoot the douche as long as Slider was standing in the mess, so I just bided my time. I'd get the fucker.

"What the fuck are you doing, Richards? You think you can come on my grounds, to my club, and start running off at the mouth? You have a goddamn death wish?" The guy opened his mouth to protest, but Slider cut him off. "I know who your father is, and frankly, that doesn't mean fuck all to me. You come here again, uninvited, and I'll let Poet have you. He'll make you wish you were dead long before he grants that wish. Now, get the fuck off my property before I fucking bury you."

I realized Brenna had walked back up next to me just as I heard the rumble of Kendra's car. What a clusterfuck. God, I hoped the bitch would be smart enough to stay in the car.

Nope. Of course not. She walked right between Brenna and me and wrapped her arms around me as if she didn't notice the fifteen guns pointed at us. God, this bitch was dense. I didn't move. I couldn't make myself put my arms around her as I stood with Brenna up against her husband. This chick was mine, and she had been for a year, and I couldn't touch her. Brenna was looking at Kendra like she didn't know what to make of her when Richards started blasting his mouth off again as he got ready to leave.

He got back in his car and took off, but I couldn't pull my eyes from Brenna. She looked as if she had shrunk into herself. I didn't know how it was possible, but she looked smaller than she had just seconds before. Her eyes were closed, and she was taking fast, shallow breaths. Her arms were wrapped around herself, and she was holding her elbows so tightly that I could see her fingers were completely flexed.

I went to take a step toward her when I remembered Kendra hanging on me. Fuck. The dickhead was right—there was no comparison between Kendra and Brenna. Even with her skin pasty white and pain written across her face, Brenna would win hands fuckin' down.

Poet walked up to Brenna and made eye contact with me. I knew he'd take care of her, so I left her standing there in the driveway while I took my old lady inside. Kendra seemed completely unaware of what she had stumbled into, and as we walked inside, she was talking about how much she'd missed me and all she'd done the past two weeks. Was she always this goddamn annoying? Her voice was like nails on a chalkboard, and I had never realized it until I heard Brenna's husky rasp again. And why was this bitch talking like a five-year-old? Did she think it was attractive? She hadn't done that shit before I left. I was going to have to put a stop to it. If she pulled that shit while I was fuckin' her, I'd go soft, guaranteed. I wished she would just shut the fuck up for a second.

Trix ran to me as soon as we sat down in some chairs in a corner of the room. I pulled her close as she called me *Papa* over and over. Her hands clenched in the neck of my T-shirt, stretching it to shit, as she burrowed herself under my cut. My girl was a little shaken up, so I just held her tight and let her do her thing.

Kendra had a strange look on her face, but I didn't give a shit. I'd tell her and be done with it. If she had a problem with my girl, she could kick rocks. Bitches were thick on the ground; it wouldn't take long to find someone else. Fuck, if I were being honest, I wouldn't go looking. There was only one woman I wanted in my bed.

I glanced back up at the door, but Brenna still hadn't come inside. Fuck, but I really wished I were out there, taking care of her myself.

## Chapter 9
### Brenna

I ended up taking a nap with Trix, and we didn't see Dragon again that night. I assumed he had taken his bitch home to make sure she didn't need to see a dentist. I was pretty sure I'd knocked some shit loose. I was having a hard time coming to terms with the fact that I had just knocked a chick out like a common club slut. It was not my finest moment.

However, as I went over it again and again in my mind, I realized that I would do it again. I was pissed that Dragon had an old lady, but that wasn't her fault. She probably didn't even know about me—not that there was much to know, except for one night five years ago. I hated the fact that he was with her, but I wouldn't have hit her for it. However, I could not and would not let her anywhere near my daughter. The way she looked at Trix still made me want to hit something. Who the hell glares at a four-year-old little girl when she thinks no one is looking?

Eh, I just hoped I wouldn't have to see her again.

After dinner that night, Slider informed me that we would be moving into the little house the next day, so I needed to pack my shit. I was relieved to get away from the tension in the clubhouse, and I couldn't wait to sleep without a flailing Trix. I missed having our own space, but I was also really nervous about being out there alone. One of the guys would always be close to our place, but that didn't keep my fears at bay.

The morning of the move was rainy and wet, and I had never been so glad that we didn't have many things with us. Pop and I packed our stuff into my little car, and I followed the dirt road to the far edge of the property. The house was nice...little but nice. It had a front porch that begged for a rocking chair and plenty of grass out front for Trix to play in. The inside had an open floor plan, and the front door opened directly into the living room with the outdated kitchen behind it. A little hallway held a bathroom and two bedrooms the size of postage stamps, but I figured they would work just fine for Trix and me. We didn't need much space.

I spent the day familiarizing myself with where everything was, making a grocery list so Vera could run to the store for us the next day, and getting our little house all finished.

Vera had rounded up the old ladies, and they all pitched in furniture and other household stuff I forgot I'd needed until I had to start with nothing, giving us things they didn't need or just didn't want. The ugly couch in the living room was still in really good condition, so I was pretty sure that was in the *didn't want* category. Nothing in the house matched, and it caused a little anxiety in my chest when I looked around. I was used to keeping things immaculate, and even when our little house was clean, it would never look the way I'd been forced to keep things before.

Trix and I both had beds and dressers in our rooms, which I was really thankful for. My queen-size bed seemed massive in my room with little space to walk around the edges. The dresser had actually been moved into the closet because there wasn't enough room otherwise. Trix's room was perfect though. Her twin bed fit perfectly against one wall, and she had plenty of room to store her toys and clothes. I couldn't wait to take Trix to pick out some character bedding and matching curtains. At Tony's, Trix's room looked like something out of a magazine, all muted colors and cream carpets. I wanted her to have a kid's room here—a room where she could leave Barbies on the floor and put those little glow-in-the-dark star stickers on the ceiling.

The rooms were situated in such a way that Trix's windows faced the front of the house and mine faced the back. I was happy with this at first because it meant that sunlight would be streaming through my windows at the ass crack of dawn and not Trix's. I could sleep through it; she could not. It took me about one minute before the fact that our rooms faced different sides of the house started to freak me the hell out. If someone were trying to get into Trix's room, I wouldn't even hear it. I'd be completely oblivious. Shit. I didn't know if I even wanted Trix that far away from me. What if something happened? I decided to push my thoughts away in favor of puttering around our new little house. I could stress about our bedrooms when it was time for bed; there was no need to worry this early in the day about sleeping arrangements.

Grease showed up not long after we got settled and pulled me out of an almost panic attack. Trix was sitting on the ugly-ass couch, playing with her Barbies, when I let him in, and I was busy trying to rearrange things to my liking. Having him in the house made me far less jumpy, and I wondered what the fuck I was going to do when he went home that night. I didn't know if he had a family, if he lived at the club, if he had a house in town, or if he was annoyed about babysitting me. It was funny how many things changed when you disappeared for five years, how life went on when you expected it to stay the same. I opened my mouth to ask him about his life when he tilted his chin to the kitchen and started to walk toward it. Once we got there, he answered some of my unasked questions.

"Fuck, Brenna. You've really got yourself in a situation this time. Tony fuckin' Richards. Goddamn, you go big when you fuck up. Fuck Dragon, take off for parts unknown, marry Tony fuckin' Richards, have Dragon's kid, come back here screaming sanctuary, and drag the whole fuckin' club into your shit. Fuck me, his dad has police in his pocket!" He shook his head.

"I didn't know he was an asshole! Yes, I knew his dad had political connections, but I never expected to come back here. I figured we would just live a normal life. You know, where you aren't afraid the police will come knocking! He seemed normal!" My voice was defensive.

"Normal? The guy's a fuckin' sociopath!"

"I was pregnant; I had to do something. I was twenty-two years old and barely graduated from college. I'd never had a fucking job, and I had a baby on the way. I wasn't exactly thinking straight," I mumbled, knowing that I couldn't argue with the sociopath statement.

"Don't *even* bring that shit up to me, Brenna! You could have come back here. Where your family is. Where the father of your child is. You completely fucked Dragon over, and you completely fucked me over. I fuckin' saw you that night, and I had to decide if I should say shit to Poet. I was fuckin' walking on eggshells for two months after you left, not sure what was the right thing to do. Finally, I think, yeah, just bury that shit. No one needs to know. You were an adult, made your own decision, right? Not my business. Then, you show up with Dragon's kid, and all that shit comes out again. *Goddamn it!*"

"I'm sorry! I'm so sorry for everything! I'm sorry I put you in that position. I'm sorry I bailed on everyone. I'm sorry I married that fuck. I'm sorry, okay?"

Shit, I was crying and trying to keep my back to Trix, so she didn't wig out. I'd known Grease my whole life. He was the kid of an Ace, just like me, and he'd gotten his cut right before I left for college. I felt like shit for taking off and leaving him to deal with everything. I just felt like shit, period. I wiped my face and looked to the floor, trying to get my emotions under control when, seconds later, I felt his arms around me. He smelled exactly the same as he had five years ago. He'd always worn the same deodorant, and the smell of it mixed with cigarettes reminded me of home.

I heard the door open behind me and felt Grease lift his head, but I didn't turn around. If there were a threat, he'd let me know. I was just going to rest where I was for a moment.

"The fuck, brother?" I heard Dragon rasp.

Shit.

I dropped my arms and turned around to see Dragon walking toward the kitchen and Trix jumping off the couch to catch him. He wasn't even aware of her though; his eyes were locked on me where Grease's arm was hanging loosely across my shoulders. His jaw was tight, and he looked far from happy. I wasn't ready for any drama, so I sidestepped out of Grease's grasp and called to Trix, who was now trying to get Dragon's attention.

"Baby, you want mac and cheese for dinner? I think we have the ingredients for homemade. I'll let you spread the cheese and crackers on top if you want," I said with a smile at my girl.

She loved helping me cook dinner, and I'd become adept at finding things for her to do that would cause little mess and had little chance for injury.

"Okay, Mama! Can I have strawberry milk, too? Macaroni and cheese is delicious, but it's better with strawberry milk. Can we have broccoli, too? With ranch?"

It amazed me how far she'd come out of her shell after only being here for a few weeks.

"Sure. How about you go play for a while in your room, get your PJs and your trainer on, and I'll call you when it's time for you to do your part?"

"Okay," she called as she turned and raced toward her room.

When I looked up from where Trix had been standing, I noticed the tension in the room was gone, and both men looked surprised.

Why did they look like that?

Grease started laughing softly. "Delicious? That kid's a trip. I didn't realize she could even talk."

"Of course she can talk, dumbass. She's four. She's been talking for like three years."

Had he never been around kids before? What was the big deal?

"Brenna, she's said about three words since you two got here. One of those was Papa, and the other two were yes and no," Dragon spoke softly beside me.

When I glanced up, he was looking down the hallway toward Trix's bedroom proudly.

After a minute, he looked back at both of us. "My girl is smart. 'Mac and cheese is delicious,' she says." He shook his head and mimicked Trix. "Fuck me, Brenna, she sounds just like you."

Grease and Dragon stayed for my homemade macaroni and cheese, and Trix was in her element. She chattered on and on about everything she did that day, detailing where she put every single toy in her new room. The guys just sat there patiently, jumping in when they could, and generally agreeing with everything she said.

It was a good night even though I was hyperaware of every move Dragon made, and I often found myself staring at him. God, he was beautiful, more beautiful now than the last time I'd seen him. He seemed bigger, more in charge of his body. Every move he made was calculated for maximum effect. His shoulders were broader, and there were more lines around his eyes. The soft look I remembered was now directed at Trix, but I didn't mind. Quite the opposite actually—it was a thousand times better when I saw it directed at my baby.

I wondered what he saw when he looked at me. Yoga had slimmed me down the last couple of years, so I wasn't carrying around any extra baby weight, but things were definitely softer. My boobs weren't quite so perky, my hips were rounder, and my stomach would never again be as flat as before. For the first time in five years, I was concerned about how I looked naked. It was ridiculous. He had an old lady, a wife. He wasn't here for me. I knew this, but it didn't stop me from worrying about the stretch marks covering my stomach or the heavy-duty bra I needed to keep the girls looking chipper.

Trix pulled me from my thoughts with a doozy straight out of Tony's mouth.

"Mama and I go to yoga. We bend and stretch and make animal shapes. We go, so we don't get fat. Nobody loves fat girls. Mama runs, too, so she doesn't get a fat ass again, but I don't run."

I had never heard her say anything like it, but I knew she had heard far worse from Tony. I gaped at her a moment before I got my shit together enough to snap, "Trix, don't say ass! That's not an okay word for kids to say! Plus, you're not fat. You won't ever be fat. We go to yoga because it's fun." I could feel my face burning in mortification, but I calmed my voice, so she didn't think she was in trouble. "Bedtime, kiddo. Head in and brush your teeth. I'll be there in a minute."

When she made a face that said she was about to argue, I gave her my I-mean-business look, and she quickly scrambled down from the table and ran toward the bathroom.

*Shit.*

I didn't want to make eye contact with either of the men at my table, but I could feel the hostility in the room, and I knew I had to get it over with. When I looked up, they were both staring at me in disgust, and I could feel my face that had started to cool down start burning again.

"You tell her that shit?" Dragon rumbled. "You tell our four-year-old that she has to work out or she's gonna get fat?"

"Of course not! I wouldn't do that! She's four for fuck's sake!"

"Well, she didn't come up with that shit on her own!" His voice was steadily rising.

"Calm down, Dragon." Grease tried to diffuse Dragon's anger. "You know that shit didn't come from Brenna's mouth."

"Brother, you got no part in this. Shut the fuck up. This is between Brenna and me. I don't even know what the fuck you're still doing here. I get here—you leave. I'm not puttin' up with another dick playing Daddy to my girl, and I'm sure as fuck not letting you sniff around Brenna."

Grease's body snapped away from the back of the ugly gray dining room chair he was sitting on. He looked as if he were about to launch himself at Dragon. I could tell that the words coming out of Dragon's mouth weren't for Grease. He was pissed, but his anger wasn't because of anything Grease had done.

Dragon wasn't going to back down, and by the way Grease was looking at me to gauge my reaction, I knew the situation would only escalate if I didn't get him to leave. He was looking at me to see if I needed him to stay, and while I was thankful for it, I could tell that it was just pissing Dragon off that much more.

"You better just go, Grease. I'll see you later, okay? I gotta get Trix in bed anyway."

He nodded slowly and rose from the table, eyeballing Dragon in a way I didn't think was prudent at the moment. He needed to get out of here. What the fuck was he trying to do, getting protective of me all of a sudden? I wasn't some helpless fucking maiden. I could take care of this shit myself. *Ugh. I wished someone would save me from testosterone and pissing matches.*

Once Grease was out the door, the intensity in the room increased until it was almost choking me.

"Okay, Brenna, we played house. Got you all fuckin' moved in. Time for you and I to have a chat. Do whatever shit with Trix you need to do, and then get your ass back out here."

Dragon stood up and went to take a seat on the couch while I sat at the table, trying to figure out how to stall. Fuck. I could try to do the dishes, but I knew that wouldn't work. There was pretty much nothing I could do to put it off, so I needed to pull on my big girl panties and just get it over with.

When I went to check on Trix, I found her sprawled out across my bed completely passed out. She had her blanket pressed under her cheek and a book wedged under her stomach. God, I loved her.

She was the best thing I'd ever done, and I'd do anything to keep her safe—even if that meant I had to leave her. That was why I needed to get back out to Dragon. If I couldn't keep her safe, if I wasn't here to raise her, he would be. I pulled the book out from under her and to stall for time, I brought it back into her room and put it away. Unfortunately, there wasn't anything to straighten or clean in there since we'd just moved in. It was time to face the music.

## Chapter 10
### Brenna

When I got back into the living room, Dragon was sitting on my couch, bent over with his elbows on his knees. I stood for a moment at the edge of the hallway taking him in. He had taken off his cut, and it was thrown over the back of the couch. His boots were sitting by the front door. It made me a bit nervous to see that he was making himself comfortable in my place. His powerful shoulders and arms were on full display in a greasy white T-shirt, and I had to consciously stop myself from imagining them naked…and braced above me. He looked dejected, sitting there like that, as if he had the weight of the world on his shoulders. I took one quiet step closer to try and get a look at his face, and that was when he noticed me standing there.

"Get your ass out here, Brenna." He didn't raise his head when he continued, "You're not putting this shit off. We gotta talk."

I tentatively walked toward him, wondering where I should sit. We only had the ugly ass couch in the living room, and I really, really didn't want to sit next to him. I guessed that put me on the floor. I didn't like it, but the alternative was standing, and I knew I needed to sit for this conversation. As soon as I got close enough to him, he reached out, grabbed my hand, and yanked me down next to him.

"Quit fuckin' stallin'!"

Now, I could see his face. He wasn't dejected; he was pissed.

I scooted as close as I could to the edge of the couch and pulled my feet up, so I could wrap my arms around my knees. "I'm not stalling," I told him wryly. "I know we need to have this out. I'm just not looking forward to it."

"Trix asleep?" His face softened at Trix's name, but it immediately went back to the stern expression I was beginning to expect.

"Yeah, she crashed out on my bed before I even got in there. It's been a busy day, and she was exhausted." I couldn't meet his eyes, so I looked over his shoulder to the kitchen as I spoke. "About what she said at the table—"

He cut me off before I could finish. "Tony say that shit to you? Tell Trix she was fat?"

"Yeah, well, I didn't ever hear him say it to Trix. He's said it to me. It's not a big deal. He's a dick. We both know he's a dick." I laughed nervously. I didn't want to discuss my relationship with Tony to Dragon. I already felt like a complete moron for staying so long. I didn't need him to think it, too.

"It's a big deal, Brenna. You're tiny. You've always been fuckin' tiny. Trix doesn't need that shit in her head. What's she gonna think when she looks at you and how small you are, and then thinks she's gotta be fuckin' smaller than that?" He looked at me incredulously. "She's got a bit of me in her, too. No way she's gonna be as small as you."

"Well, let's be honest here. If that's the worst thing she remembers from Tony, we're good." I was trying to reassure him, but I noticed immediately that it was the wrong thing to say.

The tension in the room amped up considerably, and it was emanating from Dragon. He was wearing the same look I had seen during the confrontation in the yard—complete and utter fury. My heart started pounding in my ears as I waited for the blowup.

When he spoke, his voice was so low it was almost a whisper. "You better explain that, Brenna. Right fuckin' now. Seems like tonight is the night for explanations."

I swallowed hard and curled into myself even more. "You know he had a heavy hand—"

"Trix around when he did that shit?"

"Yes," I whispered. "Not always but enough. She knew to get safe when he started, so she only saw the beginning most of the time. I tried to keep her away from it. I knew she shouldn't see it, but sometimes, I didn't have time to prepare," I continued, desperately trying to explain myself, speaking faster and faster until my words were tumbling over each other. "Sometimes, he didn't give me time to get her out of the room. She knew to leave once it started and to stay out of his way. I just didn't have any warning! There was no reason for it. Sometimes, he just came home and started in. Other times, it would be the middle of the day or at night after dinner. There weren't any signs. He wouldn't even seem angry!"

"Our daughter had to learn how to *hide*?" he questioned, throwing his arms up in the air for emphasis.

I instinctively jerked back into the couch, wrapping my arms around my head. I couldn't help it. I started sobbing. My chest started to ache with all of the pressure that had been building since I'd come back to the compound. I knew it was my fault our daughter had such horrendous memories. I'd stayed there, waiting it out, thinking Trix would forget as soon as we could leave. I'd thought it wouldn't be forever, and we could manage until I figured something else out. I'd put our daughter in danger because I didn't know where I would go if we left. I deserved Dragon's anger, but I didn't know if I could handle it. I was already on the edge of becoming useless. How much could a person take before she completely fell apart?

I was so ashamed that I had cowered like some weakling. Where was my backbone? I wasn't afraid of Dragon. What the hell was wrong with me? Once I'd started crying, it was like everything hit me head-on—the fear for Trix, the stress of our escape, the relief of feeling safe for the first time in five years, and the fear of Tony when he'd come to the compound. It all left me overwhelmed with conflicting emotions.

"Baby?" he questioned, his voice soft in a way I hadn't heard in five years. "Baby? What the fuck? I'm not gonna hit you."

He ran his hands up and down my legs, waiting for me to look at him. When I didn't raise my head, he wrapped his arms around me and pulled my still curled-up body into his lap. I couldn't get the tears under control, and I was embarrassed that he was seeing me like this.

"Hey, calm it down," he whispered as he rubbed my back in slow circles. "You're safe. That fucker's never gonna lay another hand on ya."

At his words, I took a shuddering breath, wrapped my arms around his waist, and pressed my forehead and eyes into his throat. He felt so good—big and strong and safe. I didn't ever want to climb out of his lap again, and he seemed to agree. When I pulled my legs down into a more comfortable position, his arms tightened around my back in warning.

"Stay where you are. Just 'cause you turned into a sobbing mess, don't mean you get to escape again."

I could hear the smile in his voice.

"You're such a jackass." I giggled a little in response. "I'm sorry," I whispered. "I usually don't burst into tears at the slightest provocation."

"Eh, you've had a rough month. Don't worry about it." He started rubbing my back again. "We gotta figure this shit out though, Brenna. I'm still so pissed at you for keeping her from me. That's so fucked."

"I know," I sighed. "I'm sorry for not telling you who I was. At first, I was going to, and then I was just so afraid you would stop if you knew. I figured, what was one night? And then, it all changed. You were different than I thought. I wanted more, but I knew I'd fucked-up, and if I said anything, my pop was going to kill you—"

"That shit's water under the bridge. It's over. Was I pissed? Yeah. But it's over." His hand gripped my hip as he spoke, and when he was finished, he started rubbing my back again. "I wanna know about Trix and how you ended up with that douche bag."

"I met Tony in college. We dated a bit, but I was busy during my senior year, and we sort of just stopped seeing each other. We weren't together when I met you, just to be clear." I looked up at him, and he nodded. "I thought he was hot, but there was no spark, you know? It was all sort of boring. When I got back to school, things were really busy for a while, and Tony was calling nonstop, wanting to see me. I had other shit to do, so I blew him off all the time. But then, when I realized our fun had some consequences, I needed a friend, so I called him up."

Dragon's body went completely still. "And he just welcomed you with open arms even though you fucked someone else and were carrying another man's kid?"

"I wasn't sure how he would react at first, but yeah, he just sort of stepped right in. I was thankful, you know? That he would step up like that. I was a mess. I missed you, I missed my pop, and I didn't know what the hell to do. If I should come back or not? When he asked me to marry him, it just seemed like the easiest choice."

At my last sentence, Dragon dropped his arms, leaned away from me, and pressed against the couch. "Why the fuck didn't you come to me, Brenna? I woulda taken care of you! What the fuck? You just forget about me? Just decide to pretend you didn't fuck me any way you could get me?"

Since he wasn't holding me, I stood up and took a step away. "I don't want this life! I don't want to deal with club whores and my man going out on runs and being in danger all the time. I don't want to visit you in prison. I don't want Trix to have this life!"

"Ah, so you just decided you're too good for this life. I get it. Too good for me, too good for your pop, too good for Slider and Vera. So, instead, you marry some fuckin' psychopath. Fuckin' smart move, Brenna. Genius." His voice had risen, and he was standing so that we were only a couple inches apart. "Tell me, what makes you think you're so much fuckin' better than us because it sure as shit isn't your fuckin' common sense!"

"I don't think I'm better than you! My pop is a good man, no matter what he does for a living, and Slider and Vera love me. I'm not better than them!"

"Oh, so it's just me then?" Dragon started to chuckle low and mean as he rubbed the back of his neck. "You know what your dad did in Ireland? Why he just up and moved here?"

"No. We don't talk about it, but obviously, you have something to say." I folded my arms across my chest. This was going nowhere, and he had taken everything completely out of context.

"Your Pop? You know the 'good man' you were talkin' about? He was known as the Butcher of Dublin. A fuckin' hit man."

I was shaking my head. "What are you talking about?" I couldn't even wrap my head around what he'd just said, but he was still talking.

"Your dad was a hit man, Brenna. He killed people for money. He was deep in one of the clubs over there, and when things got too hot, he came out here and hooked up with Slider's pop."

"Why are you telling me this?"

I couldn't understand why he would bring this up now. I'd always known that my pop had a past. It wasn't something that was hidden; we just didn't talk about it. This explained so many things in my childhood, and I was going to talk to Pop about it soon, but seriously, why was he bringing it up?

"You run and take my baby with you, but it's not because of your pop who was a fuckin' hit man. And it's not because of the club. What the fuck is it, Brenna? You're too good for me? Didn't want your baby growing up with a grease monkey for a Daddy? Got a problem with the color of my skin?" He was raising his voice now and was glowering down at me.

"N-no," I stuttered. I was totally shocked that he thought I saw him that way, and I couldn't get the words out to interrupt him.

"You were good, but I've had better. Those little noises you make? Damn. But that timid act you did? Not gonna lie. That shit was annoying. You almost made up for it with that sweet fuckin' pussy you've got, but now that that fucker has been in that shit? I doubt it's sweet anymore—"

He was on a roll, but I was fucking done, so I cut him off by slapping him across his face. My chest felt like it was breaking open, and I couldn't pull enough air into my lungs. The best night of my life had been one of many mediocre ones for him. One of many—that was what I was. This was why I'd left. He wanted to know why I didn't look back for five years? Then, I'd tell him, and he could choke on it.

"You want to know why I left?" My voice was wobbling, and I worked hard to control it. "I left because I was crazy about you, and I didn't want to watch you fuck around. I left because I never wanted to hear that garbage you just spewed all over me."

He raised his eyebrows at me in surprise.

"I left because I never wanted to watch you get hurt. I never wanted to visit you in prison. I never wanted to have you come home, smelling like a chick I saw at the club."

He started to interrupt, and I raised my hand to stop him.

"I was crazy about you, and you *never* said anything beyond that night. You never gave any indication you wanted more than that. I wasn't going to come back and have you tuck me away in some house while you did whatever the fuck you wanted. I didn't want you to hurt me." I chuckled humorlessly and wiped the few tears that had made their way down my face. "But I guess it doesn't matter now, does it? You've got a wife, and I'm stuck here. I left you and stayed away because I would rather be beaten to a pulp by Tony again than have you look at me and talk to me the way you just did, like I was nothing but an *annoyance*."

"Brenna—" His voice rang with remorse. He looked like he had gotten the wind knocked out of him. He looked sorry.

But I was done. "I'm going to bed. Lock up when you leave." I headed toward my room and Trix. I just wanted this day to be over with. I was exhausted and upset, and I just needed to hold my girl for a while.

I got dressed quickly in shorts and a T-shirt and climbed under the covers with Trix, wrapping my arms around her. I tried to hear if Dragon had left, but I didn't have the energy to get up and check. If he'd left, he would make sure everything was locked up tightly. I was almost asleep when I heard someone in the hallway, and I looked up as he walked into the room. He walked around the bed, and I had to twist my body in order to keep him in my sight.

"Stayin' here tonight." He grabbed his shirt by the back of the neck and pulled it off, giving me a glimpse of his broad tattoo-covered chest in the moonlight.

I was too tired to argue or wake Trix up. Honestly, part of me was kind of glad that Trix and I weren't alone. I decided to just give up and deal with things in the morning. When I heard his jeans hit the floor and felt him slide in beside me, my body tensed. He spooned my back and wrapped his arms around Trix and me, pulling us in close. I tried to stay rigid, but the warmth against my back had me relaxing all too soon.

As soon as he felt me relax against him, he whispered in my ear, "Lied. Best I've ever had." Then, he kissed my temple.

I eventually heard his breathing even out and felt his body go heavy.

The man had a wife. I knew this. I'd met her, but it didn't seem to matter. He was lying with his arms wrapped so close around me, snoring softly, and I couldn't help but feel glad that he was there. I was so confused. I had been running for so long that I didn't know what to do with myself now. Did I want to stop running? I hadn't felt so secure or at home in five years, but I wasn't sure that I wanted to be an old lady. I had the same fears that had plagued me five years ago when I found out I was pregnant. I didn't know if raising Trix here was what I wanted to do, but I couldn't take her away from Dragon now. Did he expect what he'd said to me to just change everything? That we'd start where we had left off the last time I saw him?

My mind was racing. In my head, I reminded myself that he was taken, but I couldn't get over the feeling that he had always been mine.

It was hours before I fell asleep.

## Chapter 11
### Brenna

I woke up to a rough hand rubbing back and forth across the tattoo covering my lower stomach. The white wall I was facing didn't look familiar, but it only took a few seconds for me to realize where I was and who was lying behind me. I leaned up on one elbow, brushing my hair out of my face, and turned my head to look at the man behind me. Mornings had never been my best time of the day, and I blamed that on the sleepy smile I sent in his direction. His hair was a mess, and his eyes were adorably sleepy.

I had seen him asleep before, five years ago, but never when he had just woken up. After our night all those years ago, I had left while he was sleeping to get something to drink and brush my teeth, fully intending to climb back into bed with him. The boys and their toys never woke up early after a party, and I was glad to have some extra time with him before we acted like strangers. But when I was scrambling to grab my toothbrush out of the bag in the backseat of my Bug, my pop and some of the boys pulled into the forecourt, and the opportunity for a lazy morning had vanished.

"Hey, baby. Sleep good?" he asked me in a voice even scratchier than normal.

"Yeah," I replied in a soft voice, drinking in his morning scruff and the affectionate look he was sending me. "Where's Trix?" I asked as I finally noticed she wasn't in bed with us.

"She woke up fuckin' rarin' to go, so I sent her to play in her room. You didn't fall asleep for-fuckin'-ever last night, and you needed to rest."

"What do you mean I didn't fall asleep?" I asked as I felt my face start to burn. "How would you know? You passed out right after you got in bed."

"Not gonna last long the way we live if you aren't aware of your surroundings, babe. You were up 'til 'bout three. Your body didn't relax 'til then."

The morning fog I'd been enjoying lifted as I realized he'd known I was awake and stewing for hours. I was irritated that he'd been awake the whole time I thought I'd been alone with my thoughts. My eyebrows furrowed, and I glared over at him.

"I need to go check on the baby."

I tried to slip out from under his arm, but he tightened his grip and pulled me into him. He rolled from his side to partially on top of me, and his knee slipped between mine, trapping me under him.

"She's fine, Brenna. Why don't you wipe that scowl off your face, and tell your man good morning?" he asked with an amused look in his eyes.

"I don't have a man, and I need to go check on my girl." I pushed at his shoulders, but it didn't seem to faze him.

"Oh, you don't got a man, huh?"

"No, I don't. Get off me. I need coffee. Trix needs breakfast. Why don't you head on home to your wife? She can tell you good morning," I grumbled, still trying to wiggle out of his arms.

He started laughing, a rumble that started deep in his belly. It was annoying as hell. This wasn't funny, and I wanted to get the hell away from him.

"Got no wife. That what you're pissed about? Kendra?" he asked, still looking down at me like he thought this whole situation was hilarious.

"Yeah, Kendra. I doubt she'd be real happy if she saw you lying on top of me with your hands all over me. Now, get off!"

I shoved as hard as I could, and his shoulders rocked back. As soon as I tried to scramble away, he wrapped both arms around me and leaned his chest into mine. My arms were completely immobile, and he dropped his head, so our faces were less than an inch apart.

"You don't need to worry about Kendra. I'll worry about that. Hear me?"

I glared back at him, not willing to have this conversation.

"You hear me, Brenna? That's none of your business."

His arms gave me a little shake, so I nodded, still refusing to say anything.

"You say you got no man?" He waited a minute for an answer, but I didn't say anything. "You just crawl in any man's lap and bawl your eyes out? Huh? You just let any man crawl in bed with you and my daughter, curled up like a bunch of puppies?"

I gasped at what he was insinuating. "Of course not! She didn't even sleep with Tony and me!" Then, I realized the trap I'd walked right into.

"You got any other man's name tattooed on your belly?" he asked quietly.

"It's not your name." I clenched my jaw tightly.

"You have Draco tattooed on your belly," he reminded me as if I didn't know exactly what was written there.

"Yes." I nodded. "That's not your name."

"We just pretending we don't know what Draco means?" he asked incredulously.

"I told you. It's not for you." I was beginning to panic at the direction this conversation was going.

"Yeah, okay, Brenna. You wanna pretend like you and me aren't what we are, that's fine. I'm not gonna pretend. I'm not takin' your bullshit either. Baby, I've been waitin' five years for you. That shit's never gone away. So, you can bitch and moan and make your own life miserable, or you can suck it the fuck up and get on the same page with me. I'm not goin' anywhere."

I opened my mouth to argue that he was wrong, but Trix slammed open the door and jumped up onto the bed.

"Hi, Mama! Whatcha doin'?" She looked back and forth between Dragon and me curiously.

I was trying to inconspicuously pull myself out of his arms, but he wasn't letting go.

"Morning, baby girl. You hungry?" I asked her, trying to act like I wasn't lying under a man she'd met just two weeks ago.

She'd never seen anything even remotely like this when we lived with Tony. She had known not to come into our bedroom.

"Yeah, can I have yogurt for breakfast? We have the good kind in the fridge. I checked!" She started squirming like she was in a hurry.

"Sure. You remember where the spoons are? Next to the fridge in the drawer," I answered her as she climbed back off the bed. "Sit up at the table!" I called, but she had already run down the small hallway, leaving my bedroom door wide open.

"I think she just wanted to see what we were doin' in here," Dragon said with a smile.

"Get *off* me! What the hell is a matter with you? She's four! She doesn't need to see some strange man in my bed, lying on top of me."

I finally slid away from him and crawled to the edge of the bed, climbing down and spinning around to send a glare his way. I expected him to laugh at me or be pissed. I figured with his hot and cold personality, it could really go either way at this point. What I didn't expect was for him to stand up and pull on his jeans with a completely blank expression on his face. I stood there stupidly, trying to figure out where his head was at, as he pulled on his T-shirt, and I caught another glimpse of the tattoos covering his torso. They looked like little dots all over his skin. I couldn't see them very well, but it looked like they covered his whole chest and stomach. When he finished dressing, he walked around the bed and stood, looking down at me. I was frozen to the spot by his complete lack of expression.

"I'm not a stranger. I'm her dad. She knows I'm her dad. Don't know who fuckin' told her. I'm just glad I didn't have to explain it. She'll get used to me bein' in your space 'cause I'm gonna be there a lot. She'll also get used to me in your bed 'cause that's where I'll be sleepin'. Moms and dads sleep together. It's normal. You got any other concerns, you're gonna have to bitch at me later. I got places to be."

As soon as he stopped talking, he wrapped a big hand around the back of my neck and pulled my face up to his for a quick kiss, rubbing his tongue along my bottom lip and then biting my top lip softly. His expression never changed, and before I could say anything, he had walked out into the hallway. I followed slowly behind him and watched him smile at Trix, kiss the top of her head, and then head out the door.

It was like any other family in America—the kid ate breakfast, and the mom stood there in her pajamas while the daddy headed off to work. *Well, almost the same*, I thought to myself as I watched him slide his cut onto his shoulders and then listened to the roar of pipes seconds later.

Not long after Dragon left and I got dressed for the day, we heard gravel crunching as someone drove toward the house. I'd forgotten how quiet it was out here. We'd lived in a neighborhood and then at the clubhouse, which always had people coming and going. The silence was nice and provided the added benefit of always knowing when someone was driving up. It gave me a little peace of mind; no one would get here on foot as we were too far out in the boonies. Trix ran to the window, already bored with the cartoons she'd been watching.

"Auntie Vera!" she squealed and then ran for the door.

Well, this wouldn't be pleasant. Vera had been giving me the cold shoulder since the night we had dinner at her place. I was surprised she was showing up here. Trix threw open the door, and I caught sight of Vera opening up the back door of her car and then popping the trunk.

"Brenna!" she shouted up to me. "Come help me grab these boxes!"

"Be right there!"

I ran to my room and grabbed some flip-flops from behind the door in my room. I guessed I could start leaving some by the front door, but I'd gotten in the habit of putting everything away the minute I got home. Tony didn't like clutter, and after he'd tripped on my high heels once after dinner, I never left shoes out again. But this was my house, and if I wanted to leave stuff all over, I could. But just the thought of it caused my heart rate to spike, so maybe I'd try tomorrow…or next week.

"What is all this stuff?" I asked as we brought in the last of the six boxes Vera had dragged over.

Boxes were spread out all over the living room, and I could already feel the start of a panic attack coming on. They needed to go somewhere, anywhere, but our little house had virtually no storage.

"Hey, what's your deal? You okay?" Vera asked, looking at me like she couldn't figure out what the problem was. By the look on her face, she could tell I was ready to freak out.

"Uh, what are all these boxes?" I looked around the room.

"It's all your old stuff. When your pop sold his place, I went in and packed up your room. Clothes and shoes in some boxes and memento stuff in others. I didn't bring the memento boxes. Didn't think you'd have space for 'em. I packed all of your star books in with the clothes. Figured if you ever came back, you'd want to open those first."

The quiver in her voice told me what she would never say. I'd hurt her when I took off. Now that I had Trix, I could finally understand how she must have felt.

I felt a knot forming in the back of my throat. "I'm sorry. I should've—"

She stopped me when she wrapped her arms around me and hugged me tightly, her voice muffled in the shoulder of my T-shirt. I could feel her breath stuttering against me like she was trying not to cry.

"That's okay, baby. You're here now."

I breathed in her smell of vanilla perfume and cigarettes, and my panic instantly faded.

All of a sudden, she stepped away, tugged on the bottom of her Harley Davidson tank top, and went on like it'd never happened.

"So, I brought by all of the clothes boxes. I mostly got stuff for Trix when I made that trip into town. A woman's gotta have some clothes. I doubt your ass will fit into any of your old jeans—"

"Ouch!"

"But all those skirts and T-shirts you had will probably still fit." She looked up, smiling from where she was using her pocketknife to cut open boxes. "I'll even make some sundresses for Trix if you want...out of your old band T-shirts. Remember when I did that for you when you were little? Couldn't even fit into the smallest size they had, and you still insisted on getting any band T-shirt you could get your hands on."

"You want some new dresses, Trix?" I asked my daughter who had climbed onto one of the largest boxes in the living room and was shaking her little hips. She looked like a miniature go-go dancer.

"Yeah!" she yelled as she jumped off the box onto the couch.

"Trix! Don't jump on the couch!" In that split second, I was envisioning missing teeth and a trip to the emergency room.

"Trix, you're gonna give your mama a heart attack."

Trix giggled as Vera pulled her off the couch.

"Why don't you go out front and play? Leave the door open."

I opened my mouth to protest, but one look at Vera made me close it again. I didn't know how she perfected the *Mom* look, but she'd been using it on me for as long as I could remember.

"Okay, here are the rules." I stopped Trix as she headed out the door. "Stay away from Auntie Vera's car. No climbing on anything. You can play in the grass, but stay off the driveway. And if a car comes, you get back inside right that minute. Do you understand?" I waited until she nodded and then let go of her arm. She ran outside, and I turned back to Vera. "Can you help me get these boxes unpacked?"

"Sure, you better grab a laundry basket." She started rifling through the first box as I headed toward the hallway. "These clothes are gonna need to be washed. I made Slider store them in the compound, so who knows what they've come into contact with through the cardboard."

I grabbed a basket out of Trix's room and got down to work with Vera.

Vera was a lot like a mother to me, but she was also my best friend. While we sat there on the floor, it felt like I had never left. We laughed over gaudy rhinestone tops and talked about what had happened in the club since I'd left, and I told her about life with Tony. She was pissed for me, and halfway through my story, she got up and grabbed us a couple of beers out of the fridge.

"We're gonna need fortification."

We got through the boxes quickly, putting my astronomy books on top of the TV as we found them and sorting the clothes into *keep* and *charity* piles. A lot of the clothes were far too small, but by the end of the second box, I had a load of laundry washing in the machine. It was weird going through my old clothes. I had dressed like the perfect wife for so long, and I was nervous to get back into my old gypsy skirts and sundresses. I was listening to Trix talk to herself on the front porch and rubbing an old Drop Kick Murphy's shirt between my fingers when Vera spoke.

"I've heard what you told Slider, but now, I wanna hear it from you. What the hell is going on with you and Dragon?"

## Chapter 12
## Dragon

I left the house this morning, knowing my day was going to be shit. I didn't want Brenna to worry. I didn't know where she got her tender heart from, but I knew she'd freak if she found out what today was. The nonsense from five years ago was finally catching up to me, and I was going to be in a world of hurt tonight.

When I got to the clubhouse, everything was quiet. A few of the boys were sitting around, drinking coffee, but boss man hadn't come in yet. I walked up to grab a cup just as Poet came in from the back hallway. I wasn't sure where we stood because most of my time since Brenna got here had been taken up with my trip to Boise or dealing with my girls. I was hoping we could wait to talk after my deal this afternoon, but he headed straight for me.

"Dragon. Got a minute?"

It was a question, but there was only one answer.

"Yeah."

I walked to the corner of the room to give us a little privacy, but I knew our conversation would be all over the club in a matter of hours. I sat down on one of the couches and rested my elbows on my knees. I wasn't sure what I was most embarrassed about—the fact that I had no idea who Brenna was the night we'd met or that I'd been pretty much hiding all the shit that went down for over five years.

"Shit is not going to go well for you today." Poet coughed and then took a sip of his coffee. "I can't say that I'm glad you were with Brenna. I'm also pretty goddamn angry that you and Grease kept that shit from me. Ya kept my baby from me for five years. That was Brenna's choice, but a choice she made, so she didn't see you."

I didn't say anything. I couldn't argue the point because everything he was saying was true. If I woulda manned up, Poet would have dragged Brenna's ass back here, especially if she was pregnant.

"I had no idea what was in that girl's head when she ran outta here. Figured she stayed away because she was embarrassed—maybe she didn't want that husband of hers to know where she came from. Maybe that was part of the reason but not all of it. Once she was gone, I'm thinking he wasn't gonna let her come back here anyway."

I stopped him, asking a question I'd been wondering for weeks. "Why didn't you keep an eye on her? Fuck, Poet!"

"Son, I don't think you wanna be steppin' on my toes right now," he answered calmly, but I knew by the way his accent deepened that I'd pissed him off.

I didn't care. The thought of Brenna and Trix in the world with no protection made me want to puke. "I got nothing to lose now. Today's judgment day, right? Might as well ask what the fuck you were thinkin'." I didn't care if this got me more of what I had to look forward to later. I wanted to know what the fuck he'd been thinking.

"Son, I'm gonna explain this once, and then you better never question me about it again." His face looked normal, but his eyes had gone the coldest I'd ever seen them. "I had eyes on Brenna. Always. Boys from a chapter up north kept her on their radar at all times. Eyes only. They saw her only when she left the house. None of them saw nothin' to make them think that she was in trouble. They were watching for outside problems. Didn't think to watch the husband." He shook his head. "She chose him. Figured she would come home if she wasn't happy. Took her a while, but that's what she did. Now, I'm done with fucking story hour. You want to get back on my good side, you'll get the fuck out of this clubhouse and let me forget that you just questioned me about something you got no business in."

He stood up and walked back to his room without saying a word to anyone else. I still had questions, but I figured that was all I was gonna get from him, so I left. I was anxious about today, and I needed to keep busy or I was gonna lose my mind. Plus, I had business in town that I needed to take care of.

When I got to my apartment, the door was unlocked, and I walked right in. Kendra was sitting on the couch, painting her toenails and talking on the phone. Didn't know how many times I'd told her to lock the fuckin' door when I wasn't here, but the chick never listened.

"Tracy, I gotta call you back. My man's home!" she squealed and then launched herself off the couch and wrapped her arms and legs around me. "Where have you been?"

"Takin' care of shit at the club. I told you to lock the door." I glared down at her. "Lock. The. Door."

I pushed on her thighs to get her to let me loose. She dropped to her feet and immediately started bitching that I'd ruined her toenail polish. Seriously? She was in her own fuckin' world. I was standing by the front door, obviously waiting to leave, and the bitch had no clue. I stood there for a second, hoping that she would notice that something was up and ask me about it, but she went back to painting her nails. Finally, I just jumped right into it.

"Yeah, Kendra, this is no good anymore. You need to find another place to live."

I watched as she stopped ranting and blinked at me for a couple of seconds, like she couldn't understand what I was talking about.

"What?" she asked me, all wide-eyed and surprised.

I didn't know why she was surprised. I got home from my run and avoided her for the past few days, and she still hadn't noticed anything was wrong. Usually, when I got back from a run, I would be all jacked and need an outlet. I was always here the minute I got back and checked in. I'd get some relief and then head out to be with the boys. Sometimes, she came with me, and sometimes, she didn't, but I always hit home as soon as I'd checked in with Slider.

"Yeah. You got two weeks to find a new place. Feel free to be stay here until you do, but I'm not gonna be here."

"Where are you going to be then?" Finally catching on, she was not happy. She was doing that thing women do when they were pissed—the hand on the hip with the head cocked to the side.

"Not your business where I'm gonna be. It wasn't your business before. Why you think I'd tell you now? Find a place to live, Kendra." I just wanted to get out of here. I had a couple errands to run before I headed back to the clubhouse. My head was already preparing for the rest of my day, and I was barely paying attention to what she was saying.

"What the fuck, Dragon! You're just going to dump me? Out of the blue, no explanation?" she asked and I nodded. "Is this because of your bitch of a baby mama who hid your kid her entire life? Seriously? You're dumping me for that redheaded skank?"

"Woman, you're testing my patience. It's none of your goddamn business who I'm with. That's the mother of my child, and you'll show respect when you talk about her, or I'll throw your ass out now with nothin' but the clothes on your goddamn back!"

She shut up pretty quickly when I started yelling, and by the time I was done, she was crying. I felt bad for her, but I had so much shit on my plate, and I just didn't have time for this.

"Kendra, find a place to live. You can have this place for the next two weeks. You can't find another place by then, you call me, and we'll figure something out."

She rushed to me, deciding that tears weren't going to get her what she wanted, and she was all over me before I knew what she was doing. She'd unbuttoned and unzipped my jeans before I could get a hold of her and shove her back. Normally, I'd just let her try and make her point and then leave anyway—might as well get a blow job if the bitch is begging—but the thought of her mouth on me just didn't do anything for me since Brenna had shown up. I shoved her away from me and buttoned my jeans back up easily. Even with her hands all over me, I wasn't hard at all. Fuck, I didn't want to be dealing with this drama right now.

Before she could grab me again, I was out the door and on my bike. She stood at the front door and when I yelled up, "Lock the fuckin' door!"

She smiled at me, and I could tell she was going to be a problem.

I hit a couple of stores in town before I headed back to the club. I stuffed all the shit into my saddlebags and checked my phone for missed calls. Grease had called a couple of times, but he hadn't left a message, so I figured it was nothing important. I noticed that it was time to head back to the club though, so I cracked my neck and decided to stop stalling. Showtime.

When I got to the club, there was only one brother guarding the gate, a recruit called Curly. The kid's head was bald and shiny as a cue ball and was glistening in the sun. He gave me a small smile as I rolled through the gate, but it looked like the kid was more nervous than I was. He was probably freaked that he had to stand the gate alone. Recruits weren't allowed at the house for shit like this, and the only other recruit we had was up at Brenna's house, making sure she stayed put.

I could hear everybody talking inside the main room, but everyone quieted when I stepped through the door. I looked around the room and found Grease, but his eyes didn't meet mine. It looked like he was sweating, which was fuckin' weird because it wasn't hot out today.

"Dragon, you ready for this?" Slider stepped up next to me.

"The fuck kind of question is that?" I asked him, but I was actually a little glad he came over. It gave me a little more backbone, and my chin lifted a little higher.

We walked out of the main room and headed into an empty garage bay. All the brothers circled around with Slider, Grease, and me in the middle. I looked over to Grease, wondering what the fuck he was doing when Slider started to speak.

"Dragon here's been lying to his brothers for five long years. He not only disrespected Poet, but then he hid the disrespect, so Poet had to find out five years later. Grease also knew about shit and never spoke up. Poet, Tommy Gun, Razor, and myself had us a little meeting this morning and decided their punishment. While Dragon was the one who fucked Brenna, Grease did his part in this little fiasco and helped him hide it. Each one of you gets one hit. Bare hands. I'm not taking part, but Poet goes last. Make them good, and all of you remember this. I won't be so lenient if I have to deal with this shit again."

I was stunned silent for a minute that the punishment was gonna go so easily, but then everything clicked, and I realized Grease was still standing next to me, and the other brothers were lining up.

"Boss! Wait!"

Slider slowly turned around.

"Grease shouldn't be here. He fuckin' warned me, but I didn't listen. He's fuckin' stupid, but he shouldn't be up here."

Slider stared at me a second, and then I watched his lips turn up. "You gonna take his punishment? I promised my boys two hits, not one."

I didn't even hesitate. "I'll take it—"

Grease finally looked up at me. "Don't do this, man. It's fine."

"Get the fuck outta here. But you hit me? I'll knock you the fuck out." I gave him a little shove. Still really fuckin' happy that this shit wasn't what I'd been thinking. I had one more thing to say, and I found Poet in the crowd. "No hits to the face, yeah? Don't wanna freak Trix out when I go home tonight." I held his stare until he nodded, and then I faced the boys and braced myself.

By the time there were only a few brothers left, I was seriously thinking I'd underestimated the punishment. I also figured out why Slider had smiled when I decided to take Grease's hits. The sneaky fucker had set me up. My ribs were on fire, and I'd already puked my fuckin' guts out twice. The second time, I had nothing left, and the dry heaves almost made me pass out. It was hard to not fight back when fuckers are hitting you over and over again, especially when you lived your life fighting your way to the top. After the first ten brothers, I'd pretty much blocked everything out, except breathing and staying on my feet, and at that point, I wasn't even halfway through. By the last ten, I was fighting to stay conscious.

Finally, I caught a glimpse of Poet coming toward me, pushing brass knuckles onto his hands. I thought I muttered, "Oh fuck," before he knocked my ass out.

I was out for a while, and when I woke up, the boys had dragged me into my room at the club. Doc came in to see me, but I was pretty much out of it, so I just lay in bed for a few hours, glad I was still breathing. Finally, I got up, took the most excruciating shower of my life, and went out to have a drink with the boys. That was the best thing about this club and something I'd always craved growing up. You might fuck up, but the brothers wouldn't ever act like you weren't welcome. They'd punish you, but then it'd be over, forgotten. You'd be back in the fold. After getting passed from one home to another, whenever I got too hard to handle growing up, the Aces were like a sanctuary.

Later that night, I walked over to Brenna's place. I didn't take my bike. Figured I'd give my ribs a rest for the night. The house was glowing, and I could hear some music playing. The front door was open, and before I opened the screen, I caught a glimpse of Brenna and Trix dancing around the kitchen. I felt my breath catch, and it was as if someone had his hand around my throat.

The table was pushed against the wall, and two of the chairs were in the middle of the living room. The music was loud, and they didn't notice me as I stood there, watching them. Brenna was wearing a little white tank top and a long skirt. Her shirt rested high enough, and her skirt was low enough that I caught a glimpse of her tattoo spanning her waist below her belly button. I loved seeing my name there even if she liked to pretend the tattoo wasn't for me. By the way her tits were bouncing around, I knew she didn't have a bra on. Her tits were fantastic, but the look on her face is what had me stopped and staring. Her cheeks were stretched in the most gorgeous fuckin' smile. It lit up the fuckin' room.

I hadn't seen that smile in five years.

She was swinging her hips around, but Trix was like a tornado. She was bouncing up and down and pausing with the beat of the music. She had some little cartoon pajamas on, and her wet hair was whipping around her face. She'd obviously just taken a bath. Looking at her, I still couldn't believe how much she looked like me, but now, I saw she had Brenna's smile. It was the most carefree I'd seen my baby girl since she'd gotten here.

Once the song sped up, they were both spinning around in the kitchen. Brenna's red hair and Trix's black hair were flying out in all directions as they danced. I caught a glimpse of their feet, and both of them were stomping on the cracked linoleum with the beat of the music. It reminded me of the powwows I was dragged to as a kid. I remembered an auntie telling one of my cousins to make sure her feet hit the dirt with every beat of the drum. Trix's rhythm was crazy good for a four-year-old. She had that shit down. It was like they knew exactly what the other one was doing at all times as they twirled around each other in the tiny-ass kitchen. Their eyes were locked.

My chest started to burn when I realized they were singing to each other. They were actually dancing around the fuckin' kitchen and singing to each other. Trix looked at Brenna like she was the best thing she'd ever fuckin' seen, and I was wondering if that was the look other people saw on my face when I looked at them. The song said something about belonging to each other and calling each other sweetheart with the last word dragging out as they smiled.

I'd seen Brenna doing the *Mom* thing now for the last couple of days. I fuckin' loved watching her do all of the simple things, like helping Trix brush her teeth. I loved the way she rested her hand on the top of Trix's head when they were standing together, like she didn't even know she was doing it. And I loved that she took the time to listen to every single one of Trix's long-ass rambles about nothing in particular. But this? This totally carefree dancing-in-the-kitchen thing? It blew all of that other shit out of the water.

I fucked up five years ago. Honest mistake, but there it was. Then, I was fuckin' sneaky and didn't say shit about it. If I woulda just listened to Grease and not gone down that road, life would have been fuckin' easy for me right now. A couple of times this afternoon, I asked myself if I'd do it again, if it was really fuckin' worth it. Seeing them acting like goofs dancing around the kitchen gave me my answer.

They were the most beautiful things I had ever seen in my entire goddamn life, and they worth every fuckin' bruise I had.

## Chapter 13
### Brenna

I was dancing around the kitchen with Trix when I saw movement out of the corner of my eye. I glanced over toward the front door, and just as I was about to scream, I heard Dragon's voice from the other side of the screen.

"It's just me, Brenna," he said quietly as he swung the screen open.

Trix paused mid-dance, staring at my face, waiting for the all clear. It broke my heart that she picked up on the smallest body language as if she were just waiting for something bad to happen. When she heard Dragon's voice, she spun around and ran straight for him.

"Papa!" she screamed excitedly, but as soon as she was about a foot away from him, she slammed to a halt and tilted her head up at him. "Why are you hurt? Don't worry. I'll be careful." And then, she gingerly wrapped her arms around his thighs.

I didn't notice anything off about Dragon until Trix had said something. Then, I noticed how he was holding his body. He wasn't standing straight. His shoulders and back were slightly hunched over as if protecting the front of his body.

I knew that stance.

I looked up into his face and found myself walking closer as I noticed bruising around his jaw and a split in his bottom lip. I couldn't read the look on his face.

"Trix, it's time to get ready for bed," I told my girl who was still gingerly holding Dragon's legs and was now soothingly rubbing her hand up and down the back of them. "Put your PJs on, get a book, and climb into bed. I'll be in there in a few minutes to tuck you in. You can brush your teeth in the morning." I waited for her to follow my instructions, but before she did, she tilted her head way back to look at Dragon.

"I'm sorry you're hurt, Papa," she whispered, and I could tell my tenderhearted girl was about to cry.

"Papa's fine, little warrior. Don't be gettin' upset." Dragon ran his fingers through her hair. "You better go get ready for bed like your mom told ya." He started to bend over as if to give her a kiss, but he winced and straightened back up.

I knew that if he couldn't even bend over, something was seriously wrong, and I felt my palms start to sweat.

As soon as Trix ran down the hallway, Dragon reached out and braced his hand against the wall. His entire body slumped as if exhausted. I had started to freak out when I knew he was hurt, but once he braced himself on the wall, I became completely calm. I remembered feeling something like this when Trix was a baby and started choking on a piece of fruit. I'd known I had to get it out, and I immediately did the baby Heimlich maneuver even though I hadn't ever done it before. It wasn't until after, when she was happily playing with her toys again, that I'd broken down. The same thing happened to me as I walked toward Dragon and reached my hand out to him. As soon as he grabbed hold, I led him into the bedroom.

"Can you take off your shirt?" I asked him, surprised at how strong my voice sounded.

"It's fine, Brenna. Doc looked at it earlier. I just need to get some sleep."

He started to turn toward the bed, but I stopped him with a hand on his arm.

"I didn't ask if Doc had seen it. I asked if you could take off your shirt."

He got a weird look on his face, but he tried to reach behind his neck to grab his T-shirt. He didn't get far before he dropped his hand down in pain. He didn't say anything; he just lifted his chin and looked over my shoulder at the door. I felt my eyes fill with tears when I realized he wasn't going to be able to get it off. Suddenly, looking at his wounds wasn't nearly as important as taking off his damn shirt. Looking at it gave me a strange case of claustrophobia. I needed it *off*.

"Okay, it's fine. Just stay right there. I'll be right back," I told him as I spun around.

I quickly checked on Trix, who was looking at a book, as I rushed down the hallway to grab some scissors from the top of the fridge. When I got back to the bedroom, Dragon was sitting down carefully on the bed.

"I got some scissors. I don't want to try to pull it over your head, so I'm just going to cut it, okay?" I asked quickly.

"Close the door, so Trix doesn't come in here," he ordered.

I closed the door and noticed there was no lock, so I wedged a shoe off my dresser to semi-lock it. As soon as I was done, I reached for the hem of his shirt and cut quickly up the front of his torso. What I saw on his body was worse than I'd imagined.

His chest, belly, and ribs were one huge bruise, so dark I could barely discern the tattoos across his body. I felt the tears running down my cheeks as I slipped behind him, trying not to jostle the bed, as I pulled the rest of the shirt down his arms. His back was almost completely unblemished. I leaned forward to take a look at his chest again. Yep, it was just as bad as I thought. I didn't understand how on earth only the front half of his body was this bruised.

I started to question him. "What…" Aand all of a sudden it dawned on me. "Tell me this didn't happen because of me," I whispered. My tears were no longer running down my cheeks; they were pouring. I could barely see out of my eyes. "Tell me that my father didn't do this to you."

He didn't answer, and that was answer enough.

"Oh my god. I'm so sorry. I'm so sorry. So sorry…" I was shaking in disbelief and horror.

"Hey." He reached up and brushed my hair back from my face, cupping my cheek. "This is not your fault, Brenna. You hear me? I'm an Ace. I knew what I was doing. This is not your fault."

I could barely understand him as I sat there, shaking miserably and staring into his eyes. It was like the only thing I was aware of was my colossal fuck-up and his beautiful dark brown eyes. Before I knew it, he was pulling me onto his lap.

"Dragon, don't! Your ribs!" I didn't want him holding me because I didn't want to hurt him, but I couldn't wiggle away because that would make it even worse. I was stuck there on his lap, trying my hardest to keep from brushing up against the front of him.

"I'm fine, Brenna. It's over, baby." He had one hand wrapped around my waist and the other on the side of my face, his fingers weaving through the hair behind my ear. "It's over, baby. No need for cryin'. Now, we can move the fuck on from this shit. No more repercussions. Okay?"

My tears were starting to dry on my face as I sniffled, and he gently rubbed his thumb across the apple of my cheek. It was like I was mesmerized by the look on his face, the way his body was wrapped around me.

"Baby. It's over for us. Not just me. It's over for you, too. You don't have to worry about people sayin' shit to you, Slider bein' pissed, none of it. It's behind us."

He shifted forward, so the space between our faces disappeared, and I closed my eyes as he started to slowly kiss my face.

I whispered, "Okay," as he kissed me gently across my cheek, the tip of my nose, and my forehead.

He rubbed his lips across the tears on my eyelashes, and then I felt him lick his lips. That was the trigger. I didn't know why that single movement made me catch my breath and lift my lips toward him, but it did. All of a sudden, I was begging him to kiss me. Thankfully, he didn't keep me waiting.

This kiss wasn't soft. The tenderness I'd felt just moments before was completely gone, and he instantly pushed his tongue between my swollen lips. He ran it between my top lip and teeth and then brushed it across the roof of my mouth. I shuddered. I wanted to push myself against him. My heart was beating so fast that I could hear it in my ears, and I wanted nothing more in that minute than to push him onto the bed and make sure that he was okay by tracing his body with my lips. I wanted to inhale him, to pull him into my body so deep that he couldn't ever be hurt again. I knew I was thinking crazy. Nothing was clear between us, and I didn't know what the hell I was doing, but I wanted him, right now. But he was hurt, and he was sitting on my bed, holding himself abnormally still, so I sat pliantly in his lap, taking whatever he had to offer.

He kissed me for what seemed like forever, but still, it wasn't long enough. His hand was clutched tightly in my hair, and every time he tugged on it, I felt small whimpers travel up my throat. Suddenly, he stood me up in front of him, and the minute I caught my balance, he lifted my tank top over my head. I quickly raised my arms to cover myself, but he grasped my wrists, and I was too conscious of his bruises to fight him.

"Damn, Brenna. You're more beautiful than I remembered." His voice was low, and he was staring right at my breasts.

I was totally embarrassed. Yes, he'd seen me naked before, but that was before I'd gained the massive stretch marks across my belly. I was hoping he'd be so mesmerized by my larger breasts that he wouldn't even look farther south. My stomach used to be so smooth and toned. I'd had a belly button piercing that I proudly showed off whenever I could. Now, I could barely look at my own stomach, and there was no way in hell I'd willingly let anyone else catch a glimpse. My prayers that he would ignore everything but my boobs went unanswered. He let go of one of my wrists, and I stood there, frozen, as he reached up to trace the thickest scar on my belly.

"Is this from your belly ring?" he asked me, still running his finger up and down the scar.

It felt weird. The skin was so thin there that it was extra sensitive.

"Yeah," I told him, my voice husky. "I took it out when I found out I was pregnant, but it didn't heal right away. Then, it made that stretch mark a hundred times worse."

He nodded his head and continued to stare at my stomach. When I was about to step away from him, he raised his other hand and used both to trace the silvery lines covering my torso. He was running his fingers over them, and it reminded me of the way a blind person read braille. His eyes were narrowed in concentration, resembling something close to awe. I finally managed a step away, but I paused when he looked up to catch my eye.

"I can't believe you had my baby. She was all curled up in here, and I never saw it." He shook his head. "This is all I'll ever see, Brenna. This is all I get. Let me look."

My breath caught in my throat as he spoke, and I took a small step back toward him after he explained what he was doing. He was mapping the changes like any other dad would. He didn't get the chance to watch me grow, so now, he was following the scars like a map of what he'd missed.

I wished I could tell him all about it. I wished I could explain that I was overly large, that this many stretch marks weren't normal, that I rarely got to sleep because there was always a baby awake in my belly, rolling around and kicking my ribs. I wished I could tell him how scared I was when I went into labor, how alone I felt, how much I missed him. But I didn't say any of these things because if I would've, it could open up a discussion that I wasn't ready for, and I didn't think he was either.

Pounding on the door startled me back into the present, and I quickly grabbed a nightshirt and pulled it over my head. "Just a second, Trix! What do you need, baby?" I called through the door.

"I want Papa to tuck me in tonight! Okay?" she called back to me.

For a moment, I was in shock, but quickly afterward, I was jealous. She had never asked for anyone but me. I knew he was her dad, but I'd always done this on my own. She'd never asked for Tony to do anything with her. It had always been Trix and me against the world.

Before I could answer her, Dragon did it for me. "I'll be right out, little warrior. Get in bed!" He slowly pushed himself to his feet. "Brenna, grab me a shirt outta my bag." He nodded his head toward the end of the bed where I saw a black duffel bag.

"You could ask, you know?" I grumbled as I unzipped it and started pawing through his clothes.

"You want Trix to see me like this?" He gestured toward his chest.

"No, but—" I started to grumble again.

"Are you really trying to start a fight with me right now? I gotta tell you, I'm not in the mood." He swayed a little on his feet.

I tossed a shirt at him that had snaps along the front. "Whatever. Just go tuck Trix in."

I watched as he gingerly tried to slip the shirt up his arms, but it was a struggle because the muscles in his shoulders were so broad. I watched him for a second before I went over to help him pull it up. It was hard to watch him struggle at anything; he was usually so strong and self-assured. I couldn't stand the thought of anything bringing him low. I started snapping the shirt from the bottom to the top, and when I glanced up at his face, he was grinning at me.

"You just can't help yourself, can you? You were bitchin' at me about fifteen seconds ago, and now, you're dressing me like I'm Trix." He shook his head. "So damn sweet, baby."

My face was on fire. Fuck, this was embarrassing. I *was* just dressing him like a five-year-old, and I didn't even realize it.

"Why don't you get undressed and get into bed?" he whispered as he grabbed a hold of my head with both hands. "I'll get Trix to bed and come back and trace all of those parts I haven't seen in so long." He kissed my lips softly and then finished talking against my mouth. "Remember how good it was, baby? How sensitive you are on your thighs? That sweet spot right under your ass cheeks? Fuck, I can't wait to taste you." He gave me one last kiss, his tongue rimming my lips, before he pulled open the door and went to Trix.

I stood there for a second, my body on fire and my thoughts scrambling, before I got it together. Twice in one night, he'd made me want to climb him like a tree. My panties were uncomfortably wet, and I wanted to change, but I couldn't decide what to wear to bed. It would probably be a good idea to change into some flannel pajamas, considering the fact that the man was beaten to a pulp earlier, but it was just too damn hot in the house for anything more than what I was wearing.

He was out of his mind if he thought I was just going to strip down and do the dirty with him. Shit. My thoughts were all over the place tonight. I didn't want to want him. I wasn't even sure that Trix and I would be staying here for any length of time, and there were things that Dragon didn't know, things I needed to tell him before we got into whatever this was any deeper.

I did want him though. My body ached for him. I wanted to lose myself in him and never worry about anything ever again. I was so tired of being the strong one; it would be nice to lean on someone else for a while. The problem with leaning on Dragon was that it could become a habit. I didn't really know him anymore—if I ever really did in the first place. One night together did not make a relationship. I needed to figure out my head before I had sex with him. *Mind-blowing, orgasm-inducing, wet, sweaty sex...shit!* I didn't think I was going to be able to resist him, and even though it was a very, very bad idea, I wasn't sure that I wanted to.

I could hear Trix and Dragon talking, and I decided to be a little sneaky and eavesdrop on their conversation. I was curious what they had to talk about even though I probably shouldn't have been. Trix could talk to a tree for hours and never run out of things to say. I crept out to the hallway and stood out of sight next to Trix's doorway.

"Today, Auntie Vera came over and brought a bunch of Mama's stuff. She said Mama's ass was too big to fit into her jeans."

"Don't say ass, Trix. Your mama would flip if she heard you."

"Okay, I won't say ass. Did you know that we have flowers outside? They're in the yard. I picked Mama some before our dance party."

"That what you were doin' tonight? Havin' a dance party?"

"Yup. Me and Mama have dance parties *all* the time. Mama's a good dancer."

"I saw you singin'. You like that music?"

"YEAH! That's The Lumineers. They have lots of good music. I like Michael Jackson, too, but Mama says he's dead. He's got good music for dancing though."

"Oh yeah? I'll have to check him out then." I heard a smile in Dragon's voice. "All right, little warrior, it's time for you to go to sleep. You want Mama to come in and kiss you good night?"

"Yeah." I heard Trix yawn. "Can you sing me a song first? Mama always sings me a song before I go to sleep."

"I don't know any kid songs—"

"That's okay! You can sing anything. Mama sings all sorts of stuff."

"You really want me to sing? Not a good singer, little warrior."

Trix didn't say anything, and I could imagine her snuggled up in bed, nodding her head. There were a few beats of silence before I heard Dragon start to sing. I covered my mouth with my hand to hide a giggle and listened closely to him. It took me a second to recognize what he was singing. His voice was rough, and I could tell he was a little embarrassed even though his only audience was a four-year-old. It crashed into me like a freight train, and I held my hands to my mouth for a completely different reason as the song choice sank in.

He continued onto the second verse, and I heard Trix whisper, "'Walk the Line'…Johnny Cash. Good choice, Papa."

In that moment, all of my fears and apprehension disappeared as my heart swelled with emotion. I knew what I needed to know. We were his. It was as terrifying and as simple as that.

I heard him coming toward the door, and I rushed to my room, trying to pretend I hadn't just eavesdropped on his moment with Trix. I spun around when I heard him right behind me. His eyebrows were raised to his hairline, and he was smirking at me. He knew I'd listened.

"Trix wants her mama to come give her a kiss," he told me, searching my eyes. "See, not takin' your place, baby. I'm just new and exciting."

"What are you talking about?" I shook my head like he was crazy and started walking toward the door nonchalantly.

Before I could pass him, he stepped into my space and leaned down close as his hand reached up to the side of my face. God, I loved when he did that.

"Baby, I saw your face earlier. Nobody's takin' your place. I don't want that place. I want *my* place. With you and with her. Okay?"

I just nodded.

He spoke so softly, and his hand was so tender on my face that I was frozen. It was like he'd put me in a trance.

"Go put our girl to bed, yeah?" His eyes darkened, and a wicked smile formed on his lips. "I got plans for us tonight."

His words jolted me out of the fog he'd put me in, and I snorted. "Chill out there, stud muffin. You're not getting any. Did you forget you got the shit beat out of you today?"

"None of the boys hit me in the jewels, baby. I woulda killed 'em if they did. You're so worried, you can do all the work," he said with a grin.

"Keep dreaming. I'm going to kiss Trix." I walked out the door and glanced back at him. "I'll help you with your clothes when I get back."

"Fuck yeah, you will," he mumbled as he glanced down at the cell phone he'd pulled out of his pocket.

I found myself shaking my head at him for what seemed like the eighty-fifth time tonight. It was either that or laugh. I wasn't sure how we had gotten to this point—this domestic bliss, putting the kids to bed, sleeping together point. I knew I should be fighting it.

Things were moving too quickly. I was keeping secrets, and all of this was going to blow up in my face one way or another. But I just couldn't stop myself from being glad that he was here. He made me feel safe and wanted. It was a heady feeling.

## Chapter 14
## Dragon

When Brenna went to kiss Trix good night, I popped a couple of pills Doc had sent home with me. I had forgotten that I even had them until Grease texted me to remind me that Doc said to take two. I had a pretty high tolerance for any drugs. I thought it was probably because I'd built it up over the years. Most shit I'd dealt with didn't require anything but bourbon to soothe the aches though. Today was the exception.

If I were going to sleep, I would have just dealt with the pain. It felt a little like a badge of honor or some shit like that. It was nice to have this shit off my shoulders, like I could finally have Brenna because I'd paid my dues. The pain was temporary, but it meant that no one was going to be in my way with Brenna. She was mine. She'd been mine for five fuckin' years, and now, if I wanted to be a douche, I could climb to the top of the clubhouse and shout it from the rooftop. Like I said, if I was going to sleep, I'd welcome the pain. But I wasn't going to sleep. I was going to wait for Brenna to get her ass back in here, and then I was going to taste every inch that I'd missed for five years. For that, I needed some fuckin' pain relief.

When she finally walked in, she seemed preoccupied. She was looking at the floor, and her eyebrows were practically meeting at the top of her nose. I sat there, watching her for a minute, and when she didn't look up, I caught her attention.

"Trix asleep?"

I wasn't starting shit if Trix was awake. I loved my baby girl, but she'd proven more than once that she had no sense of timing. She'd be knocking on the door right as things were getting good if she were still awake.

"Yeah," she sighed quietly as she watched me from the doorway.

"Shut the door, baby," I told her, but she didn't move.

She just stood there, looking at me, like she couldn't make up her mind. She finally nodded as if the decision was made, and she turned and shut the door. Before she could step away from it, I told her to lock it. Her eyes went wide and dark before she cleared her throat to speak.

"I can't. Lock it, I mean. There's no lock."

She sort of stuttered when she was nervous, and for some reason, I found it sexy as hell.

"We'll fix that shit tomorrow," I told her, and my voice sounded about ten times deeper than normal. "Wedge that shoe under it, like you did earlier. We'll hear her if she's trying to get in."

She nodded again as she stuffed the shoe under the door as far as it would go. She was stalling, shoving that shoe around, crouched in front of the door. She looked ridiculous in a big U of O T-shirt and the long-ass skirt she was wearing when I'd gotten home tonight. I didn't even think she realized what she had on. It was the weirdest fuckin' outfit, but the way it shifted around her, skimming her skin and swishing around her hips, made my dick twitch. I let her stall for a minute more before I called her to me.

"Need help getting this shirt off, Brenna," I told her even though I really didn't.

Whatever Doc gave me in that little plastic bag had me feeling no pain at this point. When I got back from Trix's room a bit ago, my chest was throbbing. I was glad that I was able to sit with Trix for a bit, but fuck, sitting on her tiny-ass bed had my bruised muscles screaming.

Brenna came over to help me with my clothes, and I was taken aback by how gorgeous she was. It never got old. It surprised me every time I looked at her. She used to have this confidence about her. She knew she was pretty, but she wasn't a bitch about it. Now? It was like she didn't see herself. Richards had done a fuckin' number on her. For a minute, when she'd knocked Kendra out, I thought I'd seen the old Brenna again, but she'd immediately turned back into the Stepford wife. I was looking forward to fuckin' the Stepford wife right out of her, and if that didn't work, I'd try something else.

She unsnapped my buttons from top to bottom, the opposite of how she'd put it on me an hour ago. Her hands were shaking, and I didn't know what the fuck to do to make her less nervous, so I just stood there. She licked her lips as she pushed the shirt off my shoulders, and I wiggled my shoulders a little and let it fall to the floor. Yep, these pills from Doc worked fuckin' great. I was feeling no pain.

As she reached for the button on my jeans, I stopped her and pushed her chin up to look at me. For the past couple of minutes, she'd been avoiding my eyes, and I wasn't sure why. I couldn't read her face, but she seemed really fuckin' nervous, more nervous than I'd originally thought, *Fuck it. It'd be better to just get it over with the first time, right? Like ripping off a Band-Aid.* It wasn't like we hadn't done this before. She wasn't a goddamn virgin.

Before she knew what I was doing, I leaned down and pushed her skirt to the floor, so she was standing in a puddle of fabric. Next, I pulled her oversized T-shirt over her head. Her eyes were wide, and her breathing was shallow as she looked up at me. She must've remembered my reaction from earlier because she didn't try to cover herself. She just looked me straight in the eye and kept her hands loosely by her sides.

Fuck me. I had to readjust myself in my jeans as I took her in. Her hips were wider than I remembered; her tits were bigger, too. I noticed both before, but seeing them naked was a whole different thing. When I'd had her before, her body was toned, firm, and round. I'd loved it. But her body now was unbelievable. She was all fuckin' lush with her rounded thighs, scarred-up belly, and bigger tits. I was having a hard time deciding where I wanted to go first when she made a distressed noise deep in her throat. I glanced up to catch her eye and noticed that her face was as red as a fuckin' tomato, and her eyes were starting to water.

"I know it's not like it used to be. It's all stretched out and gross—"

I cut her off from saying another word by leaning forward and sucking one of her nipples into my mouth—hard. Her hands flew up and grabbed on to my hair as I licked her and sucked her like I couldn't get enough, which was pretty close to the truth. Her skin was so soft, especially where her scars were, and I ran my nose up and down her belly, licking and nipping at her scars as I went. I didn't know why she had such a fuckin' problem with her body. She needed to get that shit outta her head.

It blew my mind that Trix had been in there, and I'd missed it. She was so tiny. I couldn't even imagine it, but I bet she was gorgeous. Fuck, she was always gorgeous. She had a scar that was different than the others, covered by her tattoo. It was a raised line that tilted slightly up at the sides like a smile. C-section scar. I didn't know she'd had one, but we hadn't talked much about Trix's birth. Fuck, if she'd had a C-section, that meant that nothing had stretched her. There was a good chance she'd be as tight as the last time I had her. The thought of her wrapping around my cock with that tight pussy just about sent me through the roof. I stood up quickly, and fuck, those drugs Doc gave me were strong. I swayed for a second, and Brenna wrapped her arms around me tightly. She opened her mouth to say something, but I didn't give her a chance. I grabbed her hand and sat. Then, I lay back on the bed.

"Take off my jeans," I told her.

I was past having any sort of tact. I wouldn't say please. I wasn't fuckin' asking. I wondered for a second if she was going to bitch at me, but the minute she registered what I'd said, her eyes dilated, and she was tearing at my jeans. She got the button and zipper down, and I tried to raise my hips, but searing pain sliced through my abs, and I dropped them back to the bed. She was looking at me like she wasn't sure about what we were doing. I looked like a fuckin' mess. Like a finger painting of a seriously fucked-up kid with blacks and purples and blues covering my front.

"Dragon, this is a bad idea. Look at you. You can barely move. I really don't see this going well—"

I cut her off. If she didn't get on my dick soon, I was going to go fuckin' nuts. "You're doin' all the work, baby. Take. Off. My. Jeans. I'm not waiting another fuckin' minute to be inside you."

She moved her lips to the side, not biting her lip, but sort of distorting her mouth. "Okay," she whispered, and I could see she was shaking.

She wasn't scared. I'd seen her scared expression too many times since she'd been back, and this wasn't it. She was as impatient as I was. So impatient, she was shaking. Fuck. Me.

I got my hands underneath myself and pushed back up, my abs and chest screaming. The minute I stood in front of her, she reached down and pushed my pants to the floor. She ended up kneeling at my feet, and she pulled the jeans away. She sat there for a second and then swept her eyes from my feet to my face, pausing for a second at my dick. The minute I met her eyes, I knew what she wanted. I remembered this. Brenna wasn't aggressive. I knew it from the first time I kissed her when she whimpered and moaned until I kissed her how she needed it. Now, she was kneeling at my feet, and I knew what she wanted. Shit, I hoped I wouldn't fuckin' pass out and topple both of us to the floor. I reached out and ran my fingers through her hair a couple of times. I fuckin' loved her hair. On my third way through, I grasped it tightly and pulled her up and forward. The minute I did, she started making the noises that haunted me for five fuckin' years. I wasn't sure how long I was going to last.

"Open," I growled and she moved her eyes back to my dick.

She reached up and wrapped her hands around the backs of my thighs, so they were brushing the undersides of my ass. God, her hands were soft. When my dick was almost touching her chin, she tilted her head down just a fraction and took me in completely until I could feel the back of her throat. I held her there until she looked back up at me.

"That's right, baby," I told her as I slid out and back in, brushing my thumb across her cheek, my eyes never leaving hers. "Take me deep, Brenna. Swallow." Fuck, that felt good.

Her throat muscles massaged the end of my dick. I kept talking to her. Told her what to do and moved her head for her. The more I talked, the larger her pupils grew until they were almost covering the green in her eyes. She was fidgeting and squirming on the floor, and her nails were digging into the backs of my thighs. She was really whimpering now and growling deep in her throat. I wasn't sure how much more I could fuckin' take, and I was pretty sure she needed some relief.

I pulled her head away from me and pushed her hair out of her face where it'd fallen since I let go. She was so fuckin' sexy with her hair all wild, wearing nothing but a little pair of panties, her lips all red and swollen, and her eyes dazed.

"Come on, baby."

I ignored the pain in my chest as I pulled her up until she stood in front of me. She was breathing really hard and searching my face like she was confused.

"Not coming in your mouth, Brenna. I'm coming when you're riding my dick with that sweet little pussy. Been waiting a long time."

Her breath stuttered, and I knew I had her. Looked like I just needed to keep talking. If she changed her mind at this point, I might kill someone. My dick was so fuckin' hard that it felt like it was going to burst through the skin.

"Get up on the bed, Brenna."

I crawled up the bed behind her and lay down flat on my back about a foot from the headboard with my head on a pillow. "Come here, baby," I called to her, and she gently moved up the bed until she was kneeling next to my hip.

"I'm not sure where to touch you," she whispered with a smile. "This is not at all how I imagined this."

"You not getting what you need?" I asked her, irritated. Fuck, I just got the shit beat out of me for her, and she was complaining. She'd been quiet this whole time, and when she decided to speak, she irritated the shit outta me.

"Baby, that's not what I mean," she whispered. "I want to touch you. I'm just afraid I'm going to hurt you, that's all."

She was looking down at her knees on the bed, and I knew it was another one of those times when I needed to actually tell her what to do. She was waiting on me. My irritation vanished.

"Climb on," I rasped at her.

My voice was doing all sorts of fucked-up shit tonight. No other woman had ever gotten to me like this one did. When she started to climb over my thighs, I shook my head at her.

"Up here, Brenna. Put your knees outside my shoulders."

She blushed, and it was cute as hell. Who knew a woman her age could still blush at shit I told her to do in bed? Once she was above my face, her blush had moved all the way down to cover her collarbone. She'd braced one hand against the headboard and the other was covering most of her face in embarrassment.

"What are you embarrassed about?" I tried to ask her without laughing.

She was just cute as fuck straddling my face, completely fuckin' mortified. She must have heard the laugh in my voice because she started to scowl.

"I haven't done this in freaking *years,* and I'm sitting on your damn face! Gimme a break!"

"The douche bag didn't eat you out?" *What?*

"Uh, no. He didn't."

"Ever?" I was completely confused. He had to have fucked her. I got that much from when he showed up at the clubhouse.

"He said it was…" She finished her sentence on a mumble; her hand once again covering her face.

"Said it was what?" I asked her. She was not getting out of this.

"He said it was gross. He never did it," she told me, and her voice was trembling.

God, I wanted to kill that fucker. He made her feel like shit, beat her, and told her she was gross? What the fuck?

"He said it was gross, huh?" I said and raised my eyebrows. Then, I licked her pussy from her ass to her clit. Just like I remembered, it was sweet as fuckin' candy. "Nope, not gross." I licked her again.

She still had her hand over her face, and I couldn't see her expression, but her eyes looked watery. I reached up and pushed her hand away from her face, pressing until it was next to the other on the wall behind my head. She looked unsure, so I told it to her straight.

"Keep your fuckin' hands on the wall. I don't want you falling. You got your hands up there, that also means I get to watch those sexy fuckin' tits bounce when you start riding my face. You look at me, Brenna. Don't look anywhere else." Then, I wrapped my hands around the back of her thighs and started eating. The first time I sucked her clit into my mouth, her head fell back, and I fuckin' loved it, but I told her to look at me, so I stopped what I was doing and called her back. "Look at me, Brenna. You keep your eyes on me, baby," I told her, and her eyes went soft.

She was so fuckin' dazed. I was pretty sure at this point she'd give me whatever I wanted. I sucked and bit and licked and pulled on her with my lips. Then, I reached farther down with two fingers and slid them inside her. She was so close; she was throbbing around my fingers. I pumped my fingers once, then again, and that was all it took for her to come all over my hand and lips. Before she was done, I grabbed one of her thighs and threw it over me, so she was kneeling beside me again. She could barely keep herself upright, and I knew it was sheer willpower that kept her from collapsing on my bruised chest.

"Sit on my dick, Brenna," I ordered her.

I didn't know how she understood me; my voice was so deep even I could barely understand it. She heard me though, and she quickly scooted down the bed, fumbling around, trying to get her bearings. When she straddled me, I could feel her pussy weeping onto my thighs, and I almost lost it. I needed to be in her *now*. I grabbed her hand to pull her toward me, and my muscles protested. Fuck, but she was going to have to do this herself.

"Baby, you're not gonna hurt me."

She was looking at my body, and the glazed look was slowly disappearing from her eyes. Fuck.

"Brenna, goddamn it! Climb the fuck on!" I snapped, and that was enough for her to make a decision.

She scooted up until I could feel her pussy at the head of my dick, and before I could take another breath, she'd taken me to the root.

"*Shit!*"

"I'm sorry!" She looked at me, her eyes wide, as she tried to scramble off me.

"Brenna, if you get up, I'll fuckin' spank your ass! Fuckin' ride me, woman!" I was almost shouting at this point.

Her eyes filled with tears, but she started to move, rolling her hips and taking me even deeper. How the hell did she get to be so damn tenderhearted, growing up at the compound?

"Baby," I called, my voice low, "look at me."

When she finally met my eyes, it felt like a sucker punch to the chest.

"You feel so good, baby. I just didn't want you to stop." I laughed under my breath. "You stop, I'm gonna lose my fuckin' mind. You're so fuckin' gorgeous up there, ridin' your man with your tits fuckin' bouncin'."

"Yeah?" she asked me quietly with a small smile on her face.

"Yeah, baby. Most beautiful thing I've ever seen."

"Dragon?" Her voice was soft, and her hips were moving slowly, taking me deep, and only pulling halfway up my dick before she dropped her weight and bottomed out over and over.

"I'm right here, baby."

"I don't have a man," she said as her smile turned from soft to something else.

"No man, huh?" I grabbed her hips and pulled her up until she was completely empty. "Gonna have to change that, I guess." Then, I pulled her down hard and listened to her cry out.

I only pulled her up and brought her back down about five more times before she was shaking and crying my name as she came. She was gripping me so tightly that I came with her. All my muscles went tight, and it was agony as I came. I didn't think this shit through. Figured if she did the work, I wouldn't even feel it in my chest and abs. I didn't think about when I came, and my whole fuckin' body tightened up.

I felt myself pulsing inside her a few times, and my eyesight started to gray around the edges. Fuck, I knew what this meant. Within seconds, everything went black, and I passed the fuck out.

## Chapter 15
### Brenna

I just barely kept myself from collapsing on top of Dragon after I came. Both of our chests were heaving, and I just knew his ribs had to be killing him. When I looked down at him though, his eyes were closed. At first, I didn't realize anything was wrong; my eyes had been closed just seconds ago. When I called his name though, I got no response. I was embarrassed that it took me a couple of minutes of staring at him before I comprehended that he'd passed out on me during sex. Seriously? That had to be some kind of record. I mean, I knew that dudes fell asleep after sex all the time, but this was mortifying. I didn't know if he'd even finished. Ugh, how romantic.

I climbed gently off the bed, so I didn't disturb him, but it probably wouldn't have mattered. As I stood up to go to the bathroom and clean up, I felt the mess we'd made between my legs. Yep, he'd finished. And we hadn't used a condom. *Fan-freaking-tastic.* I didn't know how I hadn't thought about it beforehand. No, that was a lie. I knew why I hadn't questioned it. As stupid as it was, this was Dragon. The minute he touched me, I was out of my mind for him. He'd always had that effect on me. Unfortunately. Did all thoughts completely leave my mind? No. However, when he was touching me, all other things seemed inconsequential in comparison. No condom? Eh, no biggie. Not sure of your relationship? Eh, no biggie. Not sure how long you'll be living here? Eh, no biggie. He might have an old lady still? Eh, no biggie. I was an idiot when it came to him.

With all of those thoughts running through my head, I tossed on my nightshirt and shorts and grabbed a pair of panties. I wasn't going to put them on until I cleaned up. I didn't need to keep all those sperm that close to me for any longer than necessary. Plus, wet panties? Gross.

I quietly made my way to the bathroom and shut the door behind me. One glance at the mirror above the sink had me stopping and staring. I hardly recognized myself. My hair was a rat's nest all over my head, my lips looked like they'd been injected with collagen, and my cheeks and chin were beet red with a severe case of whisker burn. But I looked happy, sated. It freaked me out. I didn't know that person anymore—the person who got whisker burn, the one who had curly hair and shining eyes. I hadn't been that person in five years.

Suddenly, a panic attack started, and I did the only thing I could do. I turned the shower on as hot as I could stand it and stepped in. I needed to look like me again. Things were getting too confusing. I had all of these old clothes to wear, Trix had started leaving toys around instead of putting them away, and Dragon was throwing his cut over the back of the couch because we didn't have a coat closet. I was having incredible sex with a guy so injured that he passed out as soon as we were finished. This wasn't my life. Was I happy here? Yes. Did it feel real or lasting? No.

By the time I finished my shower, the panic attack had subsided, but my skin was red from scrubbing. I hadn't realized how vigorous I was while my mind raced. I dried off quickly, wrapped a towel around my body, and went to check on Trix to make sure I hadn't woken her up. Thankfully, she was still curled into a ball in the middle of the bed. Since I was already tiptoeing around in a towel, I decided to check on Dragon to make sure I hadn't killed him with my sexing. I swung open the door and cringed. Shit! I'd been in such a hurry to leave earlier I'd left him laid out on the bed completely naked. I hadn't even covered him with a blanket or sheet. The odds of Trix trying to climb into bed with me were pretty high, so I knew I needed to get him at least partially covered up.

Dragon was sexy. And built. I could look at him for hours and never get tired of it. However, he was also heavy as hell. I found some of his boxer briefs in his bag, but after looking at the underwear, then back at him, then back at the underwear about fifteen times, I knew there was no way I was going to be able to get them on him. They were too snug and tight and delicious. I needed to stop handling his underwear and freaking focus. I finally decided to put him in a pair of boxers I used to sleep in. I liked to wear them with the waist rolled up, so I'd bought them big. I was still a little miffed that he'd passed out on me, so I grabbed a pair that was covered in candy hearts. The satisfaction of my joke was pretty much lost when I tried to get the shorts on him.

Dressing an adult that was asleep was nothing like dressing a child. For one, an adult was a lot heavier. For two, they were a lot bigger. You couldn't just move an adult around to get a better angle; you were the one who had to move. I had to climb all over the bed, pulling up a little here, a little there. By the time I reached his ass, I was sweaty, and I could feel my hair starting to curl around my head. I knelt, straddling his upper thighs, and reached my arms around his waist, then slid my hands from the small of his back and over his ass cheeks until I could feel the waistband of the shorts. My face was as close to his abs as I could get without actually touching the bruises. As I started to slide the shorts up, the dumbass started getting hard. So, while I was grunting quietly, trying to pull the boxers up, so he didn't flash our four-year-old daughter, his dick was thumping against my collarbone with every movement. Pull, thump. Wiggle, thump. Sigh, thump. I checked to see if he was fucking with me, but when I glanced at him, he was still out cold. Eventually, I got the shorts on.

I threw the comforter over him and crept out of the bedroom to get dressed. Once I was in the bathroom, I shut the door quietly behind me and got out my hair products. I needed my hair straight again. It took me a good forty minutes of blow drying and ironing, but I finally looked like me again. My hair was back in the sleek style that I'd been wearing since I got back to school five years ago. There was no sign of the wild uninhibited Brenna, which was exactly what I wanted. I'd been trying for the last few weeks to slowly let go of the woman Tony made me—the perfect housekeeper, the classy stay-at-home mom. I let Trix leave her toys out and come back later to play with them. I didn't wear my former regimen of makeup with precisely drawn eyeliner and lipstick. I wore peasant tops with flowing skirts and flip-flops, like a hippie. But tonight, I needed a little of the control I'd given up. I needed some of the control I'd given to Dragon. So, when I went back to bed, my hair was perfectly styled, and I'd changed into a nightgown I'd brought with me from Tony's.

I looked like Tony's Brenna, but I felt like Dragon's as I snuggled up next to him and pulled the comforter around us. I let my mind wander back to our night, the night before my life started a downward spiral that took five years to escape from.

I hadn't been a virgin when we met. I'd been with two other guys before Dragon. The first was a guy I'd met during my freshman year at U of O. He was sweet and charming and absolute crap in bed. I didn't think it was his fault; neither of us had any clue what we were doing, and it ended up being awkward and fumbling and uncomfortable. We ended up deciding to be friends, but I rarely saw him after we did the deed. I thought we were both too embarrassed to ever look each other in the eye again.

Tony was the second guy I'd slept with. He knew what he was doing. He was smooth and knew all of the buttons to push, so I always came. I always came even if I wasn't in the mood or wasn't having a good time. At the time, I figured it was a good thing. He must be really good in bed if he could always get me to orgasm, right? It wasn't until I was with Dragon that I noticed what was wrong with that scenario. Yes, Tony could get me off, but the chemistry just wasn't there. My heart didn't race, my breathing didn't grow rapid, and I didn't feel the need to claw, moan, or grab his ass with both hands and pull him into me as hard as I could.

When I'd met Dragon, I was having a shitty week. My grades were in the gutter, I'd had to buy all new tires for my Bug, which cut way into my savings, and I'd come home to whine to Pop about it, but I couldn't because he was out on a run with the boys. I was pissy and feeling sorry for myself by the time I made the rounds to all the old ladies and went out to sit on the hood of my car. I hadn't wanted to drive back to school that night, so I was debating my options of staying the night at Vera and Slider's or crashing in Pop's room at the club.

I'd had no idea that my sleeping arrangement would change with the arrival of a tall, dimpled, Native American guy with tattoos on his knuckles and bleary drunken eyes. He was beautiful. I knew guys weren't supposed to be considered beautiful—they were handsome, hot, or cute. But this guy couldn't be described as cute or handsome, and hot just wasn't a big enough word for him. His face was scruffy with a full beard that was trimmed close to his jaw, and his hair was pulled back in a ponytail with strands hanging down on each side of his face.

When he walked up to me and grabbed a hold of my thighs, I knew he didn't know who I was. I could tell by the newness of his cut that he hadn't heard about me yet, or he wouldn't have been hitting on me. I protested a little at first, but when he rubbed his beard up the side of my neck, I was done for. I would have done anything he wanted. I'd been in a weird place, upset about my grades, disappointed that I'd missed Pop, and he made me forget about everything. I wanted him with no regard for the future or worry for him. What I'd agreed to could have killed him, and lying beside him now reminded me of how thoughtless and immature I'd been then. I hadn't given him a chance to make a better decision or change his mind. I hadn't told him who I was.

We didn't just have sex that night. We had a lot of sex—really good, mind-blowing sex—but that wasn't all that happened. We talked about everything and nothing. He didn't say much, so maybe it would be more appropriate to say that I talked. I told him about school and about astronomy. Looking at the stars had always been my thing when I was growing up. My mom had died when I was small, and because my pop told me she was in heaven, I'd always had a fascination with the sky. As I grew older and went to school, the clouds and the sun were explained pretty clearly, but the stars were still a mystery. They became a mystery I was determined to solve. I told him about my favorite constellations and the brightest stars in the sky. At one point, I grabbed a Sharpie off his cluttered bedside table and drew the dragon constellation, Draco, across his chest, complete with a full explanation of the constellation. Then, he made me draw my favorite constellation, Orion, next to it.

I went into the thing with Dragon looking for a little escape from reality, and I'd gotten way more than I bargained for. He wasn't charming like Tony. He didn't tell me sweet things. He was gruff and rude, and the things he said to me made me blush. But the way he looked at me was different from the way any other man had ever looked at me. It was like he was memorizing my face. At times, he looked like he thought I was the funniest girl he'd ever met, and other times, he looked like he wanted to eat me for dinner. He'd listened to me chatter, and he'd acted like whatever I was saying was the most interesting thing he'd ever heard.

I knew I was in deep. I hadn't wanted to leave him. I'd been determined to stay as long as I could in his little bedroom in the compound, hiding however I could, so I could stay with him. Unfortunately, Pop had gotten home early. Dragon hadn't said anything about forever. He hadn't tried to make plans or even asked me where I was living. So, when Pop asked me what I was doing there, I told him I'd stayed the night in his room, but I had to get back to school.

I was afraid that if Pop looked too closely he could see what I was hiding, and a little too late, I'd worried about what would happen to Dragon if anyone found out about us. I'd left Dragon asleep in his bed, and I'd headed back to school. I planned on going back as soon as I could to explain, but a couple weeks later, I found out I was pregnant. By that time, I'd convinced myself that Dragon hadn't been as great as I remembered and that he'd only been looking for a one-night stand. So, I married Tony, and I never went back.

## Chapter 16
### Brenna

When I woke up the next morning, I was alone in bed, and the sun was shining through the bedroom curtains. As I rolled from my stomach to my back, I stretched my arms above my head and flexed my toes. I hated mornings, but if I got the chance to sleep in, I reveled in the slow stretch and burn of waking up. It was the best stretch of the day, almost nothing felt as good. I could hear quiet chatter coming from the living room, so I rolled myself to the edge of the bed and stood up to go see what Trix and Dragon were doing. Trix's voice was definitely not projecting at its normal level, and I loved it that they were being quiet for me.

I walked into the living room, smoothing down my hair and nightgown as I went. It was already a pretty warm morning, so I didn't grab a sweatshirt or robe to throw on. When I reached the living room, Trix and Dragon were sitting on the floor, building what looked like a tree house out of some pink and white Legos I'd never seen before.

"Hi, Mama!" Trix called to me, and she obviously didn't think she had to control her voice anymore as it was ear-piercingly loud.

"Hey, baby. You have breakfast already?"

"Yeah, Papa got me some cereal," she answered with a smile toward Dragon, like he'd accomplished some huge feat.

Dragon didn't even look at me when he called out, "Got you a new phone yesterday while I was out. It's on the table with your new number. Need to trash that old one."

I spun toward the kitchen to see a shiny new smartphone box sitting on the kitchen table with the phone plugged into a charger. I couldn't believe he'd gotten me a phone—a really nice phone at that. I needed coffee before I could process the new toys for both Trix and me, so I headed toward the pot on the counter.

I was halfway through my first cup and looking out the window when I felt Dragon's hand fall heavy on my shoulder. Just as I set my cup down, he surprised me and spun me around to face him. His face was set in an angry mask as he took me in from head to toe.

"The fuck, Brenna?" he rasped at me.

I looked down at myself and then back up at him. "What?" I had no idea what in the world he could be so pissed about. My nightgown was pretty modest. I didn't have coffee down the front of me. I knew there was no smudged makeup on my face from the night before.

"He buy you this?" he questioned me as he plucked at the spaghetti strap of my nightgown.

"He bought most of my clothes. What are you talking about?" I tried to pull away, but he grabbed my arms before I could get very far.

He didn't say anything else to me as he dragged me into the living room and started talking to Trix.

"Little warrior, go on and play in your room for a little bit."

"I wanna play with my Legos!" she whined back at him.

I didn't know who this child was, but my Trix would have never whined about being sent out of a room.

"You can play with those in a bit. Leave 'em out here, and go in your room. I gotta help your mama in the bathroom."

"Why do you have to help Mama in the bathroom? Mama doesn't need help in the bathroom," she prodded him with a dubious expression on her face.

"She needs help with her hair."

"But why?" she asked again.

I could feel my head darting back and forth between them, like I was watching a tennis match played by aliens. I couldn't believe what I was seeing or hearing.

"Trix," he growled, "room. Now."

She must have finally understood that he meant business because she scrambled up and, with one last look at her new toy, she ran into her room.

When Dragon started pulling me toward the bathroom, I tried to stall him. "She could've taken those Legos with her, you know."

He didn't break his stride even though I was dragging my feet along the hardwood floor. "Don't want her to choke or some shit while I'm dealin' with you."

His comment made me laugh for a second, completely forgetting that I didn't know why the hell he was dragging me into the bathroom.

"She's four. She's not going to stick them in her mouth and choke on them."

His head whipped around toward me, and I could tell he was pissed I was laughing at him.

"Well, seeing as how I haven't seen her for more than a week her whole goddamn life, how's I supposed to know that?"

My jaw snapped shut as we stared at each other, and seconds later, he turned back around and dragged me into our tiny bathroom.

"I don't know what your problem is!" I tried desperately to put a little distance between us as he shut the door, but there wasn't any place to go.

"I fuck you, and you get up and shower and put on some shit that the douche bag fucking bought you?"

"I-I—" I stuttered as I tried to find a reply to his question.

"What the fuck did you do to your hair?" He wrapped his hands around the back of my neck and ran his fingers through the hair at my nape. "My fingers don't even get fucking caught in it," he grumbled to himself.

He shook his head once to clear it, and before I could pull away from him to figure out what the hell was going on, he reached down to the straps on my tank top and jerked against them hard. My breath caught as both straps snapped, and my gown slid down my body to the floor. Then, he crowded me against the tub and reached down to turn the water on. As soon as he got it to the temperature he wanted, he took a step back and opened the bathroom door a crack.

"Trix, how you doin'?" He stood there for a second, waiting for an answer I couldn't hear over the roar of the shower. "I'm gonna help your mama take a shower. You stay in your room. I'll be out in a minute!" Then, he shut the door and proceeded to undress.

His bruises had darkened overnight and looked even more painful, but I could tell he was less sore by the way he was moving. I stood there with my arms wrapped across my chest until he was completely naked and pushing me toward the shower.

"I took a shower last night! What the hell is your problem?" I griped at him as I climbed over the side of the tub.

"Yeah, Brenna, what the fuck is that about? I pass out, and you run off to wash me off your body? Is that what you were doin'? Puttin' on your Stepford wife armor before crawling back into bed with me? Laying against me so damn tight I can barely take a fuckin' breath without moving you, yet you look like Tony fuckin' Richards's bitch?"

I gasped at him calling me a bitch, but I didn't want him thinking whatever it was he was thinking.

"It's not like that. I just...I was feeling a little out of control. I just needed a little control," I mumbled, not meeting his eyes.

He pulled me into the spray, and I relaxed into his arms, grateful he was holding me and we weren't fighting.

"I know, baby. I know you needed control. But with me, you aren't gonna get it."

I stiffened, and he kept talking.

"You gotta let go. I'm in control here. Not you. You don't need to be. I'm not gonna control *you*. Not gonna boss you around or tell you what to fuckin' wear. But I am in control of the situation. Always. That's not somethin' you need to be worrying about. Yeah?"

"I'll try," I answered him, but I wasn't convinced that his little scenario was going to work for me. I needed that control to keep from completely flying apart.

"That's all you can do. And, Brenna?"

"Yeah?" I whispered, still trying to find some steady ground beneath my feet.

"You throw out all the shit he bought you."

I started to shake my head, but he cut me off.

"I'll replace it. You need clothes; *I* buy them. You need shoes; I buy those, too. You need fuckin' perfume; *I will buy it*. You got me?"

"Yeah, I got you."

I was starting to relax because the whole time he was talking, he'd been getting my hair wet and then began running shampoo through it. He startled me when he grabbed a tight hold of my hair and pulled my face within an inch of his.

"You do that shit to your hair again, I'll blister your ass." He waited a second then jerked my hair again before biting out, "You wear your hair fuckin' curly for *me*." Then, he slammed his mouth down on mine.

I should have known that he knew what was going through my head. Five years ago, he'd seen right through me. Trying to hide my reasons for anything would be almost impossible, and it really freaked me out that any of my secrets could be ferreted so easily. My second of insight was quickly overpowered by lust as he let go of my hair with one of his hands and started sliding his soapy hand down the side of my body. I slid my hands into his hair and pulled the ponytail out, dropping it into the tub, so I could grip his hair with both hands. I was about to wrap one of my legs around his and climb him like a tree when a pounding on the bathroom door caught my attention.

"Mama, I have to go potty!" I could hear Trix yelling from outside the door.

I looked at Dragon in horror. "Please tell me you locked the door."

His eyes grew wide and panicked as he glanced down at his very impressive erection. "Shit!"

## Chapter 17
### Brenna

After our close call with Trix that morning, Dragon and I got dressed and ready for the day. It was weird for me, being out here in the middle of nowhere with nothing to do. I could only clean the house so many times without it turning into the compulsive cleaning that I was trying so hard to break myself from. I was going to bring Trix out back for a picnic, and I was hoping I could wear her out enough that she would take a nap that afternoon. I was so tired at the beginning of the day that I knew I'd be dragging ass by dinner time.

Dragon had things to do at the club, so Vera and one of the recruits were going to come over and hang out with Trix and me. I loved watching him get dressed and ready to go. I loved watching the way he moved. I'd read romance novels that described the men moving fluidly, but that was the opposite of Dragon. He moved quickly and with purpose. I watched in amusement as he pulled a brand new white undershirt out of a plastic package of three and slipped it on; it would be covered in grease by the time he got home tonight. It was so thin I could see hints of his tattoos through the fabric. Yum.

As I sat there, eyeing him from the edge of the bed, he noticed me watching, and he started to chuckle.

"Like what you see, baby?"

"What?" I was still in the fog I'd drifted into when he'd dropped his towel.

"You gonna get dressed, Brenna? Gotta say, baby, I like what you're wearin', but I won't like it if Casper sees it when he gets here in ten minutes."

I could hear the amusement in his voice, and it snapped me out of my daydreaming.

"Shit!" I started scrambling around the room, grabbing a bra and panties, while trying not to drop my towel.

Before I could get anything on, Dragon was in my space, kissing me and pulling the towel from around my body.

"Christ, woman. How do you look so damn good all the time? Wearing none a'that shit that other broads spend hours on, and you still look ten times better than any of 'em."

He kissed me one last time, squeezed my ass tightly with both hands, and sat down on the bed where I'd been just minutes before. I just stood there for a second, wondering what to do, but when I heard the roar of pipes, I rushed to get dressed. I didn't have time to worry about Dragon watching me hop around the room, trying to pull my jean shorts on. When I was finally dressed, he pulled me between his thighs with his hands on each side of my waist.

"I'm gonna take your old phone and trash it. I know that dick's been calling you, and that shit's gotta stop. You file for divorce yet?" he asked, watching me like a hawk.

"Yeah, when we first got here. Vera helped me fill out the paperwork."

"Okay, there ain't no reason for him to keep callin'. That phone I got you does all sorts of shit. I had Vera put in everyone's phone numbers last night, so you should be good to go. It's also got Internet if you want it since we don't get that shit out here. You need to use it as a hot spot. You tell me, and I'll set that shit up."

"Okay," I whispered.

He was taking care of me, and I loved it.

"Okay." He smiled back at me. "I'll be home early. You see if Vera can take Trix overnight soon. My balls are probably fuckin' purple after that shower this morning. If you woulda given me a boy, I coulda told him to piss out the damn window." He chuckled. "We need some fuckin' time to ourselves."

He leaned up and kissed me softly, still chuckling about the pissing-out-the-window comment and walked out of the bedroom. I was glad he was in a hurry, or he would have noticed that I hadn't moved an inch since he mentioned giving him a boy. I was frozen solid, my mind racing with the memories I was desperately trying to beat back. I didn't know how long I stood there after hearing his bike leave before Trix came running into the bedroom.

"Mama! Auntie Vera is here!"

"Okay, baby," I answered and grabbed her hand as we walked toward the front of the house. I needed to get my shit together before Vera noticed anything was off.

Our picnic was fantastic. Vera and I sat out on a blanket and watched Trix run around the backyard, picking flowers and spinning like a top. I loved the space we had out here; there were no houses for miles around, and as Trix got older, she'd be able to come out here and play without me having to watch her every second. The sun was high in the sky, and it was hot as hell when Trix started begging me to run through the sprinkler. Vera had the foresight to grab one when she'd went grocery shopping for me, and Trix had been playing with it and asking nonstop when she'd be able to use it. I finally gave the okay, and Vera helped Trix strip down to her underwear as I rounded the side of the house to get the hose.

The recruit that had been keeping an eye on things was on the front porch steps, knees wide with his elbows resting on them, holding a phone. He glanced up when he heard me and quickly stood up as I rounded the house.

"Hey, I don't think we've actually met. I'm Brenna." I gave a little wave.

"Yeah, nice to meet you. Casper," he told me with a nod of his head.

"Casper?"

The boys came up with stupid nicknames all the time, and they stuck. I knew this. But I couldn't figure out why they would give this dark-skinned kid the name Casper.

"Uh, yeah."

He took a few steps closer, and it clicked into place. His eyes were the lightest shade of blue I'd ever seen. They were almost white. When you matched them with his dark skin, he could have looked pretty freaky. But the way he was looking at me didn't make me feel anything but comfortable.

"Ah. Your eyes. I get it," I said with a smile.

The kid was handsome. If I were a few years younger, I would have been checking him out, but the life I'd lived the last five years left me feeling old enough to be his mother.

"Yeah. Genetics are a funny thing. My mom was Hispanic, but my dad had red hair, almost like yours. My sister and I both got all of our mom's features, but our eyes are like our dad's. It's pretty fucking weird since brown eyes are dominant." He shook his head and grabbed his phone again as I started walking toward the hose at the side of the porch.

"You can come out back with us if you want," I called with my back to him. "We've got soda and stuff back there. Lunch. Plus, Trix is going to be running through the sprinkler like a maniac, which should be fun times." I grabbed the hose and spun back around with a smile on my face that quickly disappeared by the look on his.

"I need to bring you up to the gates. Some official is up there, and they're not letting her through, but they said you need to get up there." He looked at me worriedly.

"What?" I couldn't understand what was going on.

"We have to go to the gates, Brenna. You want me to let Vera know?"

He started to walk around back, but I stopped him.

"No, I'll just bring this hose back and let her know. No reason for Trix to miss out on the sprinkler."

I hurried around the house and found Trix with her head on Vera's lap on the picnic blanket. Vera raised her finger to her lips to keep me quiet, but as soon as I got close, Trix popped up and started clapping her hands.

"You little faker! I thought you were sleepin'!"

Vera teased her as I set down the end of the hose. She was tickling Trix, making her scream and laugh, when I finally got her attention.

"Vera, I have to go to the front gate," I told her quietly. "One of the boys called Casper. They need me at the front. Can you keep Trix here?"

"Sure, darlin'. No problem. You ridin' with Casper?" she asked as I stood back up.

"Yeah, he said he'd give me a ride." My mind was racing with possibilities.

"Dragon ain't gonna like that."

"I can't argue about this right now. I have to get up there." I shook my head. "Give me a kiss, Trix. I'll be back in a few minutes."

Once I got back to the front of the house, Casper fired up his bike, and we took off toward the gate. It only took us a couple of minutes to get there, and when I saw the group there, my stomach dropped.

Dragon and Pop were arguing with some man in a cheap suit while a lady dressed in a matching suit stood by the side of a government-issued car. They seemed to be arguing about getting on to the compound as the lady watched with a scowl on her face.

"Hey, what's going on?" I called out, refusing to let my voice show my fear.

"Are you Brenna Richards?" the lady asked me in a tone that made it clear she thought I was trash.

Dragon growled as I answered her, "Yes, I am. What's this about?"

"You've been served," she told me as she handed over a manila envelope and started back toward the driver's side of the car.

I stood there, shaking, as I watched my pop say something to the man in the suit before he hurried to the passenger seat of the car.

"Fuckin' cunt. Couldn't even let the man drive the fuckin' car; she wants to have a dick so bad," Dragon grumbled as he wrapped his arms around me.

I couldn't move. I just stood there, staring at the envelope like it was a snake ready to strike. I didn't want to open it. I didn't want to know what was inside.

Dragon finally realized that I was shaken up, and he took the envelope from me as he set me on the back of his bike. "Casper! Goin' home for the night. You're off shift. Poet, you heading back with us?"

I didn't see or hear either of their answers because I had my face pressed tightly into the back of Dragon's cut, trying to keep out the entire world.

By the time we reached the house just a couple minutes later, I was desperate to read the papers in the envelope. I wasn't sure why my feelings had changed so quickly, but I had to find out what was happening. I ripped the envelope out of Dragon's hand the minute I climbed off his bike and tore it open. The sound that came from my throat when I realized what the papers entailed would have scared me if I were aware of it. I dropped to my knees in the gravel and started rocking, letting the pieces of paper flutter out around me. This couldn't be happening. He couldn't be doing this.

"What the hell, Brenna?" Pop called from across the driveway.

But I couldn't tell him. I couldn't say anything because if I did, I was afraid I would start screaming and never stop. I just knelt there as Dragon dropped down beside me and started gathering the papers, all the while trying to hold me still.

"Read this," he ordered, handing my pop the stack of papers. "Find out what the *fuck* is going on right now."

He lifted me in his arms and cradled me tightly as I started wiggling. I could tell he thought I wanted him to put me down, but it was just the opposite. I wanted to crawl inside him. I wanted to take Trix and live inside him where Tony could never get to us—where we'd always be safe. I couldn't get close enough. Faintly, I heard the sounds of Trix playing in the backyard, laughing at the top of her lungs, but I couldn't even process it. I couldn't process anything.

I barely noticed when Dragon laid me down on the bed and wrapped me tightly in the comforter we'd used the night before. He sat with me for a while, rubbing my head and whispering comforting things, until I closed my eyes. I was hoping he'd think I'd fallen asleep. Once he left the room, I heard him talking to Pop, and I knew they were trying to figure out how we would fight this. I just needed a minute to myself before I went out and got Trix dried off and dressed. I just needed a minute to wallow and worry and panic before she saw me.

The reason I left Tony was playing in the yard, and for the first time in her life, she was happy and secure enough to laugh at the top of her lungs. She was slowly coming out of her shell and felt comfortable enough to whine like any other kid her age. She was happy, and it was the most beautiful thing I'd ever seen.

It was all going to come crashing down around us, and my chest physically ached at the thought of Trix retreating back into the shell she'd been in since birth.

My nightmare, the very thing I'd been running from, had caught up to me. Tony was suing me for full custody of *my* daughter, and he had the money and the lawyers to win.

## Chapter 18
### Brenna

Trix came bounding into the room, fully dressed, before I could make myself crawl out of my cocoon. Dragon was close behind her, trying to keep her from waking me up, but he paused when he noticed my eyes were open.

"Hey, Mama. You tired?" Trix asked me, and I could see the apprehension in her eyes.

She was far too perceptive for me to play it off. She slowed down as she reached the bed and gingerly started to crawl up like she'd done a hundred times before. I didn't want her thinking I was hurt, so I quickly shoved my arms out of the blankets and grabbed her up, pulling her on top of me.

"Hey, baby girl! You have fun in the sprinkler?"

She was confused about me lying in bed in the middle of the day, but she was giggling cautiously as I squeezed my arms around her middle.

"Yeah, let's do it again tomorrow!" she told me with her eyes wide.

"If it's warm out again, we can. Maybe I'll get in tomorrow!"

She laughed as I rolled her to my side and pulled the blankets up and over our heads. The light shining through the windows let me see her face clearly, and she was once again the happy girl I was coming to expect. Once we were under the covers, she started whispering, like she was telling me a big secret.

"Papa said I get to stay the night at Auntie Vera's tonight! Can I come home tomorrow, so we can do the sprinkler?" she asked with her eyebrows lowered questioningly.

"Sure, baby. I'll have her bring you home as soon as you wake up, and we can have pancakes when you get here." I was irritated that Dragon had given permission for her to go to Vera's, but I knew it would be better for her if she wasn't home tonight while we dealt with Tony's newest blow. "Want me to help you pack for your first ever sleepover?"

"Yeah! Can I bring my Legos?"

"Sure, baby. Let's go get your stuff."

I flipped the covers down to our waist, and I was surprised to see Dragon leaning against the doorway with a small smile on his face. I'd forgotten he came into the room with Trix when I put the blankets over our heads. He was looking at me like he couldn't believe what he saw, and I wanted to lie there, basking in it, but Trix had other ideas and jumped like a kamikaze off the bed.

"Let's go, Mama!"

I climbed out of bed and watched as she raced past Dragon and out of my room, mumbling the whole way about what she wanted to bring with her. As I went to pass him in the doorway, he stopped me with a hand on my arm. Before I could even look up, he grabbed both sides of my face, tunneling his long fingers through the hair by my ears and tilting my face to his.

"Best mama in the world, and I'm the lucky bastard who knocked her up," he whispered as his eyes held mine. "We'll figure this out. Our girl's not goin' nowhere."

He waited until I gave him a small nod, and then he kissed me like he'd never done before. It was soft and tender, and I felt my eyes starting to burn until he lifted his head.

"Go get our girl packed up," he told me and slapped me on the ass to get me moving.

Once Trix was on her way with Vera, Dragon and I sat down at the kitchen table with my pop. I knew they were trying to figure out how to stop Tony, but they didn't know him or the lengths he would go to get his way like I did.

"He's not her father; he can't do this shit!" Dragon broke the silence by slamming his fist on the table.

"Yeah, you're right, but fuck, he's on the birth certificate, right? We gotta get you one of them damn DNA tests." By the tone of Pop's voice, I knew he was trying to calm Dragon down, and his no-nonsense voice seemed to do the trick.

"Yeah, I guess. They have that shit at the fuckin' pharmacy by the condoms. How fuckers ever want to get laid after they see that shit, I will never know."

"They do the test right there at the pharmacy?"

"Nah, you do it at home, and then you have to send it in to the company, and they mail you the results."

My eyes, which had been staring blankly at the tabletop, jerked to Dragon after his little explanation. He was watching me, and as soon as he saw the horrified look on my face, he explained.

"Some chick was eyein' me as she got her fuckin' tampons, and I didn't want her watchin' me pick out fuckin' condoms. Bitch was skanky as all hell." His ears had turned bright red as Pop laughed at him across the table. He rubbed the back of his neck. "Picked up the first thing I saw that didn't say 'lubricated' and acted like I was busy. She practically ran."

They were both laughing by this time, but I just didn't have it in me. I was hollow. It felt like every wall that I'd built was crumbling around me as I sat at the scarred wooden table. I'd have to go back to him. I didn't see any way for me to win this fight, and I'd never let Trix go to him without me.

I was scared—more scared than I'd ever been in my entire life even when I'd thought he would kill me. We'd been here over a month, and in that time, I had lost the hard shell that had once protected me. I felt everything. Every word and deed caused an emotion in me that I hadn't felt in years, except for with Trix. This time, I knew he could get to me, the real me. Not just my body, but my emotions. They were too raw to withstand him, and I knew he would finally break me. I was terrified of what would happen to Trix after I was broken.

I cleared my throat to get their attention. "You can't send away for anything. That'll take too long. I don't think it'll matter anyway. We were married when I had th...Trix." I caught myself and took a deep breath. "I'm not sure what the laws are, but I do know from searching online that if I was married to him when I had her, she's legally considered his."

I jumped when Dragon pushed quickly to his feet, and his chair screeched back against the floor. He started pacing back and forth in anger, and I didn't know if it was from the futility of our situation or the reminder that I was married when I had Trix.

"You had to fuckin' marry him, right?" He shook his head at my stupidity. "Had to find some suit-wearin' fuckin' psychopath to raise our daughter with. Couldn't fuckin' come home. Oh no, high-class piece like you had to have a fuckin' suit, right?" He laughed humorlessly.

"Son, sit down, so we can figure this shit out. No need to be sayin' things you're gonna regret later," my pop said quietly across the table. "Sooner we figure this out, sooner you two can figure out what the fuck you're doin'. End of the day, my granddaughter isn't going anywhere. Not while I have breath left in my body. Just gotta figure out where we go from here."

Once again, Pop talked Dragon down. It was evident to me just how much respect he had for my father by the way he listened when Pop spoke. I was, in turn, both relieved that their relationship was still solid and guilty with the knowledge that I could have messed that up.

"Sounds like we're gonna be goin' to court. Fuck me."

"You sure that's the way you wanna play this?" Pop asked Dragon with a look on his face that I couldn't interpret.

"My name is going to be on that fuckin' certificate, Poet. Do what I have to in order to make it that way." He grabbed his keys off the counter and headed toward the front door. "Be back later. You good here?" he called to my Pop, catching his nod as he walked through the front door.

He never even looked at me. The pieces of me that I'd thought shattered in the yard proved that they could break even smaller as I watched him walk through the door. I needed him, and he was gone.

"Don't worry, bonnie Brenna," Pop told me as I twisted back to face him. "He just needs a little time. He'll be back."

I knew he'd be back, but I didn't know what he'd find when he got here. I felt like I was already gone.

"He'd give his life for you and Trix, Brenna. He'd walk through fire. He'd slay a dragon. He'd go to prison." With that, he walked quietly into the bathroom.

Pop and I spent the next few hours sitting on the couch, watching movies. It would be more apt to say that Pop watched movies, and I stared into space, my mind spinning with possibilities. When I'd sat without moving or talking for a solid two hours, Pop finally wrapped his arm across my shoulders and pulled me against the side of his chest.

"Gonna work out, Brenna. You trust your old pop for that, eh?" He kissed the top of my head as I snuggled in against him.

It was only a few minutes later that the safety and comfort of my pop's arms lulled me to sleep. I barely noticed when he carried me to bed, and in the back of my mind, I hoped the bed didn't smell like sex as I fell back asleep.

A few hours later, I woke up to Dragon climbing in next to me. I tried not to stiffen when he did, but I couldn't help myself when he reached around my waist to unbutton the jean shorts I'd worn to bed.

"Know you're awake, Bren. Ya don't need to wear these to bed. Ain't gonna stop me anyway," he mumbled from behind my head.

My voice was scratchy from sleep when I answered him, "Pop carried me to bed…I'm a little old for him to put me in my pajamas."

"Oh, yeah? You fall asleep on the couch?" he asked me as he pulled my shorts and underwear down my legs.

I let him. I needed him close to me, and I didn't care how.

"Yeah, he was watching some shoot-'em-up movie. Not really my thing," I told him as I lifted my arms, so he could pull off my tank top and unfasten my bra.

As soon as he had me undressed, he pulled me close and buried his head between my breasts, wrapping his arms tightly around my waist. My hands went to his hair and pulled out the tie as his breath blew hot and hard over my skin.

"I fuckin' hate this shit, Brenna. I hate knowin' he's got any ties to either of ya. I fuckin' hate that he can still make you fall to your knees in the yard like your legs ain't got any strength left in 'em. I hate that he got to see my girl growing in you, and he got to see her growin' after that. I fucking hate it. And it's your fault."

My fingers tightened in his hair as his last sentence hit me. He squeezed me twice and then lifted his face to mine.

"But I don't hate you. I've fuckin' craved you for years. Watchin' the stars. Tattooing those constellations on before the ink you used could wear off. I'll never stop wanting you, even when I'm so pissed I could knock you across a fuckin' room."

My breath caught in my throat as I pulled my fingers from his hair and traced the three star tattoos I could see above where his body was pressed to mine.

"Holy shit," I whispered as the magnitude of this hit me.

I had thought he wanted me for me, but when Trix was added to the equation, it was hard to be sure. Lots of guys didn't feel the need to play house with the mother of their child; I knew this. Dragon had always craved a family though, and a small part in the back of my mind warned me that I was just a means to Trix.

He'd gotten these tattoos before Trix was known…to even me.

Before I could get emotional, he grunted and pulled himself higher on my body.

"Kiss your man. Been a long day, I'm fuckin' ready for it to be over."

I slid my hands back up his shoulders and into his hair as I touched my mouth to his. I was disappointed he was ready for bed, but I understood the sentiment. It had been a hell of a day. As I started to pull my mouth from his, he made a disgruntled noise and reached up to grab my hair in one fist, keeping my mouth fused to his. My nipples had been hard from the moment he'd slid naked into bed beside me, but as he bit my bottom lip, I felt the wetness between my thighs. I wasn't sure what type of noise I made, but he started murmuring to me as he ran one of his hands down my body, pausing to pinch my nipples and scratch his short nails down my stomach.

He traced the lines of my tattoo across my stomach. "I know, baby. I know what you need."

He kept speaking quietly as I thrashed on the bed, none of my movements putting his hands where I needed them. When I could finally feel a fine sheen of sweat on my body, he slammed two of his fingers into me, and I let out a strangled yell as I came.

"You needed that, yeah?" He chuckled at my throat.

Before I could catch my breath, his forearms were pinning my thighs uncomfortably wide on the bed. He had dropped his head, using his tongue to build me up again. I couldn't even protest. I was so sensitive that it was painful, but I wanted more. I wanted everything. It only took a few minutes before my body started to tense, my hamstrings burning from the pressure of Dragon's forearms keeping my straining muscles still. Before I could come, Dragon climbed off the bed and flipped me over, so I was lying on my stomach. Then, he grabbed my hips and slid me toward where he was standing at the end of the bed.

"No, Brenna." His voice was raspy with arousal. "Keep your legs on the bed. Feet at the edge."

I pulled my knees up and under me to keep my legs on the bed, but I wasn't quite sure what he had in mind until he reached under me and spread my knees wide. If I were standing, it would have looked like a crouch, but as it was, I figured I probably looked more like a frog. My feet were soles up on each side of my ass, and he'd pushed down on the small of my back, so my head and shoulders were arched toward the bed. It wasn't uncomfortable really, just a strange position to hold for any length of time.

I didn't know what all of the fuss was about until he pulled up lightly on my hips, making the position even harder to hold as my thighs screamed for relief. All discomfort was forgotten though as he grabbed one of my shoulders and positioned himself at my opening.

"Hold on, Brenna," was all the warning I got before he slid inside me in one hard stroke.

I felt my back arch at the intrusion, but soon, the surprise turned into want as I grabbed the sheets above my head for any traction I could find. It felt as if he was moving me across the bed, but he still stood at the foot, so I knew in the back of my mind that I was staying in one spot. I soon realized why Dragon had chosen this position. I was helpless with my legs spread wide with no handhold for my arms. I had to just take whatever he gave me, spread wide open and gasping for breath. He felt so good pushing and pulling that I could hear noises coming from the back of my throat, and I didn't even try to stop them. I could feel him tracing where we met with his fingers, and I was vaguely wondering what we looked like at that angle when he used one of his wet fingers to slide gently into my ass. After that, I detonated, and I was barely aware of when he came. He gently straightened out my legs and cleaned me up, but I was drowsy, floating in a sea of euphoria that I didn't want to leave. So, I just let him do his thing and curled up next to him to sleep.

I woke up about an hour later to Dragon staring up at the ceiling of our room. I couldn't read his expression, but if he was wide-awake in the middle of the night, I knew it couldn't be good. I stretched against him to get his attention, and he looked down at me with a smile.

"Mmmm," I hummed into his chest. "I liked that."

"Know you did." His chest shook with a quiet chuckle, which immediately irritated me.

"Cocky. Maybe I hated it. How would you know?"

"Bren, you came. Twice. Your thighs were fucking soaked." I dug my chin into his chest, but I quickly stopped when I remembered his bruises.

When he mumbled, "Shit, so were mine," I thought about doing it again.

He grabbed my chin before I could push my head down and held my eyes. "Layin' there, lettin' me do whatever I wanted…" He smiled slyly.

"I don't just lie there!"

"Yeah, you do."

"If I just lay there like a bump on a log, why don't you go back to that club skank you were with?" I asked with attitude, my eyebrows lifted toward my hairline.

"Brenna, you have absolutely no fuckin' clue," he told me, shaking his head.

Before I could pull myself away from him, the hand around my torso tightened.

"It's the hottest thing I've ever seen, watching you take me. Not sayin' you're a bump on a log, for fuck's sake. You trust me to give it to you. You know I will, and you let me do it. I know you haven't been with many men, but let me tell you, that ain't how it usually is. You're so fuckin' sexy layin' there, sayin' my name, makin' those noises you make. Wouldn't trade that for anything. Yeah?" He squeezed me in emphasis.

"Okay," I answered meekly, feeling like an ass for getting pissy when he was trying to give me a compliment.

"Go to sleep. Gotta get up early, so I can fuck you again before Trix gets home."

I curled back against him and sighed. Morning was going to bring the nightmare back, but for that moment, I was wrapped up in Dragon, and I could breathe easy.

## Chapter 19
### Brenna

I woke up the next morning to Dragon's hands all over my body as he slid into me from behind. The night before had been all sweaty, hard, and breathless, but this was almost the opposite. It was lazy and drowsy as we barely moved, rocking against each other. As I came, my body straightened, almost severing our connection, until Dragon pushed hard against my upper back, bending me forward and off the pillows. By the time he was finished, my head was almost completely hanging off the side of the bed, my hair pushed forward and covering most of my face.

I didn't want to move. Morning sex was awesome. It was the best way to wake up, but with Trix gone, I just wanted to sleep in a little longer and pretend that I didn't have to face the day. I lay there like a limp noodle for a couple of minutes while we caught our breath until Dragon dragged me up next to him in bed.

"Haven't talked about it…because I don't care either way…but you gonna get pregnant if we keep going at it like we do?"

Well, that sure as shit woke me up. "I don't think so. After I had Trix, I never got pregnant. I never got on birth control afterward, but nothing ever happened. I guess it could though. Will you pick up some condoms today?" I answered him, picking at the sheets with my fingers, unable to meet his eyes.

"After being with you, nothing between us, I'm not wearin' a fuckin' condom."

"Well, I'll try and get to the doctor this week then. But you're not getting any until I do. We've played Russian roulette a little too much as it is." I shook my head at him.

"You think so?" he asked me with a smile on his face as he quickly rolled us over, so he was lying between my thighs. "You think you're gonna hold out on me? You got a headache tonight, baby?"

"I'm serious, Dragon! We can't—"

My protests were cut off as he pushed back inside me, and I let out a low groan. I wasn't ready for him yet, but the sticky wetness from our earlier encounter was enough to smooth his way a little. Once he was planted deep inside me, he held still until I felt my body softening around him. As he started to move, he also started to talk, but I only caught half of what he was saying.

"Gonna give me a son…fuckin' condoms…whenever I want, however I want…beg me to fuck you…*mine*."

And it was that last word that pushed me over the edge.

After we were done, Dragon got out of bed while I dozed. He had some errands to run, so he went to get ready, and he called Casper to sit outside the house. I figured Vera would call before she brought Trix over, so I still had time to sleep some more. Sleeping past nine in the morning felt decadent, and I didn't want to give it up. I finally fell back into a deep sleep and didn't wake up for hours.

When I woke up, I looked at the clock and jumped out of bed when I realized it was almost noon. I was surprised I'd slept so long and equally surprised that Vera and Trix hadn't shown up or called yet. The house was silent as I got dressed, and it gave me an eerie feeling that I couldn't shake. I was almost afraid to walk out of my bedroom, which was silly. I knew Dragon had places to be. Casper was outside, so I wasn't there alone. But I couldn't shake the feeling. I threw on a baggy sweatshirt before opening the door to my room and walking out. The house was already warm, but I was cold all the way to the bone, and I needed a little protection.

When I went to the kitchen for a cup of coffee, I almost screamed when I saw Dragon sitting at the table. He was looking at his hands sitting on top of a piece of paper, and I couldn't see his expression, but I was relieved he was there. I laughed lightly to myself as I walked toward him, but the feeling of foreboding didn't leave me.

"Hey, honey. I thought you had errands? Did you already leave and come back?" I asked as I walked toward the coffee pot sitting on the counter.

My back was to him as he spoke, and when I heard him, the dread in the pit of my belly intensified. His voice was deep, so deep it was almost guttural. He spoke in low but precise tones that I'd never heard from him before, every single word sounding as if it were a challenge to form.

"Sit. Down. Brenna."

I didn't want to turn around. I didn't want to face whatever it was that had him so angry that he wasn't even yelling. The tone of his voice reminded me of Tony's before the beatings, and it took all I had not to vomit all over the countertop.

I slowly turned around, a fight-or-flight response surging through my body. I wasn't afraid of him, not really, but the tone of his voice and rigidity of his body brought all of my old instincts to the forefront. When I was finally facing him head-on, he moved his hands and carefully unfolded the paper lying on the table. I glanced at the paper and felt my face drain of blood as black spots danced in my vision.

"Something didn't look right when I pulled this out. Club's attorney needed it, so I went through your boxes. Took me a minute to figure out what looked different. Want to explain why this says Trix was a twin?"

I stood there, staring at him stupidly, while my mind raced. I didn't know what to say or how to explain. The word *twin* had completely shut down my body, my muscles seized, and I had a hard time catching my breath. I hadn't used that word in more than four years, and it brought back a rush of memories that I'd tried so hard to keep locked in a little chamber of my heart, only to be felt and wallowed in once a year.

He lost his patience with my silence. I knew he would. I knew he was waiting for an explanation. He was waiting for me to tell him it wasn't true, that there had been a mistake. He wanted me to tell him that he hadn't had another child that he would never know.

"Sit. Down. Brenna!" he screamed at me, slamming his hand so hard on the tabletop that the legs rattled against the floor.

My body jolted, and half a second later, I spun on my heel and raced toward the bedroom, anxious to get a door between us. I needed a barrier that would hide the look on his face and would protect me and delay this conversation.

The chair screeched behind him, and I could hear the thumping sounds of him jumping over the table as he chased me. I got to the hallway before his body hit my back, and my chest and head slammed into the wall with a cry. He spun me around by my arm and gripped both my biceps in his big hands while he shook me.

"Fuckin' explain, Brenna! You fuckin' explain that shit right now!"

I didn't notice I was crying until I felt my nose start running into my mouth. I was gasping in pain and terror as he shook me, and it took me a minute to realize he wasn't going to stop until I started talking. I could feel the skin around my cheekbone tightening as it swelled where it hit the wall, and every breath I took came out in a shuddering gasp.

"He died."

"Who died?" He jerked me again, still screaming.

"MY SON! MY SON DIED!" I screamed back in his face, my fear becoming overshadowed by anger at this man.

*How dare he bring this up to me? How dare he make me relive the absolute worst moment of my entire life? How dare he think that he has any right to my memories, to my anguish?*

He dropped my arms as if burned and searched my face with bewildered eyes. I didn't know what expression was showing on my face, but his face had gone pale at my scream.

"They were early." It was almost as simple and as heartbreaking as that. "That happens with twins…a lot. They didn't have a lot of room in there, and I didn't have the easiest pregnancy anyway. I was constantly fucking sick! I threw up every single day until I gave birth, and some days afterward." I shook my head, looking at the floor and trying to find the words I needed.

I didn't know how to talk about this. How do you describe the loss of a child? You don't. There was no explanation; there was no answer.

"His lungs hadn't developed. He wasn't ready," I sobbed. "Trix wasn't either, but she was bigger. Stronger. He was here for a week, and then he was gone. I was in so much fucking pain. I barely got the chance to hold him. I never even got the chance to breastfeed him."

By that time, I was screeching, and my throat was getting raw. My hands were in my hair as I rocked back and forth on the balls of my feet. I was so caught up in my own misery that I hadn't seen Dragon's. There wasn't room for his. My own pain made me want to curl up on the floor in the hallway. I wanted to smash things and hit someone and tear my hair out. When I brought Trix home from the hospital, I'd pushed anything I couldn't deal with to the back of my mind. I had no help, no one to lean on, no time or space to grieve. It was the first time I'd felt the full magnitude of my loss since I'd held him for the last time in the hospital, and I'd wondered vaguely if that was what it felt like to lose your mind.

Dragon braced himself with one arm against the wall, his body hunched the way it had been when he came home beaten to a pulp. "Are you telling me that our son lay dying in a hospital for an entire week, and you didn't try to contact me?"

"Yes." My answer was almost defiant.

I hadn't called him; I'd done it on my own.

At my calm answer, he swung the arm hanging at his side in a wide arc and slammed the back of it against my swollen cheekbone, knocking me to the floor.

"You fucking cunt!" he screamed, looking down at me as I curled in on myself, wrapping my arms around my head as I sobbed. "You fucking, fucking, fucking cunt."

At the change in his voice, I looked up through my arms and saw the tears rolling down his face, unchecked. I wanted to wrap my arms around him. I wanted to make this better. I wanted to console him and let him console me and do this together. But I couldn't. He didn't want me to touch him. It was all such a fucking mess, a boiling pot of emotion. I hated him, and I loved him at the same time, but mostly, I just wanted to be able to take away the agony I saw on his face.

I lay there on the floor as I watched him grab his cut off the back of the couch and slip it on. He hurriedly grabbed his keys, slipped on his boots, and walked around the living room.

Before he reached the door, he turned back toward me. "What was his name?"

"I didn't know your real name," I whispered back, my voice raw and thick with tears.

He just stood there by the front door, staring at me, waiting for my answer.

"His name was Draco," I finally answered.

Then, I watched him turn and punch the wall twice, putting huge holes in the drywall, before he left and slammed the door behind him.

I crawled on my hands and knees into the bedroom, sobbing and shaking, until I made it to the edge of the bed. I didn't have the energy to climb up, so I just pulled the comforter toward me, dragging it down to wrap around myself, as I lay, crying on the floor.

Eventually, I stopped crying and just lay there, staring at the baseboards in the hallway, my mind finally going blank when I couldn't take any more.

That was where Casper found me hours later.

## Chapter 20
### Brenna

I didn't sleep. I just laid there, the last five years playing and replaying in my mind. What I hadn't told Dragon was the agony of falling down the slick carpeted stairs in Tony's parents' house. I hadn't told him how I'd crawled to the phone and called an ambulance myself. That I'd laid on the floor until they got to me and how they had broken down the front door to get to me because, at that point, I was in too much pain to get to the door to let them in. I didn't tell him about the guilt I had about walking on carpeted stairs in nothing but my socks. If I would have just put on shoes, I wouldn't have slipped, and our child wouldn't have been born too early to survive.

I hadn't told him about how scared I was when they loaded me into the ambulance, when they moved around me using medical terms I'd never heard, but instinctually, I knew they were bad. I hadn't told him how when we'd reached the hospital, I'd told them Tony's phone number, so they could call him, but he never came. I'd been out of my mind with fear when they took me directly to the labor and delivery floor instead of keeping me in the emergency room.

I hadn't told him that my doctor was the only person in the sea of faces I'd known. I'd used her as a talisman as they'd stripped me down and got me ready for a C-section. I'd stared at her mouth as she spoke to me, but I hadn't heard a word she'd said, and eventually, they put a mask over my face, and I didn't see anything more.

I hadn't told him how I'd begged and pleaded with the nurses to go see my children on a different floor of the hospital, how they'd told me I had to wait. I didn't explain my escape from the labor and delivery floor to the upstairs nursery. The nurses had eventually given up on trying to keep me in bed, and after that first trip, I'd had a nice orderly who came to my room with a wheelchair whenever I'd asked, day or night.

I hadn't had a chance to explain how alike our children were or how terrified I was for both of them. That when I'd looked at them I couldn't see any difference in the frailty of their bodies even though I knew Trix was thriving and Draco was not. About how I'd only held him twice, and each time a nurse said he had to go back in his bed, I'd plotted murder. I didn't have a chance to explain how thin their skin had been, how tiny their ears and fingernails. How Trix's eyes had looked brown from the very beginning, but Draco's were that slate blue color that eventually turned into something else.

I hadn't had a chance to explain how badly I'd wanted my pop. How I'd never let myself cry until that final day because I knew once I started I wouldn't be able to stop. I hadn't had a chance to tell him that Tony visited me only once in the hospital. Me—not the kids. And
I'd never forgiven him.

I hadn't told him how badly I'd needed him. How I'd wanted him to show up without me having to call him. How I'd waffled back and forth about calling him and eventually came to this conclusion: I'd never see him again. He would never know that he had any children. He would never know the absolute gut-wrenching, chest-hollowing, full-body grief that I would feel. He would never feel it. As much as I needed him, as much as I wanted him to come and save us, I had to give him the peace of never knowing. So, that was what I did.

When I heard someone come in the front door, I didn't have it in me to get up off the floor. I hoped Vera wouldn't just let Trix barge in here if they were back. Dragon must have called her earlier, or she would have been here hours ago.

I heard the thick stomp of motorcycle boots coming toward me, and I didn't care. I was done. I had nothing left to give.

"Brenna, what the fuck happened?" Casper asked me as I looked up into his pretty blue eyes. He crouched down beside me and slid his arms under my body, lifting me gently. "Grease! Get in here," he called toward the living room as he walked back that way.

I'd known Grease for a very long time. He was a partner in crime when I was a kid. Though, once he started being interested in girls, that all changed. But I knew him. To his bones, I knew him. Though I hadn't seen him in five years, I knew the look on his face when he caught a glimpse of mine—fury.

"Give her to me, brother," he rumbled as he took me away from poor Casper.

The kid was probably wondering what the hell was going on.

"Call Poet and Vera and get 'em over here."

"I'm okay," I whispered as he sat me at the kitchen table and tilted my chin up.

"Baby, you're not okay. You got one hell of a shiner. I'll get some ice for it," he told me as he kissed the top of my head and headed to the fridge.

I was freezing. The comforter was still wrapped around me, but I couldn't get warm even though I could feel the sweat sticking my hair to the back of my neck. I wasn't looking forward to having the frozen peas he pulled out of the freezer anywhere near me.

"You gonna tell me what happened? Like to know why I'm killing a man," he told me as he sat in a chair, facing me. His knees surrounded mine as he reached up and held the peas wrapped in a kitchen towel against my face.

"Don't do anything. This is between him and me. It's none of your business."

"You think I'm gonna let this go? Fuck that. You got bruises anywhere else?" he asked me as he tried to unwrap the blanket.

"Quit it! No, I don't have bruises anywhere else. For God's sake, he smacked me once. That's it! Then, he took off." I pulled the comforter back around my shoulders.

"The fuck happened, Brenna? Dragon's been walking on fuckin' clouds the last couple of days even though he just got the shit kicked out of him less than a week ago. I was assuming that was your doin'. But now…" He shook his head.

"Is Casper calling my pop and Vera?" At his nod, I nodded back. "I think we better wait until they get here before I explain. I'm not doing it more than once."

I was emotionally and physically exhausted. I was so exhausted that I didn't know how much longer I could stay upright at the kitchen table. I made Grease follow me into the living room, but even though there was room on the couch for both of us, he dragged a kitchen chair with him and swung it around to straddle it backward.

I lay curled in the corner of the couch, my face resting on the bag of peas, until Vera and Pop showed up within minutes of each other. The expressions on the faces of Pop and Vera couldn't have been more opposite. Vera looked at me with a sort of resigned pity. It was the look of a woman who had seen her fair share of swollen cheekbones and tear-drowned eyes. It was a look of commiseration.

My pop's face looked like I imagined the wrath of God would. His eyes were narrowed, his lips were thin, and his hands were tapping against the sides of his legs as if playing an imaginary piano. I had only seen his hands look like that one time before—when I was eleven and a rival gang dared to breach the front gate and killed one of the recruits.

Grease spoke up, breaking the silence, as we all just looked at each other. "Still the fingers, Poet. Let's hear her out before we kill him."

"Son, you think I'm gonna let you do shit? You're outta your mind," he replied. Before I could breathe a sigh of relief, he continued, "He's mine."

As they started talking, Vera broke away from Pop's side and slid in next to me on the couch. She put one arm around my shoulders, and as she pulled me in close, she ran her fingers gently down the side of my bruised face. "I'm sorry this happened, baby girl."

I shook my head at her. "Where's Trix?"

"Tommy Gun's old lady's got her. She was at the club, so I had her come on over to the house. Trix is fine. She's playin' outside."

I nodded and started to speak, but Pop cut me off as he pulled another chair out of the kitchen.

"What's goin' on, Brenna? Ain't never seen that boy hit a woman in his life. Just don't have it in him."

I cleared my throat. "I know. I never thought he would either." I glanced at Grease, who stared back with no expression on his face.

My head was on Vera's shoulder with her cheek resting on part of my hair as she spoke from above me. "They all got it in 'em. Just takes more for some than others to make it come out."

"Yeah, I'd say this was, um…more," I told them, bracing myself for the fallout of what I was going to reveal.

As I told the story, I started at the beginning, and I didn't leave anything out. I told them about the night we met, how I'd wanted to stay, but I didn't. I told them about my decision to marry Tony and the repercussions of that. Some of the story Pop and Vera had already heard, but it was all new for Grease, who had started pacing restlessly. I told them all of the things that I wished I had told Dragon. About how much I missed my son. About how after we were home from the hospital, I'd wake up at night in a cold sweat because I'd thought I could feel him moving around in my belly.

When I started speaking of Draco, I heard Vera sob once above me, but when I tried to lift my head, she just held me closer. When I told Pop how much I missed him, he cleared his throat and walked out of the room and then all the way out of the house. Eventually, he reappeared, once again stoic.

I didn't leave anything out, even the confrontation between Dragon and me that morning. I told them everything. I wasn't sure what I was trying to do by being so transparent.

I was so mad at Dragon. I was in shock that he'd hit me and hurt that he'd left me lying on the floor. But overwhelming all of those feelings was a knot in my stomach that reminded me how badly he was hurting. I didn't want them mad at him. I didn't want them looking for retribution.

I wanted them to understand all of the things that led up to this overwhelming betrayal. This wasn't a smack because I'd looked at another man or burned dinner. He hit me because right now he was out of control, completely lost and hurting, and I was the reason. He was lashing out because it was too much to deal with. I understood it as much as I hated it.

He was like a wounded animal, and I was the hunter who'd wounded him. I didn't know if he would ever forgive me, and that hurt worse than the betrayal of my swollen face.

If he'd wanted to hurt me, really hurt me, he could've. I had no illusions that if Dragon decided to beat the hell out of me, there was nothing that could have stopped him. He didn't. He hit me once, almost in reflex, and then pulled back as if he were surprised. I'd seen the look on his face.

Even though I knew all of these things, even though I knew that there was nothing left on earth that would make him swing his arm back and bring it across my face again, I didn't know if I could ever forgive him. That hurt worse than the thought of him never forgiving me.

## Chapter 21
## Dragon

I hit her. I fuckin' hit her.

Fuck me.

When I left the house, I called Casper to come keep an eye on things. As furious as I was, I wasn't about to leave Brenna unprotected. Unprotected—what a fucking joke. I wasn't any better than her douche bag of an ex-husband. I'd seen the look on her face.

When I'd opened up Brenna's box of *important papers*, I thought I'd just grab Trix's birth certificate and head over to the club to meet with our lawyer. The suit we did business with was a good guy, but he didn't usually handle custody shit. For what we were paying him though, he could hire outside help.

I was getting annoyed with the amount of shit Brenna had in the box when I finally found it, all by itself in a brown envelope. I stuffed everything back in the box and carried the certificate into the kitchen. I wanted some fucking coffee, but I couldn't look away from Anthony fuckin' Richards's name on my child's birth certificate. It burned in my gut that Brenna had allowed it.

Something caught my eye, and for a second, I hadn't understood what I was seeing. When I realized what it meant, I thought my fuckin' knees were going to give out.

By the time Brenna woke up, I'd been sitting at the kitchen table for hours, stewing. When she ran from me, I didn't even hesitate before I followed her. I was beyond fuckin' crazy at that point. It all went downhill from there.

I fuckin' lost my shit.

So, when I left her, I just rode. I didn't have any place to be. I wasn't headed anywhere but away from the fuckin' mess I'd left behind. It took me a few hours before I realized that Casper wouldn't have gone in the house. He took his lookout post pretty damn seriously, so he would've just camped out on the porch. I didn't want to deal with the questions, so I just texted Casper to check on Brenna. He'd take care of her or call someone to deal with it. I couldn't deal with anymore shit.

My son. Fuck.

I turned my phone on silent and pulled back onto the highway.

## Chapter 22
### Brenna

Vera and I decided that Trix shouldn't see me, so I called her and let her know that she got to have another sleepover that night. She didn't know what the hell was going on, and I could tell by her voice that she wanted to come home, but she couldn't see me this way. My face was bruised, and my eyes were so swollen from crying that it was a chore just to open them. I didn't want her to see me like that. Not again.

Pop and Grease took off not long after I got done telling my story, and they must have gone to the clubhouse because shortly after, a guy in a button-down and slacks showed up at my front door. The lawyer. The reason Dragon had been in my papers.

He was really good-looking. If I were looking for another suit-wearing breadwinner, he would've been at the top of my list. His hair was a sandy brown, but it was cut short, almost shaved. He had light brown eyes and sharp cheekbones, and if the whole lawyer thing didn't work out, I figured he could probably be a salesman…or even a model. He had that look. The minute he opened his mouth, the salesman idea went out the window though; the guy was a dick. He also wasn't what he appeared to be because when he rolled up the sleeves on his dress shirt, he had tattoos covering his arms to the wrist.

We sat down with Vera, and I signed a bunch of papers for him, agreeing to the paternity test and handing over Trix's birth certificate. When we were almost finished, another thought occurred to me, and I jumped up from the table so quickly that my head spun. I ran into my room. I knew the rest of the paperwork I needed was in there somewhere. When I finally found it, I raced back into the kitchen where Vera and the attorney were talking quietly.

"Here, can you get this one changed, too?" I asked him, handing over Draco's birth certificate.

"Ah, I'm not sure. I'll see what I can do."

This guy seemed so far out of his element. It would have been funny if he weren't holding my life in his hands.

"Well, they were twins. It seems like if you could get Trix's changed, it shouldn't be hard to change Draco's, too."

"That may be the case, but…well, does it really matter at this point?" he asked me callously.

"Yes, it fucking matters!" I tried to get my emotions under control, but this guy was just rubbing me the wrong way. "Please just try and get it changed."

"I'll see what I can do," he repeated as he gathered his papers and nodded to Vera before walking out of the house.

"He's not real friendly, but he's kept the boys out of a hell of a lot of prisons the last five years," Vera told me as she got up from the table. "He's good. If he can't figure it out, he'll find someone who can. Don't you worry, baby. This'll be over soon."

"Wait, only five years? I thought I recognized his name! He's new?" I asked in alarm.

New lawyers were always on a sort of probation for as long as the club felt they needed to be. There was too much at stake to trust anyone right away, even lawyers could be bought off.

"Yeah, but his pop was the old lawyer. Wanted to retire, so Slider brought his boy in. Worked out well for everyone. You ain't got nothin' to worry about," she told me as she stepped around me, looking for her purse.

I didn't believe her, but I nodded as she got ready to leave. It was getting dark outside, and all I wanted to do was climb into my bed and pretend that the house wasn't quiet and lonely anymore.

"Casper's outside. Never left, poor kid. He's probably starvin'. I'll call ya in the mornin', and we'll figure out what to do with the baby. Okay?"

"Okay, thanks for coming. Give Trix a kiss for me," I told her as I hugged her good-bye.

It had been hard to let Trix sleep somewhere else for one night, so two days was torture. I just wanted her home.

After Vera left, I quickly made Casper a sandwich and brought it out to him.

"Hey, Brenna! You didn't have to do that. I'm fine," he told me as I set his sandwich and potato chips in front of him.

"You've been here all day. You must be hungry by now," I teased him.

It was nice that he wasn't looking at me like I belonged in a sideshow. He took the swollen face and ratty hair in stride.

"Eh, it's no big deal. I don't mind." He took a few bites of his sandwich, and we sat there in silence as the night turned darker.

"I'm sorry I didn't come in the house earlier. I figured you would want privacy. Didn't need me up in your face all day, so I just sat on the porch and waited for you to come out. I didn't even think to go in the house—"

I sat there in surprise for a minute before I cut him off. "Don't be sorry!" I blurted out. "You had no idea what I was doing in there. There's nothing to be sorry about. I would have gotten up eventually. I was fine," I told him, but we both knew I hadn't been.

"Didn't think Dragon was one of those. I've seen quite a lot of them, in and out of the club. Didn't think Dragon was like that," he told me as he finished off his food.

"He's not. He's…well, you heard the story earlier, right? I mean…I'm pissed as hell, but God!" I ran my hands through my messy hair. "I was going to tell him. I was. I just hadn't figured out how to do it yet, you know? And then, the way he found out was just…it was so fucked-up. It was out of control. I should have told him before."

"When should you have told him exactly? When your ex was showing up at the club with his fucking henchmen? Maybe when Trix was sitting with you two, eating her dinner? How about during sex—that sound like a good time to tell him? Seems to me you hadn't had a chance to tell him yet," he told me, sounding far more practical and clearheaded than anyone I'd talked to that day.

I stood up to go inside. "How'd you get so smart?" I asked him with a crooked smile on my face.

"Probably Yale," he answered completely serious.

"No shit?" I asked incredulously.

He didn't answer me, so I headed toward the front door. Right before I walked inside, I heard him say, "No shit," under his breath.

What the hell was some kid who'd gone to Yale doing becoming a recruit for a motorcycle club in Eugene, Oregon? I asked myself this over and over again as I got into bed. It gave me something else to focus on besides my life that was currently swirling down the drain. Casper was interesting. I noticed that he was well-spoken from the first time we'd met. He also didn't seem to have the same chip on his shoulder as the other recruits I'd seen over the years. I couldn't figure out why he'd chosen this life when he was obviously really fucking smart. Yale. Holy hell, I couldn't even wrap my head around it. Sure, I'd gotten into the University of Oregon with pretty good grades and average test scores, but Yale was a horse of a different color. I thought about Casper and all the different reasons he could have dropped out of school until I drifted off into a restless sleep.

I woke later that night to the covers being pulled down on the side of the bed.

Dragon was back.

I lay there, still as a statue, as he climbed in beside me just inches away. I couldn't decide if I wanted to pretend I was sleeping and roll over close to him or drag my ass out of bed and onto the couch. Both sounded equally as good, so instead, I just stayed where I was at, waiting.

I didn't have to wait long before he scooted toward me and burrowed down to lay his head just below my breasts, wrapping his arms around my waist. He didn't do anything else. He didn't try to speak; his hands didn't roam. He just lay there, snuggled into me, like he couldn't get close enough.

I wasn't sure what to do with my hands. They had been up under my head when he came in, but when I'd been rolled to my back, they sort of floundered in the air above him. Should I put my hands on his shoulders? Should I refuse to touch him and keep them up by my head? His body started to shudder, and my answer was made. I pulled the tie from his hair and ran my fingers through it softly, quietly comforting both him and me. God, we were a fucked-up mess. I had no idea where we would go from here.

"I fucked up, Brenna. Shouldn't have hit you," he told my stomach.

"Yeah," I whispered back.

The night was stifling around us, and I was afraid if I raised my voice, the spell would be broken, and we'd be at each other's throats again.

"Fucked-up. I'm so fucked-up," he told me, and his body relaxed into sleep, never moving from mine.

"Me, too," I told him, but he didn't hear me.

## Chapter 23
### Brenna

When I woke up the next morning, Dragon was gone. His side of the bed was still warm, so he had to have just left, but I was in no mood to follow him. The last couple of days had made me leery of getting out of bed at all, but I eventually got up and gathered my clothes and a towel, so I could take a quick shower. I hadn't showered in the mess that I liked to think of as *the day of reckoning,* so I was getting pretty rank. I needed some shampoo and scented body wash, STAT.

When I made my way into the hallway, I could hear Dragon and Pop talking in low voices in the kitchen, and I paused outside the bathroom door, trying to hear what they were saying.

"You don't have to do it this way, son. Duncan says he can get custody with the photos I took of Brenna when she got here. No need for you to get involved." My pop's voice was compelling, but Dragon brushed him off.

"Getting my name on that birth certificate one way or another. Not arguin' about this shit anymore. Have him send the papers."

"Yeah, I hear ya. But—"

Pop's voice cut off when I leaned against the bathroom door, and it banged open. I'd thought it was closed when I leaned against it, and after the loud noise, I scrambled inside before they could see me. I didn't know what was going on with Pop, but that was the second time I'd heard him trying to talk Dragon out of getting the

DNA testing done. I decided I'd think about it later as I spun around and locked the door. It wouldn't keep Dragon out if he really wanted in, but I doubted he would come barging in anyway. If his absence in bed that morning was any indication, he was as leery of me as I was of him.

I took a longer shower than I had planned on, taking the time to shave my legs and carefully wash my face before I got out. Long showers were a luxury that I hadn't had in four years, and it was kind of nice to take my time. I eventually stopped dawdling, knowing that if I took any longer I'd look like a coward. I climbed out of the shower and got dressed in a summer dress that I'd found in the boxes Vera brought over. It was a little tight across the chest, but I thought it looked okay anyway. It was loose and flowing, perfect for a hot summer day. I also liked the irony of dressing up a little when my face looked like the Hunchback of Notre Dame. The swelling on my cheekbone hadn't gone down much, but I was pretty sure the brunt of the trauma was when I'd hit the wall. Dragon's slap had just added the little bit of extra it took to make me look like a monster. I didn't even try to cover it up with makeup; nothing was going to help.

When I got to the kitchen a few minutes later, I took a deep breath and tried not to look at Dragon sitting on the couch, alone, with his elbows resting on his knees. He looked how I felt, uneasy. I got my cup of coffee and turned around, leaning against the counter, to catch my breath. I didn't know what to say to him. I didn't know what to do in this situation.

When I was with Tony, the beatings were nothing like this. He liked to hit me. There was no purpose, no anger in it. He got off on it. The next day would be business as usual, and he would expect me to act like nothing happened. With Dragon, he'd hit me once. He hadn't beaten me. He'd been angry and devastated, and the underlying reason was still stretched between us like a foul-smelling moat that I didn't know how to cross.

He didn't say a word to me. He just sat there, looking at the floor, like he had all day to do so. The tension in the air finally caused me to take a few steps in his direction, and when I did, his head snapped up. All at once, I saw everything he was feeling. He wasn't angry anymore. There was no censure in his gaze, no fury in the lines of his face. The pain I saw was enough for me to take a ragged breath and another step forward, but it was the guilt in his eyes that led me to sit next to him on the couch.

When I got there, he turned toward me, and I flinched as he raised a hand to my swollen face.

"God, baby. I'm so sorry," he whispered, and I knew that he was.

I knew he was sorry, but whether that mattered or not remained to be seen.

"I know," I told him quietly, but I couldn't tell him he was forgiven. I couldn't tell him it was okay, and I was fine. I wasn't fine.

"I don't know what the fuck I was doing. Fuck. Fuck!" He searched my body as if looking for any more bruises, and I knew the exact moment he noticed the ones on my arms. "Shit, look at your arms, baby." He rubbed them gently with his fingertips as if to finger paint them away.

"Those will be gone by tomorrow," I told him, and they would. I bruised easily. I always had. "I'm like a peach. I bruise easy. Those ones aren't the problem."

"I know," he told me as he wiped his hand down his face. "God, I was fuckin' dyin' when you told me about him. I was so fuckin' angry with you. I thought, maybe there was an accident or somethin', you know? Like maybe something happened to him. That's why I waited, why I let you sleep. I thought we'd just talk about it. I knew it had to have been fuckin' bad for you. I knew. But fuck, when you said you knew he was dyin', and you never fuckin' told me." He shook his head and cleared his throat. "Fuck, Brenna. I never got to hold my son."

He looked at the floor again, not touching me, not moving, and for a while, I just sat there, staring at him.

"I'm sorry." I was so sorry that I hadn't had a chance to tell him, to soften the blow as much as I could.

"What are you sorry for, Brenna? I hit you in your goddamn face for Christ's sake!"

"I'm sorry I didn't tell you sooner. I'm sorry you didn't get a chance to hold him. I thought I was doing the right thing."

"You don't need to be sorry. I told you before that all that shit was over. I told you that you were fuckin' safe here. That nobody would lay a hand on you as long as you were with me. Fuck. I blew that all to shit, didn't I?"

"Yeah, I guess you did."

I could feel a lump in my throat growing as I watched him berate himself. Did I want him to be sorry? Hell yes, I did. But I didn't want him to take all the blame for the clusterfuck that was our lives. I'd done my part, and my part was a doozy.

He must have heard something in my voice because when I finished speaking, he put his arms around me and gently pulled me into his lap. The action was enough to put my overused tear ducts to work again, and I could feel my cheeks getting wet as he buried his face in my throat.

"I'm so sorry, baby. Fuck. I'm so sorry. I won't hit you again. Ever. Fuck me. I can't believe I fuckin' hit you," he repeated again and again into my throat, kissing me between words.

I didn't know who moved first, but our lips met, and everything from there was a frenzy of movement. I slid my leg around, so I was straddling his hips, and his hands slid underneath my dress, pulling at my underwear until the strings holding the sides snapped and he pulled them away. I was equally as impatient, digging my fingers into his belly, as I tried to get his jeans unbuttoned. When we were both finally naked from the waist down, I lifted up with my legs and brought him inside me in one move that had us both groaning. We weren't making love. It wasn't sweet or soft. We were fucking, hard. Every movement was rough and needy, and for once, Dragon wasn't talking me through it. We just needed to be as close as we possibly could before the world came tumbling around us again. I was headed for climax, my body stiffening with impending release, when he grasped my hips and slowed me down.

"What are you *doing?*" I griped as I tried to move against his hands.

"Baby, look at me?" he asked, but I shook my head as I pulled at his hands.

I couldn't do this right now. I just needed him to fuck me. I couldn't deal with anything more. My face was finally dry, my emotions in check. I just needed him to fuck me.

The first time was a question, but the next time was a demand. "Baby. Look. At. Me."

I tried to shake my head again, but he ran his fingers up the uninjured side of my face and lightly tangled his fingers in the hair behind my ear, and I finally met his eyes.

"I am so goddamn sorry, Brenna. I'm sorry I lost it."

"Okay," I told him and tried to move my hips again, but he was holding me still.

"I'm sorry that I hit you. But I'm more sorry that I didn't come for you."

My breath whooshed out of me at those words.

"I'm sorry I didn't get to hold him, and I'm sorry I didn't get to hold you, that I didn't get to take care of you when you needed me. And I'm so goddamn sorry that you told me our son was dead, and I fuckin' scared you and hit you, and I didn't hold you tight and love you. I'm sorry."

It was more than I could take. I leaned forward and rested my head against his neck below his ear and cried as he rubbed my back in slow circles, our bodies still connected. I finally lifted my head and nodded at him, wiping my nose on my dress, as I pulled it off.

"Okay," I told him. And I was.

The last couple of days were a hell that I would never want to go through again. It was agony, all of it. But I loved him, and I needed him, and I didn't want to be without him ever again. So, I would work through it; we would work through it.

As soon as my dress was off, he reached back and unsnapped my bra.

"Not supposed to wear a bra with that hippie dress," he told me, rubbing the lines on my breasts from the seams of my bra.

"I don't ever go without a bra. The girls are too big."

"Good, nobody needs to be starin' at your tits. You're home with me and Trix though, you go without," he grumbled as he took one of my nipples into his mouth.

He let it pop out with a small smack of his lips and then looked up at my face where I sat, unmoving.

"Not ten minutes ago, you were fucking me like you couldn't get enough, and now, you just sit, not movin'. You need me to talk to you, baby?" he asked with a tender smile.

I hadn't realized that I was frozen above him until he'd pointed it out. It was true. I had stopped. Normally, I needed that little bit of dominance from him. The little bit of direction helped me feel comfortable and safe. In our mad dash to be connected earlier, I hadn't thought about it, but once the frenzy was over, I was still, too still. I felt my face burn with embarrassment.

"That's okay, baby. I'll give you what you need," he told me before he took my nipple between his teeth.

He squeezed my ass in his hands, and I knew that he wanted to slap it, but with the day before looming above our heads, he was afraid to.

"Ride me, baby," he growled at me, squeezing again.

When I didn't move, he raised his head from my breasts to look me in the eye. I just looked at him, too afraid to say what I needed. I didn't want this hanging over us, even in bed. I wanted him uninhibited, so I felt free to be uninhibited with him. I needed him to get past it.

So, I just waited, challenging him with my eyes, for him to do what we both needed. I knew the moment when he understood because his eyebrows raised and a small smirk lifted the side of his mouth.

"Okay, baby. I'll give it to you." Then, he slapped my ass once, barely enough to sting, but it was there. "Ride me, Brenna. Now."

And I did.

We spent the rest of the day, lying in bed, talking. I told him all of the things I'd wanted to before, and he listened quietly while I laughed and cried. It was good for us. We planned on getting Trix the next day, and I really hoped that my face looked good enough to cover with makeup. The swelling went down considerably as the day went on, and Dragon frequently reached up to touch it softly as if reminding himself what a dick he'd been. We only left the bed for food and bathroom trips, preferring to spend our time cocooned together, away from the outside world. If Trix had been there, it would have been perfect.

I knew that it was going to be a process for us to put things behind us, but I was willing to be patient. When I looked at him, I saw everything I wanted. That was enough.

## Chapter 24
### Brenna

The next few days were a revelation. Trix came home the next day, and although she could tell something had happened, she never said anything. The swelling went down on my face pretty quickly after those first couple of days, and the bruising faded to a putrid yellow color I could cover with makeup. Tony hadn't ever hit my face hard enough to bruise, but more than once, he'd grabbed it hard enough to leave fingerprints, which meant I was pretty damn good at covering things with a little foundation and some powder.

We slept late in the mornings, no morning sex, but Trix came in with the rising of the sun and snuggled up in bed with us. It was heaven. Dragon was able to take off a week of time that he spent mostly with us. There were a few times that he had to go out on club business, but for the most part, he was home with us all day. I knew my pop had a hand in that, and I was grateful.

We spent time getting to know each other on a level we never had before. Little things that other people took for granted, I relished. Dragon didn't like any cereal that wasn't sugary or didn't have a cartoon character on the box, but he was really health-conscious otherwise. I'd always been pretty careful with what I fed Trix, but he took it to a whole new level, making sure she ate plenty of vegetables and nothing out of a box, except cereal.

I knew he would eventually grow more complacent, but the fact that he worried so much was endearing. He let me lounge in bed in the morning while he got Trix fed, but he was in, slapping my ass to wake me up to get her dressed. He liked metal music and anything to do with an engine that he could work on with his hands.

Spare parts soon came to rest on my kitchen table or by the front door, and I eventually got him a crate to put things in, so they didn't clutter up my house. He used orange-smelling cleaner to scrub his hands and a little nailbrush to make sure he never came to bed and put his hands in me while they were covered in grease.

We lay out on a blanket in the grass, his hand holding mine or wrapped around my waist for hours, while we watched Trix run through the sprinkler in her underwear. He always made sure both Trix and I were slathered in sunblock every time we left the house.

He was concerned about things that I had never imagined would matter to him. The way he took care of us relieved every concern I had about him in the past. He cared about everything. He tried to protect us without stifling us, and Trix and I blossomed.

One night, when Trix was playing on the floor and Dragon sat polishing some sort of engine something or other, I started flipping through the music on my iPod. He was grunting with every selection, like I was turning it on just to torture him. He never raised his head, but after a while, I started to pick music just to annoy him. Maroon 5, Janet Jackson, anything pop-related that I could find, I played, and every time, he made a noise of disapproval. Finally, I chose one of my favorites, a song I used to sing to Trix as a baby. It wasn't pop, but it definitely wasn't heavy metal. When I didn't hear a noise from him, I raised my head and watched him polishing the engine part.

"Seriously? Nothing to say?" I asked him, my eyebrows rose in surprise.

He never looked up from what he was doing, but he answered me anyway, "Babe. The man's a poet."

"You like James Taylor?"

"Just said I did, didn't I?"

I felt the smile forming on my face as I found the greatest hits on my iPod and set them on shuffle. I'd found our musical common ground. To other people, it may have seemed insignificant, silly even. But we were building a life, starting from the ground up. I loved learning new things about him, finding how we fit. When he looked up and winked at me, my smile widened until I felt my cheeks cramp.

We made our first forays into the outside world, and it didn't seem as daunting with Dragon by my side. I knew he wouldn't let anything happen to us. We grocery shopped and went to dinner, and we even went shopping for summer clothes for Trix. Nothing too short or with any thin shoulder straps made it into our basket. He was very particular about what she wore. It seemed a little over the top to me, but if it was important to him, we could wait until Trix was old enough to complain before we discussed it.

Normal things felt like trips to an amusement park. They were all new and exciting. Even settling into a routine was something that

I found myself daydreaming about. This was a life I'd never wanted, and now, suddenly, it felt completely right.

If Dragon would have treated me like spun glass those first few weeks, I thought things would have been much harder to move on from. I would have been aware of our fight every moment of every day, like an albatross hanging around my neck. But after that first day, he didn't bring it up again other than the small kisses he dropped on my cheek daily, even after the bruises had faded. It was a reminder that he hadn't forgotten; it was a promise. He went back to being the man I'd dreamed about, gruff and blunt and completely enamored with me. He undressed me with his eyes at the dinner table and grabbed my ass as I left a room, and I loved it. I loved him. I wasn't sure when it started—long before the day he found out about Draco—but it felt so much more real once he knew everything. All our secrets were out in the open, and I reveled in it.

For once in five years, I wasn't in control, and I loved it. I hadn't had a panic attack since I got the papers from Tony, and I felt stronger by the day. I knew Dragon and Pop wouldn't let anything happen to Trix, and it was a heady feeling to not have to worry about every single little thing. I was just living, playing with my girl during the day and playing with my man at night. It was bliss.

Eventually, life changed into a more normal pattern with Dragon leaving in the mornings and sometimes not getting home until Trix and I were in bed. I didn't like it. Of course, I didn't. Most nights, I lay awake, waiting for him to get home, my insecurities screaming at me. But he never gave me any reason not to trust him.

He'd come home smelling like the clubhouse—smoke and a mix of whiskey and beer. It didn't matter if he'd left only hours before, the minute he got home, I wanted him. I simmered all day, my body sore, but with an underlying arousal that never went away. We wanted each other with an urgency that never wavered.

The club had a barbeque every few months, and about three weeks after *the fight*, they had another. It was mid-summer. Everyone was outside in the sunshine, and a band was playing on a platform built every year once the sun came out. It was a tradition to have one of the local bands play, and it'd been the same one since I was a kid. The guys in the band were honorary members of the club although none of them had ever been patched in. They were old and grizzly, and I loved every single one of them. It was like seeing a bunch of uncles for the first time in years, and I proudly showed Trix off while she stood shyly, trying to hide behind my legs.

It was fun to see Dragon in his element, drinking beer with the boys and giving the recruits a hard time. I'd never had the chance to see him interact with the boys before, but I wasn't surprised by the respect he seemed to have inside the club. It gave me a feeling of family that I hadn't had in a long time.

I was sitting on Dragon's knee, my arms wrapped around his shoulders, while he talked to Grease when the band started its first set. I was familiar with all of the songs they sang. Not only were they covers, but they hadn't changed much over the years. There were newer versions of some of the songs, but for the most part, they stuck to what they considered the classics. It wasn't until they paused after "Crazy Train" and the lead singer Jimmy started speaking that I paid any attention to what they were doing.

"Now, we've been missing someone for five loooooong years!" Jimmy exaggerated into the microphone, and my forehead dropped as I groaned into Dragon's shoulder. "Brenna, my darlin', I need you! Make an old man happy!"

All of the old club members hooted and hollered while the newest looked at me in confusion, including Dragon. There was no way I was getting out of it, so I just gave Dragon a quick kiss and stood up.

"I'll be right back. If they don't let me go, please come save me."

The yells got louder the closer I got to the stage, and the minute Jimmy grabbed my hand and pulled me up to stand with him, the air was filled with cheers. I leaned into his microphone and smiled ruefully.

"I haven't done this in five years. Be kind!"

The whole crowd laughed, and a piercing whistle came from the picnic table where Dragon and Grease were sitting. When I looked over, Grease had a huge smile on his face, and Dragon was watching me closely. I looked around for Trix in the crowd of kids, and I found her standing still in the midst of the chaos, watching me. I gave her a wink, and she smiled huge before I walked to the back of the stage where Harry was sitting.

"You ready to go have a beer, old man?" I asked him with a grin.

My hands were sweating in nervousness, and I wiped them on my thighs before I sat down behind his drum kit.

When I was about six, I wanted to join dance class. I was in heaven when Pop let me go. Vera was my chauffeur, driving me to and from class twice a week for two weeks, while Pop was on a run. When he got back, I was so excited to show him what I'd learned that I'd dragged him to class. I'd had no idea the drama it would cause. I had no reason to think that anyone would have a problem with my pop. I didn't notice the dirty looks the country club mamas gave him as he sat on the edge of the floor, watching me twirl and prance. I'd been completely focused on him and the proud look on his face. I'd felt like I was walking on the clouds.

The next week, it was back to Vera driving me to and from class, but everything else was different. The other children didn't talk to me, and the dance teacher spoke to me like I was a pesky fly she couldn't get rid of. I was devastated but determined, and this went on for three more weeks before Pop had had enough and pulled me out.

I was heartbroken, but Pop thought if I liked dance, then maybe music would be a good outlet for me. Instead of twice a week lessons at the local dance studio, Vera drove me over to Jimmy's garage where the band practiced. At first, I was pissed. I wanted to be a pretty ballerina. I didn't want to try and work my fingers around the frets on a guitar neck. It wasn't long before the boys knew guitar wasn't going to be the instrument for me. I picked up the rudimentary chords pretty quickly, but I was bored. Wayne, the bass player, was the only member who was classically trained, but he said he'd be damned if he was going to buy me a fucking flute or clarinet. A few weeks went by where they tried to get me interested in the piano, but they eventually gave that up, too. It wasn't until I stepped behind Harry's drum kit that I found my place.

I was too small to sit, so I stood behind it as I beat on the drums the first time. Only my eyes and the top of my head showed over the set of toms, but it was love at first beat. It turned out that I had an affinity for percussion. I sat quietly while Harry explained what sound each piece made, and from then on, I was hooked. I was by no means some child prodigy, but I was good, really good. I played with them on Tuesdays and Thursdays for ten years. My skills improved rapidly, but steadily, over the years until one day I was as good as Harry. My recitals were club barbeques, and I had a captive audience of family every time I climbed on stage.

I probably could have applied for a music scholarship when I went to college. Wayne had taught me to read music, and I could play anything he put in front of me, but I had been reluctant to turn something I loved to do into something I had to do. I'd been afraid it would take the magic away. I'd played at random barbeques I went to during college, but when I left the club, I never played again.

It had been over five years since I played, and my fingers felt stiff and awkward at first, but within the first few beats of "Paradise City," it was like I was reconnecting with an old friend. I sat behind the kit, the world around me fading away, as I played song after song with the men who'd taught me more about music than most people learn in their entire lifetime. I pounded my frustration and pain of the last five years into the drums, and by the time I was finished, my hair was sticking to my neck and the sides of my face with sweat.

I stood up at the end of the set and met Pop's eyes across the yard. The things I'd done, the pain I'd put him through, the frustration and the anger—none of that mattered. He still watched me with the same proud smile on his face that I'd seen when I was six years old, twirling around that dance studio. Those mamas, the ones who'd acted like I was trash? They had no idea the family I'd had growing up. They wouldn't understand the support and love that surrounded me every day of my life. Pop may not have been the best man. He was the vice president of a motorcycle club, a killer, and a thief, but when he looked at me, all I saw was the man who'd loved me unconditionally from birth. Nothing would ever change him in my eyes.

It wouldn't be until a week later when I would see the part of my father that I'd been sheltered from, the man who had left Ireland under a cloud of suspicion and was welcomed into the club with open arms for a reason that only the old president had known.

## Chapter 25
### Brenna

When I got done with my fifteen minutes of fame that turned into an hour of beating Harry's drums with everything in me, Dragon was waiting. He stood at the edge of the stage, and my feet didn't touch the grass before he hoisted my legs around his waist, and he was kissing me hard. Our breath was ragged when he lifted his head to the catcalls and whistles filling the air around us. The smile on his face was wide and bright, crinkling the corners of his eyes, and his dimple was just barely visible underneath his close-cropped beard.

"That was one of the sexiest things I've ever seen. Why didn't you tell me you could do that?" he asked while kneading the cheeks of my ass with his hands.

I just shrugged my shoulders. "It's not a big deal. I've been playing since I was six."

"No wonder you and Trix dance like you do. You're fucking drumming with your feet!" He laughed in my face.

"What do you mean?" I asked him, confused.

"When I watched you guys dancing in the kitchen, your feet were fuckin' pounding the floor with the beat of the music!"

My face got hot.

"You didn't know you did that?" He laughed again at my embarrassment.

"Ah, no. I don't do it on purpose. I've never noticed," I told him.

"Well, it's cute as fuck, and Trix does it, too. That girl can keep a beat like no kid I've ever seen," he replied with a proud smile on his face.

He started walking through the crowd where shouts of vulgar suggestions were made to our retreating backs, but Dragon never put me down. When we made our way around the corner, he pressed me up against the wall of the building and kissed me again, his hands roaming my body.

"You're gonna keep a beat for me tonight, yeah?" he whispered in my ear, biting the lobe gently.

I wasn't sure exactly what he was talking about, but it didn't matter. Anything he asked of me in that tone of voice, I'd give him.

We walked home after the sky had grown dark, and Trix had finally fallen asleep, sticky and covered in dirt, sitting on Dragon's lap. Neither of us were drunk, but we were feeling the effects of the whiskey and beer we'd drunk. I hadn't had more than a glass of wine since the night Trix was conceived, and I was giddy with it.

When we got into the house, Dragon turned to me, "Get undressed, Brenna. Gonna put Trix in bed. Want you naked when I get to you."

Then, he walked quietly down the hallway toward Trix's room as I locked up the house. I raced into the room, flinging clothes off, with a desperation that bordered on ridiculousness. When I was finally naked, I lay down on the bed and waited as I heard him walk toward the front of the house. He came back, carrying a kitchen chair and my iPod dock, causing me to sit up in surprise.

"What are you doing?" I asked, my face creased in confusion.

He didn't answer me, but he went around the side of the bed and plugged in the dock. Then, he set the chair at the end of the bed and locked the door before sitting down and grabbing the neck of his shirt to drag it off.

"Only set up two songs, but I figure I won't make it much longer than that." He looked at me, his nostrils flaring, and he finally told me what was going on. "Get down here and dance for me, Brenna."

"Uh, dance for you?" I asked nervously.

I wasn't a stripper. I didn't know any sexy dance moves. I could just envision myself trying to be sexy and ending up looking like the kid from Napoleon Dynamite.

"Baby, you'll do fine," he told me, correctly interpreting the look on my face. "Come 'ere."

I climbed off the bed and went to stand in front of him as the beginning strains of Awolnation's "Sail" filled the room. I felt my breathing grow heavy as I remembered the song's thumping rhythm. He grabbed my waist gently and pulled me so that my thighs were straddling his.

"Not much to it, baby. I want a lap dance. All you need to do is move with the beat and use your imagination. You know what I like."

I stood there awkwardly until he pulled me down, grinding his jean-clad hips into my bare ones.

"Come on, baby. Don't you wanna show off for your man?" he asked me on a thrust. "Give it to me."

It didn't take long for the beat of the music to release my inhibitions. I was using my hips with the rhythm of the song, his hands roaming my body, touching anything he could reach. I ran my fingers through his hair and then dragged my nails lightly down his chest, bending my head down once to take a nipple into my mouth. He made a sound low in his throat and dragged my head up to meet his, so he could kiss me deep, but my hips never lost rhythm. The kiss was enough to have him unbuttoning and unzipping his jeans as I writhed above him.

When the song transitioned from "Sail" to "Radioactive" by Imagine Dragons, he was already inside me. I moved with the beat of the music, my eyes never leaving his, as I ran my hands over my breasts and up into my hair. When my hands rose above my head and my back bowed, I thought he was going to have a heart attack. We didn't last long after that.

We lay in the bed hours later, neither of us ready for sleep.

"We'll get this shit taken care of, Brenna. Don't worry. If I'm not here, Poet and Vera will help you take care of things. Our lawyer's a douche, but he knows what the fuck he's doing," he told me quietly.

"What!" I raised myself up on my elbow, alarmed. "Why wouldn't you be here?"

"You know how Slider is. He's not gonna be easy on me just 'cause we got family shit. Got runs to make...can't be sittin' at home forever," he told me like it was no big deal.

"Well, maybe he'll be cool. He knows all of the shit that's going on. Come on, I'm his goddaughter. He's not going to send my man out when I need him here," I told him logically.

He grunted. "Not your plaything, Brenna. I'm a brother. I do my job, and I'm good at it. I'm not takin' favors from the boss because I'm fuckin' his goddaughter."

"That's a shitty thing to say," I groused.

"True, ain't it? Just fucked you twice in the last two hours." He sounded annoyed.

"You could have said you were 'with me' or something. You don't have to talk like I'm a piece of ass." I was getting more annoyed by the minute.

"Brenna, I'm gonna say whatever the fuck I want. Not sugarcoating shit, so you don't get your panties in a twist. I ever treat you like a piece of ass?"

"No," I grumbled.

"Then, don't put words into my mouth." He shook his head in frustration. "How the fuck did we even get on this conversation? You're fuckin' crazy, you know that?"

He sounded baffled, and I giggled into his chest. He wrapped his arm around me and pulled me on top of him, so my arms were crossed, resting on his chest, with my chin leaning on my forearms, our entire bodies aligned to our toes.

"You do what I say," he ordered me gently. "If I'm not here, you lean on your pop and Vera. We'll get it taken care of. You gotta trust me, baby."

I didn't know what was going on, but I knew he needed me to answer him, so I did. "All right, honey. I'll trust you and lean on Pop and Vera if you're not here."

"That's good. I'm always gonna take care of you," he whispered, running his fingers down the side of my face, and then rolling us, so we were lying side by side.

He searched my face for a minute, and the look in his eyes made me instantly apprehensive.

"Is everything okay?" I asked him anxiously, dreading his answer.

"Everything's fine. Nothin' to worry about. Gonna be smooth sailing from here," he assured me with a slow kiss on my lips.

Then, he tightened his arms around me and tilted his head above mine, closing his eyes as if to sleep. I lay there in the dark, safe and warm in our little nest, but I couldn't shake the feeling that something bad was looming on the horizon. Dragon had assured me that everything was fine, but something was off. He wouldn't look me in the eyes as he said it.

## Chapter 26
### Brenna

Life evolved into a pretty familiar pattern. Dragon spent most of his time away from the house, but knowing he was in town was enough to keep me from completely panicking about our conversation after the barbeque. In the days after the party, I felt like the hairs on my neck stood up constantly in reaction to a force that I couldn't see. I knew something was coming, but I couldn't tell from what direction it would come.

Tony had been quiet, and we learned four days after the barbeque that our custody hearing had been pushed back in light of recent events. Dragon's paternity suit had done its job, and I was almost giddy with relief that this would all be over soon. I no longer received any calls from Tony. Dragon had taken care of that weeks ago with the new number he'd set up for me. But I'd still had to deal with Tony's lawyer calling the club and leaving messages constantly, always promising the same thing. If I went back, Tony would be willing to go to couple's counseling, and he would drop the custody suit immediately. The thought made me shudder. The attorney for the club finally took over those calls, too, telling both the attorney and Tony that we weren't interested.

Trix had made friends with some of the club kids, giving us more to do during the day, as old ladies and their children stopped by to play. Casper still spent time watching out for us when Dragon wasn't home. Dragon didn't feel comfortable leaving us alone until the dust had settled on the custody battle, but Trix and I didn't mind. Casper was becoming the brother I'd never had; he was a part of our little family, and we loved having him around. It was everything I'd been looking for when I left the club. It was a community where Trix and I felt comfortable, where we could have play dates, and I could chat with other mothers without worrying that I would let something slip that would give a hint to our home life.

It was amazing to me, the difference in my perspective from a child of the club to an old lady of one of the members. I had been so sure that the life I'd wanted was outside the gates of the club where I didn't have to worry about the stares of outsiders. I had taken for granted the community I'd grown up in. Like an extended family, there was always someone to listen or help out. I'd been so anxious to leave that I hadn't realized what I was leaving. I was sure that there was a sense of community on the outside, that there were people living the straight and narrow who had the connections I'd wanted, but I'd never found them. The club was where I was comfortable. These were the people I trusted, and I was finally finding my place.

While lying in the grass one day with Trix asleep next to me, I realized that the traits I so dreaded in a man from the club weren't present in Dragon. He didn't sleep around. I didn't always know where he was, but I was learning that I didn't need to know. He had business that I wasn't a part of, and I was perfectly fine with that. He didn't party long into the night and come home smelling like club whores the way I'd envisioned in my nightmares. I knew he was doing things that could get him put away for a long time, but I trusted him to be as careful as he could. He'd never jeopardize our little family if he could help it. I figured it was a lot like a military wife must feel when her husband was out doing things that she knew put him in danger. Thinking about the dangers didn't do anything except make her miserable. We had to make the best of a shitty situation. It made them who they were. Of course, military wives had husbands on the right side of the law…but who was I to quibble over semantics?

When I realized that this was where we were supposed to be, I felt a peace that I'd never felt before. Everything became simpler. The obsessive compulsive cleaning jags stopped almost completely, and dishes in the sink became just dishes in the sink, not a mountain I had to climb at the first possible instant. I was feeling comfortable in my skin again, free to be myself, the self I'd lost so long ago.

Dragon noticed the change in me, and it changed the way he acted toward me in simple ways. He pushed me. He teased me, knowing I wouldn't burst into tears at some perceived slight. We fought. He didn't hold back when he was pissed, and for once, I didn't either. We never crossed any lines, emotional or physical, but we fought, balls-to-the-wall arguments, which usually turned into the best sex we'd ever had.

Dragon became messier, and it was then I knew that he'd been on his best behavior before. He left shit all over the house that I'd find throughout the day—socks by the couch, a grease rag hanging on the back of a kitchen chair. He wasn't tiptoeing around the house anymore; he was leaving his mark, mostly in the form of dirty laundry. All of his furniture was still in the apartment he'd shared with Kendra, but I didn't care. I didn't want any of that stuff in my house. The thought of sitting on a couch they'd had sex on made my stomach turn. So, we made a home with the hand-me-downs and castoffs we'd accumulated, and I loved it.

Life was good.

Until it wasn't.

Dragon left early in the morning on the Friday after the barbeque. It wasn't normal for him to leave before the sun came up, but it wasn't abnormal either. I stayed in bed with Trix, snuggling up close next to her, her breath hot on the side of my neck. These were some of my favorite mornings, the ones where I was just barely awake as Dragon kissed me slow and deep before he said good-bye. It left me in a half-dreamlike state where everything felt cozy and warm. I relished the feeling of kissing my man good-bye as I cuddled our baby close. I fell back asleep not long after I heard Casper pull up, the roar of Dragon's retreating bike fading in my ears.

My phone woke both Trix and me up at eight that morning, making me groan in frustration, as she jumped out of bed to grab it.

"Hi, Papa!" she answered and then paused for a moment. "Nope, we were sleepin'. Mama's still layin' in bed. She looks mad!" She giggled for a minute and then handed the phone to me.

I'd noticed that she started using Dragon's mannerisms the week before, dropping her Gs and gesturing with her hands as she spoke. She'd never before been so animated.

"Hey, babe," I mumbled into the phone as I watched Trix bounce out of the bedroom.

"Hey, baby. Sorry I woke you up." I could hear the laughter in his voice.

"It's not funny! Someone kept me up late last night."

"Yeah, and you loved it," he answered me. "Got the results back this morning."

I sat straight up in bed, his news waking me up instantly. "What does that mean? I mean, I know what it means, but what do we do now?"

"Well, we do nothin'. We wait to hear from the lawyers. But I'd feel better if you and Trix got up and got dressed," he informed me, sounding distracted.

"What's going on? Why do we need to get dressed?" I asked, climbing out of bed to follow his directions even though I didn't understand why I was doing it.

"The douche just got papers in black and white that say Trix isn't his to fuck with. He knew it, but now, the courts know it. Man's like a cornered animal now, yeah? I'd feel better if you two were awake and dressed. That's all I'm sayin'." The tone of his voice never changed, but it was almost as if I could feel the tightness of his body from across the phone.

"All right. I'm getting dressed now. I'll go help Trix in a minute. Are you at the clubhouse? Should we come over there?" I asked, beginning to feel a sense of urgency that I didn't understand but didn't fight.

"Yeah, baby. Do that. I'm here. No need to worry," he soothed. "Everything's fine. You're fine. If I thought you weren't, I'd be there. Casper's out front. Let him know when you're heading over. Okay, Mama?"

Mama was a new endearment he'd started using last week, and every time I heard it, my stomach filled with butterflies.

"Okay," I told him quietly as I pulled my jeans up my legs.

"You take that test before you leave. No more puttin' it off. I wanna know what it says when you get over here," he told me before he hung up.

Last week, I'd noticed that I hadn't had my period since the first week I'd been at the club. It hadn't concerned me for a while because the thing came and went with no rhyme or reason. But by last week, my boobs had started magically growing, and I'd seemed to be popping out of my bras. When I told Dragon, he'd given me a small smile and then dragged Trix and me into town. We grabbed a pregnancy test at the drug store that day, but I'd been putting off knowing for sure until this mess with Trix was finished. I didn't want anything else clouding my head, and I was sort of hoping that all of our good news could come at once—after the stress was gone. Obviously, Dragon had a different opinion, and my reprieve was over.

While Trix played quietly in her room, I went in the bathroom to take the test. Morning pee was apparently the best, and I'd been jumping around while getting Trix her breakfast, trying to hold it, until I had a minute to get to the bathroom. I took it and set it on the edge of the tub, pulling my hair into a ponytail and brushing my teeth while I waited. The sense of urgency that had plagued me during my conversation with Dragon never left, and I found myself pacing the bathroom. Two steps forward and two steps back—there wasn't much room to lose my mind in the tiny room. I finally decided to dress Trix before I came back to check, and I left the bathroom, shutting the door behind me as I went.

She was sitting on her floor, playing with some little plastic horses, when I got to her room. I overlooked the toys spread across the floor as I grabbed shorts and a shirt out of her dresser and tried to remember where she'd put her sandals the night before.

"Trix! Where are your purple sandals?" I asked her as I pulled clean underwear and shorts over her tiny little bum.

The horse distracted her, and I quickly snatched it out of her hand and flung it on the bed. The hair on my nape was standing straight up again, and my stomach was in knots for a reason I couldn't figure out. I was starting to feel panicked, and there was no clear reason for it.

"MAMA! Why'd you throw my horse?" she sniped at me as I tugged her T-shirt over her head. "I was playing with that! I don't throw your stuff!" She stomped one foot. "It's not nice!"

I was strung so tight, spots of sweat were standing out on my forehead. "Baby, I'm sorry. Mama's in a hurry. Now, where did you put your shoes?" I asked her urgently as we heard a car pull out in front of the house.

Her face was screwed up in confusion, her skills at reading my body language impaired from the peace we'd lived in these last couple of months.

"Someone's here!" Trix told me as she ran to her window that faced the front of the house. "Whose car is that?" she asked as I came up behind her at the window.

Before I could answer, the sound of a silenced gunshot pierced the quiet morning, followed by something big hitting the front porch. Hard.

I didn't know why they said that a silencer lessens the noise of a gunshot. It didn't. The shot I'd heard was by far the loudest thing that had ever reached my ears.

# Chapter 27
## Brenna

In the movie *The Matrix*, the fight scenes slowed down to an impossible level, so you could see every single movement. I'd always thought when movies slowed it was for the viewer's benefit, a chance to see all of the action in perfect detail. What I hadn't known, what I wish I'd never learned was the fact that it happened in real life.

As soon as I heard the sound on the front porch, I slammed my hand over Trix's mouth and dragged her away from the window toward her bedroom door. Once I knew she would be quiet, I let go over her mouth and lifted her up into my arms and squeezed her tight. Her little body was trembling in fear, but there was no time for me to comfort her, except to make small noises in my throat as I rubbed her back and hurried across the hallway.

My mind raced.

In a split second, I remembered that the front door was locked. Dragon always locked it when he left. It didn't matter if Casper was on the front porch or not. He always locked it. It was an assurance of at least a couple more seconds of time.

I carried Trix into my room, knowing I had less than a minute before Tony shot the deadbolt and got inside. I could hear the beat of my heart in my ears as I set Trix down in front of the open window next to our bed. I was glad that Dragon hadn't gotten around to fixing the screen even though we'd had a fight about it the day before. He slept really warm. This meant that without air conditioning in our room, we had to sleep with the window open, or we'd both wake up in a pool of sweat. I had bitched that he was letting bugs in, which he was, and he'd told me to stop bitching because he killed all the damn bugs anyway, so it wasn't like I had to do anything.

Fortunately, this meant that the window was completely open to the outside, and it was only about six feet off the ground.

Every mother plays the what-if game. What if a car ran over my child, and I had to lift it off her? What if my house got broken in to, and I had to hide my child somewhere? Where would I hide her? What if my car crashed into a river? How would I get my child to the surface? What if there was a national emergency? How would I keep my child safe? What if? What if? What if?

My what-if was happening.

I'd thought about it. Of course I'd thought about it. I'd had escape plans hatched in my head since before we'd left Tony. They'd changed depending on where we were, but they were always there in the back of my mind. What if? What if? What if?

How would I keep her safe?

Doing the thing you know is best doesn't make it any less scary. I was terrified as I kissed the silent tears on her face, memorizing her. I knew I had only seconds before Tony made it in the door, so I quickly explained to her what I needed her to do. I grabbed the sides of her face with one hand, so she knew I meant business, and then I started to speak quickly and quietly.

"I'm going to drop you out the window." I shook my head at her as she whimpered. "You'll be fine, baby. It's not very far. As soon as you hit the ground, you start running for the clubhouse. Do you understand me, Trix?"

She sobbed as I jerked her once and then kept on with my directions. "You DO NOT stop. Understand? I don't care what you see. I don't care if you step on a rock. I don't care if you're afraid. KEEP GOING. You absolutely do not stop until you get to Papa, Gramps, or Vera. Do you understand?"

The heartbeat in my ears was growing louder by the second, and I was terrified that Tony was going to barge in, and all this would be for nothing.

"I love you to the moon," I told her fiercely as I propped her on the window ledge, kissing her once on the lips. I heard the gun go off again as I leaned out the window as far as I could, pried her arms from around my neck, and dropped her to the grass.

"Run, baby! Go!" I whispered urgently.

I had only a moment to make sure she was okay and running before I spun around and walked toward the bedroom door. I made it all the way into the hallway before I saw him. He was standing in the living room at the end of that hall, looking around in disgust. I'd known it was him, but the shock of actually seeing him after all that time must have caused me to make a noise because he immediately swung the gun in my direction.

"Wife." He nodded, moving the gun in a come-here motion like he saw me every day, and he didn't just break into my house.

"What are you doing here, Tony?" I asked him, sliding forward slowly, trying not to antagonize him.

I knew I didn't have a chance. He was here, pointing a gun at me, and my guard was on the front porch with a bullet somewhere in his body. As I got closer, I prayed that I was giving Trix the chance she needed to get away. I prayed feverishly that she wouldn't stop, and that Tony wouldn't look out the window and see her running to the clubhouse, her hot pink shirt like a beacon in the tall grass. I couldn't even think of Casper.

"It's time to go, Brenna. You've had your fun. Get Trix. We're leaving." He spoke to me like a parent to a child, both frustrated and amused.

"Trix isn't here, Tony. She stayed the night at a friend's house," I told him calmly, hoping he couldn't see the artery fluttering quickly in my neck.

He didn't notice my panic, but it didn't matter. He didn't say a word. He just calmly punched me in the face hard enough to shatter my jaw. I saw stars, but I didn't fall down. The pain was excruciating, and I could no longer move my mouth. I grabbed the back of the couch for support as the agony in my face threatened to drop me to the floor. It couldn't end this quickly. Trix couldn't be to the clubhouse yet. I needed to keep him inside until I knew she'd made it. Then, he could do whatever the hell he wanted.

"Don't lie to me! She told me you and Trix were home with the spic last night!" he yelled at me, spit flying from his mouth and landing in my hair.

"Who told you?" I mumbled, trying to keep my eyes on him as my vision clouded. It was a mistake.

Tony always had a pet peeve when we were together. He didn't like to be questioned. About anything. He expected his word to be law. This meant that I was expected to keep my questions to myself; he wouldn't clarify things for me. If I had the audacity to question him, I was always sorry for it. I'd learned to nod politely while my mind raced with questions.

My confusion over his informant must have triggered his ire because the next thing I knew, I was cowering against the couch as he punched me repeatedly in the chest, stomach, and back, asking over and over again where Trix was.

I was beyond any sort of control of my body and curled into a ball as he hit me. I whimpered repeatedly that Trix wasn't home, begging him to stop until I lost consciousness.

## Chapter 28
## Dragon

I was sitting at the bar inside the clubhouse when I heard one of the boys yell my name from the forecourt. Normally, it wouldn't have made me leave the conversation I was having, but the tone of his voice was off, so I immediately stood up.

"Kendra, I've told you. You can stay there a couple months, but you need to be lookin' for some place to move."

I was so fuckin' annoyed at the bitch. If Brenna saw her hanging around here, she'd flip her lid. We hadn't heard anything from my ex until last week when she was supposed to move out of my fuckin' apartment, and instead, she'd started showing up at the club with a couple of the other women that came for a good time. I had no interest, but that didn't seem to stop her from eyeballing me whenever she was anywhere in looking distance. She was being passed around like a pool stick, and every time she headed toward someone's room, she turned to look at me like I was going to stop her.

"Stop fuckin' comin' around. No need for you to be whoring yourself out in some twisted way to get at me. I. Do. Not. Care. Fuck anyone you want. It doesn't make a damn bit of difference to me," I told her as I walked toward the open door.

Before I stepped into the sunshine, I heard her call out behind me, "It will!"

But I kept walking.

When I got outside, the first thing I saw was two of the boys looking toward my house, so I automatically looked in that direction. When I did, I noticed what they were staring at. Trix was limping toward me about fifty yards away. Her face was covered in snot and tears, but she was completely silent. As soon as I registered what I was seeing, I ran to her, the chain on my wallet slapping against my leg and jingling against the keys sticking out of my pocket. I reached her in seconds.

"Papa!" she gasped, not able to catch her breath. The strength of her sobs had her body trembling against me as she tried to speak.

I jerked my head to one of the boys. "Go get Poet. Now!"

"What happened, little warrior? Are you okay?" I asked her, searching for a wound or injury of any kind.

She seemed to be whole, but I couldn't understand what she was saying, and I was wondering where the hell Brenna was. Something was going on. The feeling that had been bothering me all morning got stronger.

"Loud noise…Mama was scared…she dropped me out the window!"

Poet, Slider, and Vera came jogging out of the club as Trix tried to explain, but I was no closer to a straight answer.

"She says there was a loud noise, and then Brenna dropped her out the window? I don't know what the fuck is going on. I need to get over there," I told them as I kissed Trix and handed her to Vera.

I was about to climb on my bike when I glanced one more time at Trix and really recognized the look on her face. She was terrified.

As I held her eyes, she whispered one word that made my blood run cold, "Daddy."

Slider, Poet, Grease, Tommy Gun, and Butcher followed me to the house. They'd all been in the forecourt and decided to follow me as I roared out of the yard. I saw Kendra's convertible driving where the club's driveway and ours met, but I didn't think about it as I drove up to the house. My gut clenched as I saw Casper on the porch. There was a huge smear of blood in an arc across the floorboards, like he had dragged himself after he was shot. One of his arms was hidden behind the doorframe inside the house, and his head rested about six inches inside. The screen pressed into his side, and it looked like that was what had stopped him from making it any farther.

I noticed all of that as I ran to the front of the house and onto the porch, yelling Brenna's name.

The house wasn't disturbed. Everything was in its place, but I saw Brenna right away. She was facing away from me on the couch and flinched when I called her name, but she didn't turn to look at me.

The back of the couch faced the front door, and I had to walk all the way around it to get to her. I was afraid to walk around the couch because she was so still. That didn't slow me down though. Tommy Gun and Butcher were lifting Casper off the doorframe when I reached her, and at my moan, both heads shot up.

"Mama. Baby, you're okay. You're gonna be okay," I told her as I dropped to my knees in front of her.

If I didn't know her…if I hadn't kissed her good-bye this morning and traveled every inch of her body last night, she would have been completely unrecognizable. Her face was covered in blood, tears, and snot. It was swollen larger than I'd ever seen in my entire life. One side seemed to be worse than the other, and when I reached up to brush my hand against it, she made a noise like a wounded animal, but she didn't move. God, there was blood all over her clothes, and I couldn't figure out where it all came from.

"Baby, where are you bleeding?" I asked her, but she just stared at me, her green eyes dilated with pain and fear.

"POET!" I yelled for her Pop, but there was no need. He was standing right behind me, his fingers thrumming on his legs. "Get a towel out of the bathroom, would ya? Someone needs to call an ambulance!"

As he walked out of the room, I tried to find out where all of the blood on Brenna's body was coming from. I spoke quietly to her, the entire room dissolving around us, as I checked her out. I was going to find out where she was hurt. I was going to fix it. I promised her. There was barely any blood on her legs, so I smoothed my hands up her torso. When I reached her ribs, she moaned, but I couldn't find any cuts or wounds. I grabbed my knife out of my front pocket, and her eyes went wide.

"Always ready, just like a boy scout," I told her with a wink, trying not to let the panic I felt show on my face.

I cut the front of her shirt open from the waist to her neck, and that was when I saw bruising on her ribs. It wasn't as bad as I'd thought I would find, but it was still pretty fuckin' bad. She still wasn't talking, but her hand had reached up and was resting on the side of my neck while she watched me.

"Okay, baby, I'm gonna have to lean you forward? How's your back? Is it worse?" I asked her, and I knew it had to be.

Her body was too still. I was missing something. She started to say something, but when she did, she started choking, blood and spit pouring out of her mouth. Fuck. Her jaw had to be broken. I'd seen this before. I leaned her body forward gently, letting the blood drip from her mouth onto both of us, as I pulled the shirt down her arms.

I knew it. I knew they'd be there. Bruises the size of fists were spread all over her back. Before I could do anything more, Poet came back carrying a towel and something else in his fist. He set down the pregnancy test on the arm of the couch and stepped around behind me, speaking quietly to Brenna where her face showed above my right shoulder. His accent was so thick that I could barely understand what he was saying, but Brenna didn't seem to have the same problem because I felt her body relax the longer he spoke. I couldn't do anything but look at that positive pregnancy test sitting on the arm of the couch. Fuck. It might be over before it even really got started.

I was waiting on the ambulance with Brenna when we heard vehicles pulling into the front yard. She still hadn't said a word, but her hand grasped mine tightly, never letting go for a second. It felt like we'd been waiting for hours, but it had to have been less than twenty minutes since Trix came running across the grass to me.

I wanted to clean Brenna's face, but she made this keening noise any time anyone got near it, so I just left it how it was. I wasn't a fuckin' doctor; I couldn't have done a whole lot anyway. In the back of my mind, I was aware of my need to kill Tony Richards, but most of me was completely caught up in Brenna and getting her some help. I was fuckin' terrified that she was bleeding inside, that the fuckin' paramedics wouldn't get to her in time to help her. So, when I heard the vehicles outside, I gingerly leaned forward and slid my arms under her legs. She made a sound of protest, but we had to move her. She didn't have a choice in that.

"Brenna. I'm gonna pick you up."

She barely shook her head from side to side.

"Baby, we gotta get you outta here. I need you to wrap your arms around my neck, so I don't have to touch your back. Okay? Grab a hold."

And then, I lifted her up, a low moan coming out of her swollen mouth.

When I got outside, I was surprised to see four cops but no ambulance in sight.

"Daniel White?" the officer closest to me asked.

"Yeah, what's this about?" I asked them, not sure what the fuck was going on but pissed as hell that they hadn't brought a fucking ambulance with them. "Where the fuck are the paramedics?"

"Sir, I'm going to need you to put the woman down and walk down here with your hands above your head."

It was then that I noticed all of the officers were eyeing the boys on the porch, especially Casper, who was lying near the rail using Tommy Gun's cut as a pillow. All had their hands on their weapons though none had drawn on us.

"I can't fuckin' put her down! We're waiting on a goddamn ambulance for Christ's sake!" I told him sharply, but it didn't seem to matter.

"Sir, I'm not going to ask you again to put her down. We're trying to be peaceful here, but you need to walk down here with your hands above your head," he told me again as I thought of all the ways to kill him with my bare hands.

I didn't know if they just couldn't see Brenna's face or if they just didn't care, but they weren't going to fuckin' stop until I put her down. Poet started across the porch toward me, and all of the officers drew their weapons.

"You! Stop right where you are!" the one who seemed to be in charge yelled at Poet.

"Boy, none of us are gonna cause you any problems. No need for you to be pointin' guns," Poet told him calmly, his face as innocent as a baby. "That girl ain't gonna be standing up no time soon. You want him with you, gonna have to let me go get her."

"What's wrong with her? What the fuck is going on?" the cop finally asked belligerently.

"Well, now, we just called you boys. Someone came in, shot that boy lying on the porch, and beat the hell outta that girl. We're waiting on..." He pointed to the ambulance and another cop car pulling up the road. "That ambulance and the police."

The cop's face turned bright red as he looked between Poet and me. Finally, he told Poet to come get Brenna, and I felt her arms tighten around the back of my neck.

I whispered to her, "It's okay, baby. We'll get this straightened out. You go with your pop; he'll take care of you."

She squeezed even tighter, her breath wheezing out of her mouth fast and hard.

"Remember what I told you, Brenna? We talked about this. I said if I was gone, you needed to lean on your pop and Vera. Remember?" I felt her chest stop for a second as she finally understood our conversation. "You do that now Brenna. I love you." Then, I handed her to Poet gently, prying her fingers off my neck.

Poet's eyes met mine in understanding. "I'll call the suit. Don't say shit," he told me as I walked off the porch, hands above my head, passing the EMTs as they spread out to help Casper and Brenna.

When I reached the driveway, two of the cops started searching me, but I was completely focused on the sounds happening behind me.

The cop who'd called me off the porch stepped in front of me, his eyes remorseful. "You have the right to remain silent..."

Then, the sound of my Miranda rights were overwhelmed by Brenna screaming my name.

## Chapter 29
### Brenna

I had been right. Tony had broken my jaw. He'd also bruised my ribs and sprained my wrist. There was a warrant out for his arrest, but no one had seen him since he left my house in Kendra's car. Nobody had seen her either. I wasn't sure what had spooked him, but he'd set me on the couch and was ranting and raving, and then all of a sudden, he'd taken off like a bat out of hell. I didn't care why he'd left. I was just grateful that he had. Only minutes after he'd left, Dragon and the boys had pulled up to the house.

I didn't remember a lot of that day, but I did remember the sound of Dragon calling my name. It was the best sound I'd ever heard. I knew I was safe when he'd gotten there. I'd known Trix made it to him. The rest of the day, I remembered in flashes, like the moment I watched from my gurney when they pushed a handcuffed Dragon into the back of the cop car. I hadn't known what was going on, but I was in agony that they were taking him away from me. I thought I'd screamed.

I spent three days in the hospital while the doctors ran tests and wired my jaw shut. I had to wear the wires for about six weeks, and the first day I had them, I knew they were going to be a huge pain in the ass. Drinking all of my food through a straw sounded like a special form of hell.

I was really sore, but the doctors were hesitant to give me any heavy-duty drugs.

I hadn't lost the baby.

The doctors said to be cautious but optimistic. The little bean was still so small that he or she was pretty well-padded in there. They said that trauma could cause miscarriages though, so they told me to prepare for the worst. I was trying. Every day that I didn't bleed, I said a prayer of thanks and then tried not to think about it more than that. Worrying about what would or wouldn't happen was too much to handle on top of everything else. I was grateful. My injuries could have been so much worse; I was lucky he didn't kill me. The baby was like the cherry on top—an extra thing to be thankful for.

Casper had been shot in the shoulder, but they didn't think there would be any permanent damage. When he was hit, the impact pushed him into one of the posts on the porch, and he'd knocked himself out. The boys gave him shit constantly for that, but he was digging the attention. Behind the jokes and jibes was an underlying respect. If I had to guess, I'd say he'd be patching in really soon. The fact that they'd found the trail of blood from where he landed to the doorway of the house was a pretty clear indication he was trying to get to me. He'd passed out before he could reach me though, and I was thankful for that. Tony would have killed him.

I missed Dragon more than I thought was possible. The days dragged on without him, and I wondered what he was doing as I lay in bed and counted the ceiling tiles. I ached to hear his voice or feel his fingers in my hair. I was at my lowest point, and I needed him with me.

My second day in the hospital, Pop brought Trix into see me. She'd been scared. I could tell she wasn't sure where she could touch me, so I'd lifted her hands in mine and set them on my belly. She chattered nonstop about running through the grass and asked if she did okay. It was hard for me to talk through the wires, but I assured her that she did exactly what she was supposed to. She giggled uncontrollably at the way I spoke, and Pop had to pull her off the bed to keep her from jostling me.

"Trix, where's your game?" he asked her once she was on the floor. "Get up in that chair, would ya? I wanna talk to your mum."

She frowned at him. She didn't want to leave my side, but she turned and walked to the corner of the room, pausing to put little headphones on, before she climbed into the chair.

"What's happening with Dragon?" I asked him or tried to through my teeth.

"That's all going well. The lawyer doesn't think he'll be in there long. Might be a couple months though for skipping out on a court date," he told me as he sat on the edge of my bed and held my hand.

"What court date? What happened?" I didn't know why they had even arrested him. Every question I'd asked since I got to the hospital had been ignored or talked around. I was going crazy with the possibilities that ran through my mind.

"Well, now...back before he got his cut, there was a little altercation in a bar," he told me, and I rolled my eyes at him.

"Dragon wasn't a part of it, but he took the rap for another brother. One who had a sheet."

I raised my eyebrows as he explained.

"And?" I garbled at him.

"Well, he didn't show up for court. So, there's been a warrant out for him, seeing as how he never showed up, and the guy had been stabbed..." he told me.

I felt my eyes close in defeat. Assault with a deadly weapon. Fuck.

"He got his cut right after that, and by that time, we'd started callin' him Dragon. So, he pretty much dropped off the map. When he filed those papers for Trix, his name was flagged," he explained to me apologetically. "I knew it was gonna cause problems, but the boy wouldn't listen to me. So, that's where we're at." He patted my hand. "The suit says he'll have him out soon. The witnesses aren't talkin', and they've got nothin' else. We just gotta be patient. He's an Ace, and that's makin' wheels turn a little slower."

"Okay," I told him, nodding my head decisively. "We'll just wait then."

"Wanted to come see ya. Vera's gonna come get you when they let you outta here tomorrow." He leaned forward and gave me a kiss between my eyebrows. "She'll take care of ya until I get back or Dragon gets out. Don't you worry about nothin' but that. You're safe."

He stood up and motioned for Trix to come and say good-bye.

She came and stood next to the bed while I ran my fingers through her wispy hair. I watched Pop closely. Something was off.

Trix kissed my leg in good-bye, and as they walked out the door, I called out to Pop.

"Where you goin'?" I slurred to his back.

When he turned back to me, he looked like a different man. His shoulders straightened. His chin tipped up, and the fingers not holding Trix's hand started tapping a tattoo on the leg of his jeans. The look in his eyes was frightening, and I felt the muscles in my body tighten against my hospital bed.

"Hunting," he told me with a nod. Then, he was gone.

## Chapter 30
### Brenna

Vera took me home when she picked me up from the hospital. When I walked in, Casper was sitting on my couch, watching a movie, and I glanced at Vera in surprise.

"Got two of ya to look after. Boy's got no family around here to take him in, and he's not patched in, so he can't go to my house," she told me as she brought my flowers from the hospital into the kitchen. "Sit down, and I'll get you some iced tea. Or, you want a nap?"

"No, I don't want a nap," I slurred at her through my teeth.

Ugh. She'd already coddled me the whole way home, forcing me to sit in the backseat of the car so I could *rest*. I'd been home for five minutes, and I already wanted to leave.

"Hey, stranger." I smiled at Casper as I sat beside him on the couch. "How'd you get out before me?"

"Damn, Brenna. I can barely understand you!" He laughed. "Not sure why I was home before you. They let me out yesterday. Just said I had to wear this." He wiggled his sling at me.

"Yeah, yeah." I rolled my eyes at him. "Where's Trix? I thought she'd be here."

"Nah, she went with Tommy Gun's old lady and her kids. They were going to hang out over there for the day."

I missed Trix, but I was kind of glad that I had the rest of the day to relax. I'd called the club's attorney when we'd left the hospital, but I'd had to leave him a voice mail. I wanted to see Dragon. It'd only been three days since I'd seen him, but it seemed like a month. I was hoping that the attorney could get me in to see him sooner than the visiting days, which Vera said were Thursdays and Sundays. I didn't know if I could wait.

It took a few minutes. I didn't realize right away where I was sitting. Casper was enough of a distraction. But once he turned away from me, it hit me. Flashes of sitting in this same spot while Tony screamed in my face came flooding back, and immediately, I was afraid I was going to throw up. My head pounded, and my stomach cramped as I tried to get my frozen limbs to lift me off the couch.

By the time I was standing, Vera and Casper were standing with me, speaking in low voices.

"You're okay, baby girl. You're okay," Vera reassured me, rubbing my lower back where I had the least bruising.

"I can't throw up!" I told them desperately, pulling my lips back as far as I could as if to remind them of my broken jaw.

"You're not going to throw up," Casper told me calmly. "You do need to calm the fuck down though."

I raised my head to call him every name I could think of for being so insensitive, but when I saw the look he was giving me, I paused. His eyes were filled with concern as he searched my face.

"I've heard the way Dragon calms you down," he answered the question in my eyes with a shrug of his shoulders.

"You listen to authority. If I tried to comfort you, it would have made things worse...be glad I didn't threaten to spank your ass," he told me with a lopsided smile.

I made a small chuckling noise in my throat and shook my head. I did feel a bit better now, but I wasn't sitting back down on that couch. We were going to have to move it or something. Maybe if we rearranged the furniture it wouldn't bother me as much.

The doctors had talked to me about post-traumatic stress disorder. They'd warned me that I might have some of the symptoms, but I'd brushed them off. I'd been in pretty bad situations with Tony before, and I hadn't had flashbacks or anger problems. They thought the fact that he had violated my sanctuary might change things though, and I guessed they were right. If that little memory on the couch hadn't been a flashback, I was the Queen of Sheba.

I decided I was going to lie down for a while, and I asked Vera to make sure the window in our room was closed before I stepped inside. I didn't think I could deal with any more reminders. When I climbed into bed, I was instantly comforted by the scent of Dragon on my sheets, and I inhaled until my ribs protested. It was exactly what I needed.

"I didn't wash your sheets," Vera told me from the doorway. "When we were younger, Slider was inside for about six months. I didn't change the sheets until I couldn't smell him anymore." She laughed. "Probably couldn't smell him anymore 'cause they were so rank from never getting washed!"

I smiled back at her in thanks before she left the room, closing the door behind her. I wasn't tired. I just wanted to lie in our cocoon and pretend that Dragon was in the living room with Trix, playing Legos and letting me take a nap. I missed my family. After everything that had happened with Tony, I needed Dragon's arms around me. I needed the reassurance that the life we'd built over the last couple of months wasn't just a dream.

I tried to stay strong, to tell myself that he'd be home soon, and that I didn't have long to wait. But, within ten minutes of Vera closing the door, tears were running down my face and soaking into Dragon's pillow.

I fell asleep at some point and woke up to Casper calling my name from the doorway of my room. When I opened my eyes, he told me that the attorney was in the kitchen and walked away. He seemed a little abrupt, but I was in a hurry to talk to Dragon's attorney, so I did a quick check of my clothes and hair and headed toward the voices in the front of the house.

The attorney, I thought his name was Duncan, was sitting at the kitchen table, chatting with Vera when I walked in, eager for news. I sat across from him and tried to read his face, but it showed little emotion. I didn't know if he had good news or not.

"Mrs. Richards, I hope it's okay that I stopped by—" He started speaking, but I cut him off.

"Brenna," I gritted through my teeth.

We'd had this conversation before, and the douche continued to use my married name whenever I saw him.

"Brenna." He nodded his head once. "I have a couple of things to speak to you about. First, let's get the questions you left on my voice mail out of the way. I can't get you in to see Dragon this week."

"Why?" I interrupted him again. Pop and Slider seemed to think he could move mountains. It seemed like a very little thing to get me into the jail.

"Well," he paused. "I'm just going to tell you. I talked to Daniel White today, and he doesn't want to see you."

I felt like the wind had been knocked out of me, and the absolute lack of compassion on his face made it ten times worse.

"Why?" I asked again.

"Mr. White didn't give me his reasons, but he was adamant that if you showed up, even during regular visiting hours, he wouldn't see you," he told me impatiently. "Now, regarding the custody suit, that's been dropped due to the death of the plaintiff."

"What?" I cried.

He was going too fast; the information he was giving me was making my head spin. I felt Casper come up behind me and lay his hand on my shoulder as I looked at the attorney in bewilderment. He acted like we were wasting his precious time, like he had better things to do than sit and try to explain things to me.

"Mr. Tony Richards was found dead in a hotel room on the California border this morning. Of course, nothing is legal yet, but without a plaintiff, it's all a matter of paperwork at this point," he told me offhandedly, gathering the paperwork on the table into his briefcase. "I'll still work on getting those birth certificates changed though, but I don't foresee any problems with that."

I looked over to Vera for verification, and her face was like stone. I opened my mouth to say something, I didn't know what, and she shook her head at me once. Not while the lawyer was there. That little shake of her head reminded me of Pop's visit the morning before. He'd said he was going hunting. Holy God.

## Chapter 31
### Brenna

Dragon never changed his mind about letting me visit.

I had to learn about how he was doing from the brothers who visited him every Thursday and Sunday. I gathered their news like a hoarder, thinking about it over and over again, as I lay in bed at night with Trix cuddled into my side. The attorney was still a complete asshole, but he seemed to be doing his job. Dragon got three months, and by the time they'd decided, he'd already finished a month.

Trix and I continued with our regular routine even though most of the club's kids returned to school at the end of the summer. I decided to homeschool Trix for preschool that year. We'd had too many changes and upheavals as it was. I didn't want to add to the things she would have to tell her therapist as an adult.

Thankfully, the weather cooperated, so we were able to spend most of our time outside, which left us both with golden tans. I'd actually never had a tan before. I'd either burned or stayed pale, but I guessed Dragon was on to something when he'd slathered us with sunblock this summer.

I missed Dragon the worst at night after Trix had gone to sleep and the house was quiet. I missed his hands on me, and the scruff of his beard rubbing against the back of my neck as I fell asleep. I missed falling into bed, exhausted, after he'd worn me out with a sweaty round of sex. I missed falling asleep with the window open and his hot body keeping me warm. I missed it all.

My belly grew, and Trix helped me rub lotion on it every night, laughing as we drew faces with the white lotion. I wanted her to feel like she was a part of things, so I included her in anything I could when it came to her little brother or sister. We both felt the hole in our lives, but just like every other time we'd been alone, we just grew closer. We played games, watched movies, and shopped for baby things. It was a relaxing way to spend my time while I healed and grew round.

Dragon's ex, Kendra, never showed up at the club again. The boys had feelers out all over the West Coast, but nobody had heard from her. We weren't sure if Tony had dumped her somewhere or if she'd just skipped town, but her whereabouts were the last on my list of worries. I had enough on my plate.

Pop never came home.

I'd gotten the full story from Vera after the lawyer left, the day he'd told me Tony was dead. Apparently, Tony was found in a luxury hotel suite, his throat slit by the steak knife that had come with his room service dinner. The security cameras in the hotel hadn't caught a glimpse of anyone near Tony's hotel room the night he was killed. There was no forced entry, and there were no prints to be found because it was such a high-traffic area. The murder case was still an open investigation, but the police had no leads. It was as if he'd slit his own throat.

Only a few of us knew the truth, and we weren't talking.

Nobody had seen Pop since the day he'd dropped Trix off with Vera after they'd visited me at the hospital. I was worried. It wasn't like Pop to just take off with no word. Slider didn't seem to have the same concerns though. I finally asked him about it, a few days after I'd had the wires taken off my jaw.

"Brenna, your pop left that life behind him when he came here. That kinda shit..." He rubbed the back of his neck. "It leaves marks on a man, even if he feels it's justified. He'll be back when he gets here," he told me as he started to walk away.

"Yeah, but where is he?" I asked in frustration.

"Your man has a hard day. What's he want when he gets home, Brenna?" he asked me with his eyebrows raised in question.

"Oh," I answered him faintly.

"Yeah." He nodded. "He's got a woman near Salem. I've met her a couple times...got some weird-ass fuckin' hippie name and long-ass dreadlocks. Nice broad though...he'll be here when he gets here."

"His room...why's it yellow?" I asked, the picture becoming clearer.

"Yup. That was her doing. Said it would help his aura. Whatever the fuck that means," he told me and then walked out, leaving me standing in the middle of the clubhouse.

For the first two months without Dragon, I was weepy and lonely. I missed him, and I couldn't understand why he wouldn't see me. Did he not miss me as much as I missed him? Did he decide I was just too much trouble? Did he regret filing the papers for Trix? My mind spun 'round and 'round, each scenario worse than the last.

I was a mess. I used the baby as my excuse every time Trix saw me crying for no reason.

"I'm okay, Trix. Sometimes, when mommies are making babies, it just makes them cry a lot," I told her.

Dragon sent a message home with Casper after a visit one Sunday after he'd been gone almost two months. He loved me and missed me. He loved the babies. He'd be home soon.

I cried for two days.

Once I recovered from Dragon's message, my attitude changed. With each day my belly grew, so did my anger until I was afraid I'd explode. How dare he tell me I couldn't visit him! What an asshole! I'd just had the shit beat out of me, my Pop freaking assassinated my ex-husband, and my jaw was wired shut during the first queasy month of pregnancy, and he couldn't even see me? I was livid. My indignation got me through the last month of Dragon's incarceration. It was ironic, really. The anger I was finally feeling made the days pass quickly.

When it was almost time for him to come home, I cleaned the house from top to bottom. I didn't know if it was because I wanted him to come home to a clean house or because I had way too much nervous energy. The entire place freaking sparkled when I was through with it. I also went with Vera and bought all new bras and underwear—frilly, lacy, silky pieces of nothing, which I knew he'd love. I'd only fit into them for another month before I had to start shopping in the maternity section. I even went to a salon and got my hair dyed back to its original bright red hue.

My anger hadn't abated. I could still feel the fire in my gut every time I thought of Dragon, but that didn't mean that I wasn't counting the days until he got back. I was almost giddy when the day finally arrived.

I refused to go with Grease when he went to pick up Dragon. I was still pissed enough that he was going to have to come to me. The asshole.

I was pissed at him, but I still helped set up the food for his welcome-home party. It was sort of a tradition to have a welcoming party for the brothers as they got out of jail. A little weird, sure, but it was their thing, so I didn't judge it.

Vera and I spent all day shopping for food and beer, dragging Casper and Curly with us to load anything heavy into Slider's huge pickup. The sheer amount of food we needed made our shopping trip take forever. By the time we headed back to the clubhouse, I thought the boys were going to fall asleep from exhaustion on the back of their bikes.

The wonderful thing about having an extended family meant I was never lacking babysitters, so Trix was off to stay the night with one of the old ladies. I knew it was selfish of me to send her away on Dragon's first night home, but I honestly didn't care. We needed one night that was just for us. I didn't even tell her that he was coming home yet, and I couldn't wait to see the look on her face when we went to pick her up the next day.

By the time Grease left at about four o'clock, my stomach was in knots. My hands were shaky, and I frantically checked the food and the plates and the toilet paper in the bathrooms. I couldn't stop moving. I was a nervous wreck.

My belly wasn't huge. I was only about four months along, but it was already making itself known through my clothes. He knew I was pregnant, but I wondered if he would be surprised when he saw me. I felt like I had changed completely in the three months he'd been gone.

When the time finally came and I heard the bikes roar into the forecourt, a sense of complete calm settled into my bones. When he walked through the door, I started toward him, noting the leanness of his face as he searched for me in the crowd. When his eyes finally found me, they lit up, and a huge smile spread across his face. I didn't smile back. I just kept walking toward him, my hips swaying. I knew I looked good. Vera and I had bought a welcome-home outfit that I'd known he would love, and my larger boobs gave me killer cleavage. By the time I reached him, his smile had turned into a frown, and he was looking at me in confusion.

"Baby, what's goin' on?" he asked me, completely unaware of the looks everyone was giving us.

"Welcome home, Dragon," I told him, my face completely blank. "I washed all your bedding in your club room and made sure everything was clean before you got back. I hope you enjoy it." I nodded once and then turned as if to walk out.

"The fuck are you talkin' about, Brenna?" he asked me and grabbed my arm. The look on his face had changed from confused to pissed.

"You didn't want to see me for three months?" I asked him. "Well, now, I don't want to see you!" And then, I tried to walk away again.

"Stop right where you are!" he called after me, but I kept moving.

I knew he'd follow me. I knew we'd make up. But I was going to make him freaking work for it. My attitude was solid until he came up behind me at the edge of the forecourt and wrapped his hands around my waist, spreading his fingers over the small mound of my belly.

"Baby…" he whispered, moving my hair away from my neck with his chin. "You know I wanted to see you. I thought about you every goddamn second. Wonderin' if you were all right, wonderin' if our babies were doin' okay."

He started kissing my neck, and tears began to roll down my face, but my back stayed straight.

"Then, why didn't you let me come see you?" I asked him in a wobbly voice.

"Because, baby, I don't want you seeing me in there. Wearin' a fuckin' jumpsuit, fuckin' tennis shoes with no laces. I'm your man. I don't want you ever seein' me as anything else," he told me as he walked around me and tilted my face up to his. "You can be pissed all you want, Brenna. But don't ever tell me again that I won't be sleepin' in our bed. Got me?" he asked, and the dominance in his voice made me feel like I was coming home.

"I got you," I whimpered back.

His hands on my body and his face close to mine after so long made me feel like I was going to spontaneously combust. I hoped that he would always affect me that way.

"That's right, baby. You got me," he whispered back as he took my mouth in a hard kiss. "God, baby. I was goin' crazy without you," he told me when we finally stopped kissing, and he started dragging me through the tall grass toward our house.

"Dragon!" I laughed up at him. "We can't leave! You have a welcome-home party going on!"

"Baby, any of those boys inside won't expect us back for a couple hours. Neither will their women," he answered me, never veering from his course.

I reached forward to run my nails down the back of his arm, and it stopped him in his tracks about ten yards from the house.

"Brenna, you keep doing shit like that, and we ain't gonna make it in the house," he groaned.

Before I knew what he was doing, he'd reached down and lifted me up, so my legs wrapped around his waist, and the little skirt I was wearing was pushed to the top of my thighs.

"Fuck, Brenna. You can't be wearing a skirt like that with no underwear," he ground out as he squeezed my ass in his hands.

"Just being prepared." I kissed him lightly on the lips. "Now, take me in the house."

We stumbled our way to the house, and he had to put me down to fumble with the front door lock. My hands were all over him—unbuttoning his jeans, sliding under his shirt to trace his abs, scratching lightly down his back. By the time we made it into the bedroom, I was on fire for him.

"Damn," he mumbled once he'd stripped me naked and laid me on the bed. "Look at you, Little Mama. All fuckin' ripe and swollen."

I felt my face flush at his words. He'd seen me so many times before, but I was still nervous like it was the first time. Three months was a long time.

"I'm going to get a lot bigger," I whispered in warning as he pulled his shirt over his head. "In about two more months, it's not going to be so attractive."

He smirked at me as he pulled off his boots and jeans. "That right? Your smile gonna change? Your hair? The way you respond to me in bed? The way you take care of my kids? Any of that gonna change?"

I shook my head slowly as he crawled up the bed and laid his body on top of mine. "You could gain fifty fuckin' pounds, all that in your ass, and I'd still think you're the sexiest woman I've ever seen," he whispered before he leaned down and kissed me right above my left breast. "I love you, woman."

"Love you, too," I replied with a smile as I pulled the rubber band out of his hair and ran my fingers through it.

"Now, kiss your man," he ordered in a gruff voice.

I kissed him and whimpered as one of his hands pinched my nipple gently before exploring the roundness of my belly.

"Everything okay in here?" He lifted his head and asked me gently.

"Yeah, honey. Everything in there is perfect," I reassured him, and that must have been the opening he was looking for.

After a quietly grumbled, "Good," he leaned back on his knees and draped my thighs over his legs. He sat there for a minute, watching me, taking in my rosy lips and nipples and sliding his gaze down between my legs.

"Ah, baby. Look at how wet you are for me. Fuckin' drippin'," he groaned, his voice taking on the sandpaper quality that I'd come to expect when we were in bed.

He dipped his hand between my legs, and before I could prepare for it, he slid one finger inside. My back arched off the bed as I let out a wail that would've embarrassed me if I had any idea what I was doing. It had been so long since I'd felt him.

He added another finger, watching my face as he did so, and I found myself begging him incoherently while he told me to slow down. I couldn't slow down, and I didn't understand why he would want to either. He'd had the same dry spell as me! I was needy, digging my nails into anything I could reach, and he finally lost patience with me.

"Brenna!" he barked, pulling me out of the spell I'd been under. "Slow the fuck down! You want my dick? I'll give it to you! But I can't do that when you're fuckin' outta control! One of us has gotta keep our head, and the second I get inside you, I'm gonna fuckin' lose it!"

His breath was bellowing out in big gusts, and I finally realized why he'd been teasing me.

"You're not going to hurt the baby." I curled up, so I could put my hand against the side of his face. "Come inside," I whispered.

He turned his head and kissed the palm of my hand before laying me back on the bed, following me down, and sliding inside me with one smooth thrust.

"Ah fuck, Brenna!" he groaned into my ear as he started to move. "Not gonna last long, baby. You feel so fuckin' good. Shit."

He was right. He didn't last long, but I still got mine.

The second round was a lot slower, and I got two more.

Eventually, we crawled out of bed and headed back to his party. He grabbed a tiny pair of jean shorts for me to wear, and when I complained about not being able to button them, he made me wear them with a rubber band holding them together. I was pretty sure he just wanted me to wear something that showed off my small belly. He was trying to play it cool, but I could tell he was proud as hell that I was pregnant.

As we walked back to the clubhouse, I tried to imagine what our lives would have been like if I'd told him when I was pregnant with Trix and Draco. Five years ago, we'd been in completely different places in our lives. He'd been newly patched into the club, and I'd been running as fast as I could. Who knows if we would have been able to make it work?

I had no doubts now. We'd been through more than most couples dealt with in their entire lives, and we'd survived. I couldn't picture the rest of my life anywhere but by his side, raising our babies, and ignoring the sideways looks we'd get from the outside world.

## Chapter 32
## Dragon

Brenna and I were walking back to the clubhouse the night of my party when a car came up the drive, swerving and spitting gravel. We were pretty close to the doorway of the club, so I called out to the boys inside as I pulled Brenna behind me.

I didn't recognize the car as it pulled to a stop about fifty feet away from us, but the chick who climbed out looked familiar. It was starting to get dark outside, but I could see her face just fine, and she was pissed. She was tiny, even smaller than Brenna, and she had pitch-black hair that was cut to her chin in front but shorter in the back. I glanced down her body, but I couldn't see much as she yelled and raised one of her arms around, waving what looked like a pistol in the air.

Before I could push Brenna toward the door, brothers came rushing out in a wave into the yard, taking in the scene quickly. I felt Brenna jerk behind me as the woman looked at us and pointed her gun our way.

"You fucking *dick*!" she screamed. "Where the *fuck* is my brother?"

I was about to yell back at her that I didn't know what the fuck she was talking about when Grease took a step forward, so we were standing almost shoulder-to-shoulder.

"The fuck are you doing here, Callie? You're outta your goddamn mind!" he yelled back, walking toward her.

"What did you do with my brother?" she yelled again, retreating a little every time Grease took a step forward until her back was against the side of her car.

I could feel Brenna shaking behind me with every step closer that Grease got to the woman with the weapon.

"Your brother's fine. Now, put that fuckin' thing away before you get your ass shot," Grease told her calmly as he reached her and pulled the weapon from her hand. "Fuckin' idiot. What did you think you were gonna do with a fuckin' Taser in a clubhouse surrounded by armed men?" he asked as he dropped the black thing to the ground.

All the boys in the forecourt breathed a sigh of relief. None of us wanted to take out a woman, but nobody moved.

As soon as the Taser hit the ground, she went batshit fuckin' crazy. She was swinging her fists and her legs, intent on hitting Grease anywhere she could reach. He grabbed her around the waist, but she didn't stop. I could see her trying to bite him, and I winced as she got a hold of a good chunk in his shoulder. That had to fuckin' hurt.

I couldn't understand what she was yelling about, but I could hear Grease just fine, and the way he was talkin' to her made me wonder where the fuck I'd seen her before.

"It's okay, baby. He's fine. He's fine. It's okay. Shhh," he told her softly as her struggles finally ceased, and she went limp in his arms, her mouth falling off his shoulder where her teeth marks had caused blood to run down his chest. "Fuck, baby, what were you fuckin' thinkin'?"

I shook my head and turned Brenna toward the clubhouse. I knew the crazy bitch from somewhere, but I wasn't gonna waste time trying to figure it out. Grease could take care of it. I had more important shit to do, like making up for lost time with my woman.

# Epilogue
## Brenna

My pregnancy went really well. I didn't have any of the problems with this baby that I'd had with the twins. My blood pressure stayed steady, my hips didn't ache, and my feet didn't swell. The doctors told me it was the difference between carrying twins and a single baby, but I thought it was Dragon.

He still went on runs, and when he did, Casper stayed with us. Tony was no longer a threat, but Dragon didn't want us home alone for an entirely new reason. I didn't know if it was the baby's uneasy beginning, our history with the twins, or just Dragon's overprotectiveness, but he wouldn't leave until he knew someone was going to be around the house. It drove Slider crazy, but I loved it. I loved that he was taking care of us. I never felt stifled or annoyed. I felt protected, cherished.

We'd wanted to find out the sex. I was too anxious to wait, but every ultrasound had been a bust. I'd been really annoyed. I'd wanted to start planning early, but Dragon just laughed when we never got a clear indication either way. I thought he was just relieved that the baby was healthy. We never fought about things even though I knew half the time I was being a total bitch. Dragon would just shake his head at me like I was crazy and go on doing whatever he was doing at the time.

It wasn't until I decided I would try to have the baby naturally, rather than a C-section, that Dragon put his foot down. He'd sat with me during the consultation when the doctor gave us all of the worst-case scenarios, and he was pissed as hell that I was willing to take any chances. The fight went on for weeks, but it finally came to a head when I was about seven months along.

"Brenna, there is no fuckin' way that I'm gonna let you put yourself in danger just because you wanna commune with motherfuckin' nature or whatever the hell it is you got in your head," he told me one night as we were lying in bed.

"They can get the baby out in like sixty seconds if something goes wrong. The chances of anything happening are slim. Baby, seriously, they know what they're doing." I laid my head on his chest and traced my finger over where he'd gone in and had Trix's star enlarged on his Orion's Belt tattoo.

"They give you all of these things they say could go wrong, make you sign a fuckin' paper that says you're not gonna sue them, and you don't see nothin' wrong with that?" He shook his head. "You're not doin' it, baby. You're havin' a fuckin' C-section, like they advised you to fuckin' do. Not gonna lose you. End of story."

And that was that. I'd been willing to give him the peace of mind that he needed. It wasn't like I'd been looking forward to hours of labor anyway. I'd just have to let my fears of another C-section go.

So, there I was, lying in an operating room, surrounded by doctors and nurses, waiting for them to cut me open and get our child out. I didn't sleep last night because I was too anxious, but when we got out of bed this morning, I was completely calm. I could do this.

My arms were strapped to the table by my head, and it was scary, but Dragon was there holding my hand. His face was covered with a surgical mask, and he was dressed in scrubs, the sleeves so tight around his chest and biceps that he looked like a stripper. All he needed was a stethoscope and a boom box. The thought made me smile.

"How you doin', Little Mama?" he asked me quietly, his face close to mine.

The doctors were speaking around us, but it felt like we were in our own little world.

"I'm okay. I'm ready for this to be over," I whispered back as I felt them tugging on my torso. I didn't know if they had already cut me, and I was trying not to pay attention to what they were doing on the other side of the little curtain.

"You're doin' so good, baby." He brushed the curls that had escaped my ponytail out of my face. "It's almost ov—"

His words were cut off by the screaming of an infant, and he immediately raised his head over the curtain.

"Hey, Daddy, you want to let Mom know what she's got?" my doctor asked with a smile in her voice.

I looked around, trying to get a glimpse of anything, when Dragon's face leaned back down over mine.

"Thank God. Another fuckin' dick in the house. Gettin' tired of all those fuckin' Barbies," he told me, a huge grin on his face. "We got a boy, Mama."

The doctors were rushing around us, and tears were running down the sides of my face as a little wrapped bundle was set in Dragon's arms. He was no longer crying. He was asleep. I could barely see his face, and the doctors were still working on me on the other side of the curtain, but I was completely content in this moment.

"You did good, baby," Dragon told me as he pushed down his mask, a tender look in his eyes. "Now, give your man a kiss."

# Acknowledgments

Holy cow, I don't even know where to start.

To my girlies—Mama did it! But, as excited as I am right now, nothing will compare to the two of you. You are my biggest accomplishments, and no matter where life takes us from here, you always will be. My cup runneth over. I love you to the moon and back.

Mom and Dad—I love you. Thank you for keeping me sane, providing me with coffee, watching the girlies, and loving me. You guys are my biggest cheerleaders, and there is no way I could have accomplished all I have in the last year if it weren't for you.

To my sisters—You guys are the best friends a girl could ever ask for. Thank you for being so excited for me every time I couldn't wait to call you with every single detail of this writing process. You've been with me during every exciting step. Let's drink wine and celebrate. I think we've earned it.

To my brothers—You'll never read this, but I love you, and I could never leave you out.

To Genelle and Becky—You two were my first sounding board and the very first people to read my work. I can't ever repay you for that. Without your input, I don't know how far I would have made it. You kept me going and built me up. I love you, girls, and I'm so happy to have you as friends.

Madeline—Anything I say to you in here will have you rolling your eyes. Don't think I don't see you. You act like you didn't do anything big, but I can't even explain how much you've helped me. You answered my questions, you didn't bullshit me, and you introduced me to an entire writing community that I didn't even know was there. Thank you.

To the girls in ANGTFD—Thank you for listening to me complain and worry and bubble over with excitement. I didn't even know I needed you guys until I met you and now I can't imagine going through this without you.

Ana—You know what you did. I think I love you. Thank you.

Lb and Lisa—Thank you for reminding me of what's real and what isn't.

Madison—Thank you for letting me bug you at all hours of the night, answering question after question, and fixing my atrocious tenses. This book would not be what it is without you.

Jovana—You have an eagle eye. I'm so glad I sent my baby to you. Thank you for your help.

Scandal the Superblogger—Did you know that I dreamed of having my book reviewed on your blog? I almost passed out when you agreed to do my blog tour. You fulfilled a dream. I can't even begin to thank you enough.

My Betas—I loved having you yell at me. No, really, that was my favorite part. If you're not feeling anything, then I'm not doing my job. Thank you for your feedback!

And to the bloggers who decided to take a chance on an unknown author—
"*Did you ever know that you're my hero?*" That's right, I'm singing. "*You are the wind beneath my wings.*"